GLIMMER OF HOPE

Whispers of Conspiracy

Other Books
by
François Sigrist

Fiction

Glimmer of Hope

Boomerang Justice

Boomerang Justice II
What Goes Around
Comes Around

Nonfiction

Secrets of a Master Chef

GLIMMER OF HOPE

Whispers of Conspiracy

FRANÇOIS SIGRIST

First Edition: January 1998
Second Edition: September 2021

This novel is a book of fiction. Names, descriptions, and incidents included in the story are the products of the author's imagination. Any resemblance to actual persons or events is entirely coincidental.

ISBN: 9798546835941

Cover Design: Brent Meske

Dedication

A SALUTE TO OUR VETERANS , POLICE
AND FIRST RESPONDERS

PROLOGUE

Tearing the t-shirt off my back, my instinct was to continue to rip the skin off my bones—it felt too tight, and the panic was making my heart visibly leap out of my chest. My breathing was painfully difficult. I was frozen and could barely stand on my rubbery legs—my knees buckling from running. My mind swirled. *What is this place? Where am I? How long had I been wandering in the maze of the city?*

My legs had carried me to a surreal part of the city that was totally unfamiliar to me. Not knowing how long I had been running made it impossible to know how I had ended up in this questionable neighborhood.

It was pointless trying to figure out the answers to the endless string of questions running through my mind—what mind? With my memory diminishing daily, how could I put my thoughts in any kind of order? I felt fortunate if I remembered my own name in the web of mishaps thrown at me by the universe. *How could someone play with my life without consent or knowledge?* The insanity of the thought defied explanation.

The streets were dark as far as I could see. The only cars were permanently parked with parts missing. I broke the silence only by my footsteps as I crushed the glass or paper under my shoe.

A siren in the distance. No one to notice my appearance—sweat pouring from my face, dirt glued to my skin, t-shirt hanging from my waist, hair tangled and matted, a dazed look in my eyes. I could barely shuffle my feet with legs weakened from running.

Heaps of smelling garbage littering the street. As I passed an open door, the reeking smell of alcohol and stale smoke nauseated me. When three men staggered out of the door, I had to fight to keep from losing my balance and steadied myself against the damp, slippery wall. Instinctively I knew that I had to find a lighted, crowded street for safety.

As I pushed myself away from the wall, my legs finally gave out and folded beneath me. My body lurches forward with my knees hitting the asphalt followed by my face crashing to the ground. Lying in the street with gravel deeply embedded in my face and both knees bleeding from the fall, I felt one eye starting to swell. The burning sensation of the open wounds made me realize that I had no more strength to run. It crossed my mind that I could die here in the street with no one to hear my plea for help.

Crawling over to the curb I could hear my life force leaving with a whistling from my lung. I shut my eyes and thought that maybe this was the end. I was exhausted and could not even imagine getting to my feet.

I came to with the feeling that someone was standing over me. Opening my eyes, I could not see, but heard.

"Get up Alex. I'll help you." I felt the silent force getting stronger, pouring vitality into me, propelling me forward, picking up speed, defying the reality of my exhausted body, and pushing my lung to the brink of exploding.

There were lights in the distance. I could see cars. The lights and noise were real. I was back to civilization. The pain was entirely too real now that I had involuntary slowed down, but I felt safe for the moment.

I am bloody mess, I thought as I stepped back into the shadow of the building. Across the street in an open mall I saw a drop box for donated articles. *Just what I need.* I crossed the street limping from the pain in my knees. Going through a couple of boxes, I found my new wardrobe—a clean t-shirt and a baseball cap. Whipping the blood and gravel from my face with the remain of my torn shirt, I slipped on the clean shirt and place the cap on my head, and I felt like a new man.

~~~

The heat from the coffee brought me back to reality with no idea of how I ended up here or how much time had gone by, I glanced around the small restaurant filled with the smell of fresh, crisp French fries. The waitress taking an order a few tables down while exchanging kind words with two truck drivers looking for a short route to the interstate. A full cup of black steaming coffee sat in front of me with a glass of ice water on my left. Slowly I crumpled my paper napkin and dabbed it into the water and with gentle strokes, I bathed my lacerated face, carefully removed the remaining gravel. Grabbing a piece of ice, I place it on my swollen eye before rubbing the remaining ice on my neck.

I must remain calm and try to remember back to when all of this started was my first thought as I continued to sit with the hot coffee in front of me. After three or four more sips I relaxed a little and acknowledged that I was feeling better.

Looking around I quickly assessed the situation still wondering where I was. None of the customers looked threatening, and the waitress seemed awfully pleasant. Had it not been for the stinging of my scraped face and hands, I might have thought all this was a dream—no, a nightmare—that I would not wish on my worst enemy.

"Can I freshen up your coffee?" A smiling face wearing a t-shirt with a Florida Everglades logo was standing right in front of me holding a pot of steaming brew.

That is a place I would rather be right now, I thought to myself, but instead I answered while returning her smile with.

"Why not? The coffee is great."

"Let me know if you need anything else. My name is Sharon," she offered as she poured another cup.

"Hi Sharon. I am Alex. Thank you for your kindness. Do you know what time it is?"

"Four AM," she replied as she moved away.

Four in the morning. Another reality checks. I must have been totally out of my head, running all night with no recollection. I needed to get home, soak in a hot bath, and then try to make sense of the last twenty-four hours.

As I extracted myself from the booth, I left l a buck and some change on the table and waived at Sharon and walked outside to a car not too far from here where I had stopped for coffee and doughnut at this same place. Talk about selective memory, *why would I remember this dump?* Just another question without an answer. Oh, well, the street was deserted and quiet, and I could find my way home from here.

In less than an hour I arrived at my apartment, climbed the three flights of stairs with difficulty, opened the front door and staggered inside. Closing the door behind me, I leaned against it and breathed a huge sigh of relief.

Rick was sitting on the sofa talking to One Eye, I saw them talking, but their words did not cut through my haze. Can't stop now, as I used the absolute last of my energy to make it to the bathroom, turned on the hot water, dropped my clothes in a pile in the middle of the door where I stood, and eased myself slowly into the healing liquid. I felt the warmth seeping into my tired and battered body. I was safe at last.

What had happened to me?

~~~

CHAPTER 1

The remaining fragments of my memory made it a difficult task to remember the details of my childhood. Only the highlights of my youth remained, and those were somewhat vague. There was no rhyme or reason, no emotions attached to my memories, and worst of all no reliability of their presence from one day to another. I was born nineteen years prior to the incident I just related, just five minutes after my twin brother Adam. From that day forward nothing could separate us. Our mother died after delivering us.

"Complication," was all that the doctor had told my father. He, of course, took her death extremely hard, and even after we were old enough to understand what complications were, Dad still could not talk about her. So, I never really knew what happened.

With twins to take care of, he had turned over the day-to-day operation of his business to his partner. We never experienced a mother, so we never felt deprived. Plus, we had each other.

My father believed in positive thinking, and to me it seemed as if everything came easily to him. He seldom got upset, and if he did, he stayed calm, never raised his voice, and made everything a learning experience. Patiently he would take the time to explain, and I do remember early in my life seeing him as a source of strength and security. His wonderful sense of humor and his habit of playing practical jokes were kind of his trademarks.

One memory that stuck in my mind was a warm spring day when he jumped in his car and rolled down the window as he was backing out of the driveway and said.

"Okay, you two, behave. I'll be back in a couple of hours." He waved as the car pulled away.

Sure enough, after three and a half hours he came back with a man named John. They laughed like kids and old friends as they exchanged stories and sipped their drinks for the next few hours.

When John left, we asked, "Who was that man?" Dad just laughed and told us that he had just had an 'accidental' meeting with John. As he was driving along, obviously daydreaming, he had run into the rear end of John's car. That was the only explanation we could get out of him before he broke into laughter again about the whole incident. We grew up in a small valley off the beaten path. Half a mile behind our back porch was a lake. We loved to fish and went down to the lake with our fishing poles several times a week. We were healthy boys with dark hair and eyes, curious natures and both good athletes, so every season meant a different sports activity.

Adam and I became known by our mischievous behavior. We would chase Megan our neighbor or wait behind a bush or in a ditch until she came by so we could jump out and scare her. I am not sure if our neighbors ever understood our antics and mischief, but I guess they learned to tolerate it as the years passed.

Even in school our arrival each day alerted teachers, janitors, and all the student that trouble was on the scene. Our stunts were never destructive or dangerous. It just felt good to stir things up, and besides, I am sure we knew on some level that our father would always be there to iron things out. His visits signaled to everyone that we had done something wrong again. The worst punishment that we received was detention after school, but I feel sure that was due entirely to Dad's skill in diplomacy and advocacy for his two sons who had lost their mother so long ago.

Fifteen years of living, and yet I had to struggle to recall these few happy experiences. W*hat a shame* I thought, but what really hit me *was What a waste.*

On a very warm July day, Adam and I decides to go bass fishing on the lake. Armed with our rods, bait, lotion, cooler, and bathing trunks, we headed towards the lake. We knew it was too hot to catch any fish at eighty-seven degrees in the shade, but it was a perfect day to lay back and take it easy.

We got in the boat with a full tank of gas and took off across the lake keeping close to the shore. We laughed about girls we had met the day before while our lines drifted alongside the boat. Then Adam decided to dive in the warm water.

"Wait, Adam. Let me pull my line in and drop the anchor," I was saying. But Adam, who was by nature impatient and like to be first at everything, dove right in. He never knew what hit him and died instantly when he hit the tree stump just below the surface of the water.

~ ~ ~

CHAPTER 2

I do not remember the rescue or how I got to the shore. I guess I blocked certain parts out completely. In one split second the brother I loved so completely was gone.

The next month was grim—to say the least. Overwhelming feelings of pain, sadness, and grief erupted uncontrollably rendering a vacuum in my mind so that I still do not remember the wake and funeral of my twin brother. My father and I ceased living and moved into a routine of painful existence. Life, as I had experienced it, had been put on the back burner, and my future had been changed forever. I guess our neighbors occasionally checked in on us because we were too out of touch to take care of things, and really did not care anyway. Father took Adam's death extremely hard, and this man who had once believed in positive thinking made no effort to shake himself out of his private grief. He grew more and more into himself and seldom talked to anyone. His wonderful sense of humor left and was replaced with anger, impatience, and insomnia.

I was just as hurt, and for the first time in my life my father refused to talk to me. After a while, my sadness changed to resentment. Yes, he had lost a son, but I had lost my best pal—someone who always knew what I was thinking and lots of times said it to me before I got the word out of my mouth. From the beginning we had done everything together, and suddenly—he was gone. Dad never said a word of blame, but I felt his eyes on my back which felt very cold, steel blades piercing my heart.

Being fifteen years old, losing my twin brother, feeling the blame from my own father and the guilt that I inflicted upon myself, it took less than six months for Dad and me to cease all communications. The loss of Adam was too great for both of us to talk about. He was becoming a stranger to me, and I felt like a boarder in his house, nothing more.

One evening I went to sleep, which was no small affair in the state of mind I was during those days. I considered it a bonus to drift off to sleep for even a short nap anytime of the day or night. Suddenly I was awake sitting in the middle of the bed shaking, soaked in my sweat and my heart pounding out of control. *It was not a dream nor was it a nightmare,* I thought. I panicked. I did not know what had happened. All I knew was that I felt totally paralyzed by a feeling that gripped me and would not let go. Slowly I began to remember.

I had dreamed of this place that I could only describe as a void. I could not feel anything. I mean nothing. No joy, no pain—all feeling vanished. It was as if someone had yanked out my heart and everything with it. It was eerie. My heat felt empty, and I felt like a child who had to learn everything over again when I woke up.

After that episode I did not sleep for four nights. I would dose during the day, but the night absolutely terrified me. Every time I did sleep at night, I would remember the void and knew that slowly, but surely, my memories were disappearing. Gone were my memories of my childhood, school, church, trips, and laughter. They were replaced by fear, rage, and anger. I could not think of anything good or happy that occurred in my life. These feeling got so bad that I refused to sleep at night entirely. I napped during the day and became more and more agitated, dreading the dark. To top it off, my father who was no longer my father, kicked me out.

In my anger after the last confrontation with him I had thumbed my way to the city. There I was, fifteen, and on the streets. No parents, no skills, no place to live, no memories, no money, and scared out of my wits every time it got dark. I will never forget that first night. The security of my home was gone, I had no bed to crawl in, and all the familiar sights and sounds had changed to new and threatening ones. These thoughts did not come immediately but over the course of the long night. By dawn, all I had from thinking was a massive headache and a fierce hunger. I still had no answers to the numerous questions that kept popping in my head, but it seemed vital to hold on to the bits and pieces left to keep myself going.

I was still pondering recent events when I became aware of the flow of traffic around me, and the noise revived me a little. Finding a restaurant across the street I headed over to it, entered and found a booth on the back, I was in no hurry. I had all the time in the world in front of me and no clue of what I was going to do next.

After ordering a hamburger and a soda, I found myself looking around the place observing the activities of the people working there. The bartender behind the bar with his sleeves rolled up moved with ease as he grabbed the frosty mugs with one hand and longnecks in the other. A waitress was yelling in an order to the line cook while a busboy meticulously wiped the table that he just cleaned off.

None of this felt real, and I felt like a little boy visiting in a strange place. I counted out the money for my bill and stood up and walked over to the jukebox putting in my last quarter. I pushed a button—any button, it really did not matter. A CD flipped out of the stack and was placed in the player. A Tejano melody floated out of the jukebox loudly.

The music immediately took me away as I return to my booth. I found myself staring at a lone cactus growing in a pot near the entrance. For just a moment I was in an open field feeling the wind in my face with the crunch of dried grass under my feet.

"Do you need a refill?' her voice snapped me out of my dream.

"Yes, please." I sat in the restaurant for quite some time watching the flow of customers. *Finally, I got up and left, walked the street until it started to drizzle, Great, what is next*

I found a little alcove surrounding an old forgotten doorway. It seemed as if it has been boarded up for at least twenty years. The hours crawled by. The oppression of the weather and my fear of the night was magnified as the cold began to sink in, beginning with my feet and working its way up my whole body.

The drizzle continued, and after a while I became numb to it and could not feel anything. What was I doing here curled up in a cold dark corner like a beaten dog? I could not and would not sleep. All my muscles were stiff.

The drizzle stopped and was replaced by a bitter cold wind. I could tell that it was from the north, it hit me like a whip. I felt the life in my body start up again if only to shiver against the cold. It was dawn. Never had I been so glad to see the light of day.

I forced myself from the corner I had adopted as my bedroom. When I stood up, I had the distinct impression of my bones creaking like dry timber. Ouch, I was stiff. Little did I know how tough the next couple nights were going to be. I was cold, miserable, hungry, and I was in a city I have maybe visited ten time in my lifetime. The next few days I walked endlessly through the streets. A menacing feeling constantly hung over my head.

I have stumbled past a donation box and added another shirt and sweater to my wardrobe, but the shivering which had become part of me came from deep inside. Not knowing what I was looking for I instinctively knew that I had to keep moving. I found water occasionally from spigots in the alleyways but could not bring myself to rummage through the smelly garbage. By the third day I did try begging out of desperation.

"Do you have some spare change?" I asked politely while my hand was reaching in the direction of passing stranger.

"No." Each person said, the same thing again and again as they hurried by avoiding even looking at me. *When you live in a parallel world, one might as well be invisible,* I thought.

One morning I was sitting in my home in a deserted alley between broken cardboard boxes and torn garbage bags. Too weak to move, with the smell of rotting food all around me making my empty stomach churn, I must have fallen into a stupor because the next thing I remember was hearing something whirling above my head. I thought,

What is going on?

I looked up, and there was this bird. The flapping of his wings had brushed my head. I could not tell if the bird was hungry, but he wanted to rest like me. I did not want to scare him, so I kept very still as he hopped around on the pavement without ever noticing me. The listlessness engulfed me again, but the welts and blisters on my feet kept me from falling asleep. The pain was excruciating. This, added to the despair from the cold, hunger, and nightmares that haunted me night after night, had me pretty beaten down. This was a new game with nondescript trials.

Amazingly, my pride was still intact, which made going back home out of the question, and it was about all I had to hold on for the moment. But I was slowly conscious of a thought that kept returning to my mind, *Help me! Somebody helps me!*

~~~

CHAPTER 3

On the fourth day of wandering the streets with no prospects, a scream jolted me out of my absorbed mind. I looked around. The neighborhood was deserted except for the litter. Down the street was an old, empty movie theater. Between the ticket box office and entry doors I saw two shapes. As I walked closer, I could make out two kids shouting at each other.

The bigger kid was obviously bullying the small guy, pushing him up against the door. Suddenly he started shaking him like a willow tree and banging his head against an oversized chain and padlock on the cinema doors.

When the victim saw me, he instinctively shouted out, "Help me Doug for god's sake!" The bully jumped back like a startled cat caught with the canary halfway down his throat. He dropped the fellow and swung around, looked me right in the eye and automatically decided that it was not worth it. He turned and ran like a wild rabbit, never stopping until he was out of sight.

"Hey, man, sorry I called you Doug. It was all I could think of. My name is Tony. What's yours?" asked this kid still crumpled on the sidewalk.

"Alex."

"Well, Alex, thank you for helping me," Tony said as he picked himself up off the concrete. A trickle of blood was running from behind his ear, and a glob of spit ran down his chin. He was shaking as badly as I was.

When Tony stood up, I got a better look at him. Man, was he dirty and smelling? He was scrawny and his clothes were tattered, but he had a look of defiance on his face. He looked younger than me with grubby, ash blond hair and some chipped teeth. What was most peculiar was that he had only one eye. The other one was covered with an old black patch as dirty as his clothes. "Do you have some spare change?" Not missing a beat as he was dusting himself off.

"No, I left my last quarter in a jukebox a few days ago."

"Yeah, right. You 're all dressed up, clean, and you're telling me you ain't got any money? Don't give me that bull."

"No, I swear. My dad kicked me out four days ago, and I do not even remember how I got here. I have been sleeping in the street, and wandering around, drinking out of spigots in alleys. I have got nothing. You've got to believe me," I was begging.

"Okay, okay. I believe you."

"I don't know where to go," I admitted. Tony stunk, but since he was alive, he must know something about survival. I had to trust someone.

"Welcome to the streets, man. First, call me One Eye. Everyone else calls me that," he added with a hint of a smile.

"You got it, whatever you say."

"Second, stop shrinking your nose at me. After two or three weeks you will have the same stink," he said, starting to act tough again.

"Me? Never." I was not ever going to smell that bad.

"Want to bet?"

"Bet with what?" as I showed him my empty pockets, turning them inside out.

"Hey, stop with the 'poor me.' You help me, I help you." Tony, I mean One Eye, he saw our situation that simply.

"Lucky me," trying to sound tough like him.

"Hey! Smart, clean guy, have it your way. It is rough out here. Do not waste time. Follow me if you want. It's no skin off my teeth." Talking as he turned down the alley behind some warehouses, stray cats running away from him.

I needed all the help I could get. So, I hurried behind him. "Tony where did you say you live?"

"I told you to call me One Eye. I didn't say, but you'll see if you can keep up." Tony was proud of his 'home.' Last winter he discovered a crawl space on the roof of a print shop. It was fine for one person to get out of the rain and cold cramped against the AC unit. Piece by piece he accumulated lumber in the middle of the night and enlarged the area for a couple of his friends. It was noisy, but warm and dry, and secure from the street.

"Man, I could have used it last night. That drizzle soaked me to the bones, and I shivered all night."

"What do you mean by last night? You are still shivering. Hurry up, Alex, we got to get different clothes for you, or they won't believe you're homeless down at the shelter," With new blisters on top of my old blisters I was going as fast as I could.

"Not so fast. My feet are killing me—I haven't taken my shoes off in five days."

"That will be as event to be missed, but I'm not about to skip a meal! So, move it."

"I am coming, your sarcastic weasel," was all I could muster now.

He did not even bother to reply. He was already twenty feet ahead, silently gliding by the building walls. We turned left behind a great big dumpster which concealed a narrow alleyway.

"Normally I do not come here during the daytime, but you look too clean in your clothes. Don't make any noise." One Eye looked nervously around the alley.

A rope ran alongside the wall was covered by some trash. One Eye pulled it with his frail body. Suddenly, it happened. The rusty fire escape came down with ease.

"Hop on it," He whispered

I literally flew up the wall to the roof. "Hey, neat. No one will find us up here."

"Shut up," he hissed.

Once we were on top of the roof, One Eye stopped. He looked around and proceeded to walk toward a small shed covering the AC Unit. He went in and I followed. To my surprise this place was warm and cozy, as well as full of junk.

"What is all that stuff?" I asked.

"It's how I make a living. Over in that box is everything you need. Sneakers, jean, radio, blankets, t-shirts, toys, socks, shoes, pants, and a lot more." One Eye showed me around with a touch of pride.

"Where did you get all of this stuff?" was my next question.

"People leave things in boxes for the homeless at the shelter and drop-boxes. I have no home so that makes it legal to help myself, right?" he reasoned.

Boy this kid was smart. I am lucky to have met him. A friend, shelter, clothes, and the possibility of a meal, all wrapped up in one skinny package. I picked a shirt, a pair of pants, and some sneakers. When I had changed, he said. "Let's go eat."

~~~

CHAPTER 4

We took the fire escape back down. I felt good. I was dry, and the future looked better already. Imagine one hour ago I was freaking out. We arrived at the mission after everyone had come and left.

Tony waved madly at a woman who was closing the door.

"Hey, Peggy! Wait! My friend and I need to eat."

"Tony, how come you're so late?" a middle-aged woman with light hair asked. She looked tired but kind, her question showing concern rather than a gripe.

"We got held up. Do you have anything left to eat, please?" One Eye asked.

"I got chicken, roast potatoes, corn, and bread, of course" she rattled the menu for a feast from what I heard.

"Who's is the new kid/"

"Alex. He helped me this morning. Rich was trying to kick my butt when Alex showed up as my friend. He scared Rick off, and the jerk ran away like a whipped puppy." He put a hand on my shoulder and smiled genuinely.

"Hi, Alex. I am Peggy. Sit down, and I will fix you up. Hot tea is all we've got left to drink." She smiled at us and went back to the kitchen area.

"Good enough," I replied. The smell of real, safe, warm food made my stomach rumble like thunder, and I felt weak from starvation. *Just a few more minutes,* I told myself.

We sat on folding chairs while Peggy prepared two plates piled high with food. It was the most beautiful sight I have ever seen.

"It's ready," she finally announced.

I jumped out of my seat and grabbed the plate from her hands. I quickly sat down at the table and began to wolf the food. One Eye acted cooler and gave a little laugh while watching me. "Slow down," Peggy said. "If you haven't eaten in a while, you'll get sick eating like that. Take your time. Nobody's gonna steal the food."

She was right. Halfway through my plate I had to stop so I wouldn't throw up. I stopped for a moment and took a sip of tea, and let my stomach acknowledge that, yes, this was real food. After fifteen minutes the wave of sickness had passed, and I could take another bite. I was going to make it after all.

"You look happy," One Eye smiled, but this time giving me his best chipped-tooth grin.

My mouth was full, my stomach getting there, and looking at my new buddy, I answered,

"Best meal I've ever had in quite a while. Thanks.

Familiarizing myself with the neighborhood over the next few days, learning the ins and outs of the streets and alleys, I discovered that this neighborhood had a lot of poverty. Most of the people living here were doing only a tiny bit better than One Eye and me on the streets Almost all the cars in the streets that were still running were at least ten years old, if not older.

I heard footsteps coming behind me. I turned around to look and got punched in the nose. A symphony of stars appeared in my head.

"Remember me, your stupid punk?" the voices said. I was flat on the ground. I opened my eyes to see Rick, the bully, this time with three of his friends. Blood was pouring from my nose. I had better not let them see how scared I was.

"Oh, hey, it's you. The moron. What's up?" I asked.

Without warning all four guys started beating the crap out of me, kicking me between the punches. I tried to fight back, but there were too many of them. I curled up to protect my head as my only defense before I gratefully passed out from the pain.

When I came to, I realized those idiots had left me for dead between some stinking garbage bags in a slimy gutter. Even though I was conscious, I couldn't move. I was beaten to a pulp and retching from the pain, *I could die here, and no one would even know to tell my father, I thought half-hardheartedly.* Then I lost track of time once again.

It was already dark when One Eye and his pal Jack found me. They told me how long it took them to drag me up the fire escape and into the hideaway, though I don't remember any of this. One Eye also told me how delirious I was, going on and on about some void and the nightmares which sucked out my memory.

He nursed my injuries the best that he could for three days and fed me soup that he had gotten from Peggy. He also brought some bread, but apparently my lips were so swollen that liquids were all that I could handle. For the first time since my brother died, I had a friend and that felt special.

One day as I was lying curled up against the air conditioner listening to the motor purring, I was thinking about the rage of the guys that had beaten me up, when I noticed something out of the corner of my swollen eye. At first it seemed like just a mist in the corner of the shed, but as I sat there and watched, it took form --- kind of like a human shadow. I dismissed it as my imagination or better yet delirium from my injuries. But then the form whirled around me a couple of times. I watched in awe. It became still for a moment, then disappeared.

Talk about being unnerved and rattled, I must have been hit harder in the head than I thought. The shadow had startled me, it wasn't scary or threatening. It almost had a friendly feeling about it.

Different from the nightmares that had returned with a vengeance since my injuries. Sleeping at night had become out of the question with the void sucking my memories at an ever-increasing rate. My childhood was vanishing bit by bit with less to hang on to every day.

I finally went outside after seven or eight days, and experiencing the wind blowing through my hairs and the warmth of the sun on my face felt good. Feeling alive again made me smile through my pain.

~~~

CHAPTER 5

O ne Eye showed me how to commit my first crime. We went to the backdoor of a small produce store. One Eye grabbed a trash can and, with all the strength from his skinny body, threw it against the back door.

Of course, the owner wondered what the hell all the noise all about was and came out back to investigate. While he was checking out the noise in the back, One Eye and I ran up in front and in the store, grabbed a couple of apples. Our crime was accomplished in a few seconds.

We ventured down to another corner store, and this time Bill was with us. He had no trouble lifting a full trash can and flinging it at the door. We all ran up and grabbed a few fruits while the owner went back to see what was going on.

All three of us took off running, down the alley and through the narrow passages, leaping over trash cans like crazy. We were gone before anyone knew what had happened. We all came to a stop as soon as we felt safe. The uneven pavement was rough under our feet. My heart was pounding, trying to leap out of my chest. What a rush! We trembled, laughed, jumping up for high five exchanges.

After we came down and ate the apples, I started to feel a little guilty. I knew that what we had done was wrong, dead wrong. But I had this other feeling as well. It's hard to describe, but it was the only real sensation I had experienced since the terror of my nightmares had started. I felt like I was here and could feel the blood flowing through my veins. After that, the rules of the ruled of proper society became irrelevant when it came to be surviving in the streets. Staying alive and taking care of your buddies were the basic rules of the streets.

One particularly grim morning I was still walking around after wandering the streets all night. I was feeling especially sorry for myself, walking down a dark alley looking at the holes in my shoes, in no rush to get anywhere. At the corner I collided with a stranger.

"Hey! What's is the hurry, young man?" He asked.

"Who wants to know?" I had learned from One Eye to act tough with everybody. That way no one would think that you were a wimp.

"No need to give me an attitude, after all you bumped into me."

"Yeah? Sue me!" I started walking away

"Hey? What is your name?"

"Who want to know?" It was strange having a grownup ask my name. To most of the public, I was just a smelly, faceless piece of trash.

"Simon, that's who wants to know. My name is Simon. What you don't know your name?" He was following me in the street.

"Hey watch it. Besides, why would you care?" Why was he so interested? Bill had told me about scummy guys who were selling drugs to the street kids and others who would try to make other kids have sex with them. No way was I going to fall into those traps.

"Chill out. You look like you could use a cup of coffee."

"Are you buying?" If he tried anything, I could at least throw hot coffee in his face was my thinking.

"Sure, you pick a place, any place," he answered, which coming from even a stranger sounded safe enough.

"You include a doughnut with the coffee?" You don't

get it if you don't ask—another rule from the street.

"Can do."

"You're on, and Alex is the name." I figured a hot breakfast was worth telling him my first name.

Looking at this man, I noticed that he was tall and slender with rough hands. His pants were old with baggy knees. He had a small mole on the right side of his neck, just below his chin. His tie was nothing special and his shoes were old. He had brown hair that he had pulled back and secured, his unshaved beard was at least three day's old. It took me only half a second to size him up. He wasn't rolling in the dough. There was something peculiar about his eyes, but I brushed the thought away and out of my mind.

"Alex, please to meet you."

"Yeah, yeah, what about the doughnut and a hot java?"

"Hey, take it easy," he said with a smile. "Do you know a place around here?"

"There is a place up the block good enough for coffee. Let's go." He and I didn't say another word until we sat down in a booth.

"Tell me," we said the same words at the same time, it made us laugh.

"Go ahead," said Simon.

"No, you go first."

"What will it be guys?" Maggie the waitress had snuck up on us. She winked at me. She had given me coffee from time to time, when I was broken or cold, which was just about all the time.

"A coffee, two donuts, and lots of cream," Simon ordered.

"Same for me." Smiling to myself. Wow! An extra doughnut and hot coffee for breakfast!

The next few minutes were spent in uneasy silence. I didn't mind. It was a free breakfast.

I broke the silence, "So, what bring you in this neck of

the woods?"

"Actually, I've been looking for you for the last four days."

I made the motion to get up and split. Someone looking for you always meant trouble, cops or someone looking for revenge, or worst.

"Hey, slow down and let me explain." Simon said.

"I don't even know you. Why were you looking for me?" still standing ready to bolt at one wrong word or movement.

"One Eye and Jack told me about you."

Nobody had said that they were trying to connect me with anyone.

"How do you know that I can trust you?" I continued.

"Butterball said you were the best at stealing cars."

"Butterball?" If this guy was a cop, I had better play dumb. "Who's Butterball?"

"You know very well who Butterball is," he snapped.

This guy was really persistent, "Yes, you do, His real name is John. When he was four years old his mom put the Thanksgiving turkey on the top of the stove after taking it out of the oven. John tried to check out what was smelling so good and pulled the turkey on top of himself splashing hot grease all over himself and leaving a huge scar on his forehead."

That was his nickname, but very few people knew the real story. In the twilight of misery, no explanation is necessary in the streets. If Simon knew about Butterball, maybe he could be trusted. But he still made me nervous. I sat back down.

'Who are you exactly? I finished the question just as Maggie brought the donuts and coffee. Waiting for his answer I started making them disappear.

"I told you, Simon."

"So, but what else? What do you do? Again, I put my intuition on a back burner ignoring the warning signs.

Simon waited until Maggie was behind the counter again. "I 'recycle' hot cars."

"Oh. That Simon. We call you the ghost."

"Ghost it is then," Simon acknowledged.

~ ~ ~

CHAPTER 6

Ghost started to persuade me to steal cars for him. I was long past feeling guilty for committing crimes to survive, so I listened. After I told him I would never have anything to do with drugs, he outlines a plan that would make some money for both of us.

At the beginning, I got some impressive money by street standard for my skills, and other street kids wanted to jump on the gravy train. Soon Ghost had a small army of kids picking pockets, shoplifting, stealing cars, whatever—whatever crime Ghost could think up to get the profits from and keep his own butt out of jail. It was understood that he would get us out of jail if needed, I never knew anyone who called him on it. We were streetwise and didn't count on anyone except our buddies. Some kids did act like slaves to him think that they needed him to take care of them.

No matter how much of his dirty work we did, his plans never got anyone off the streets.

I lost track of the outside world. No radio, newspapers, or TV. Not that my street buddies or I really cared, but when I heard about politics, or a new car, or a new song it was already old to everyone else. Most of the time I slept during the day and beat the pavement at night. The nightmares persisted, also it kept that shadow from appearing from time to time, never distinctly, but always at the most inopportune times, always without warning.

If it hadn't been for One Eye, I don't know how I would've survived. I don't think I would have made it. Jack also was a great friend. He was big and stringy and didn't take crap from anyone. Then there was Butterball. He was a little slow in everything that he did, to his advantage, he knew every trick when it came to find a place to hide or how to locate a shelter or food. He was constantly looking for a better place to live.

One day he found an abandoned building. We could enter through a manhole size opening, squeeze around these huge pipes, and then walk down a hallway into a big room. We covered the floor with flattened cardboard boxes, stacking three or four to create our bed. Some of Eye's stuff was piled in a corner, there were plenty of blankets and brick pillows, and more than enough room for the four of us. The roof didn't leek, and that made it all the easier to stay warm in the winter and cool in the sizzling summer heat.

We did a lot of crazy things during those times, but we all agreed that drugs were off-limits. We even took an oath that we would never do drugs. The money we made barely fed us, let alone wasting it on chemical garbage. We had no leader, we just stuck together somehow. When an idea came up, we all talked about it and developed a plan to achieve it.

One day Jack and I were looking for something to do when we saw this kid. He had a hole in one of his sneakers, only one shoelace, his shirt half tucked in, and was trembling from the cold, probably no food in his stomach. He looked like one of us.

"Slept outside, I recall," Jack said to him.

"Yeah, man, what a bummer. I nearly froze my butt off, I covered myself with cardboard." He talked fast. There was something about him that intrigued me.

"My name is Alex, and this guy is Jack. What's is your name?"

"Randy, but everyone calls me Lips."

"Lips. Why Lips?" I asked before I thought.

"Because I never shut up."

"Where are you from?" Jack asked.

"Small town in South Dakota." Wow, this kid was a long way from home, and couldn't be over fourteen or fifteen. I continued. "What are you doing so far from home?"

"Nothing better to do. Beside my parents died in a car crash when I was nine years old. None of the family wanted me, so I got sent to the state slime pit and then a bunch of foster homes. Those foster homes suck. Man, the kids pick on you, and the grownup are just in it for the check, no one cares. One day I got fed up and took off as soon as I could and ended up here," he rattled on.

"Hold on. Slowdown. You do talk fast—you're making my head spin. Want something to eat? I've got seventy-eight cents," as I checked my change.

"Hold on. Slowdown. You do talk fast—you're making my head spin. Want something to eat? I've got seventy-eight cents," as I checked my change.

"What have you got Jack?" his hand was open and loose spare change is in it.

"Don't know, let me look," He started to go through his pockets.

"Three dollars and four cents. Man, we're rich! Let's get soup and bread then we share with the others, come on, Randy."

~~~

CHAPTER 7

Back at the building, Bill warmed up the soup in a pot he had found in a garbage can in a residential neighborhood and a steno can that he had found behind a restaurant. We all eat out of the pot with our plastic spoons. Randy was so hungry that he wiped the pot clean with his bread.

"When is the last time you ate?" Asked Butterball.

"Five days ago. That's when I ran away."

As the afternoon wore on, we all realized why Lips could talk your ears off. He knew lots of facts about politics, cars, boat, cats, building house, countries, and even mountains. All he did for five years was to read to escape the foster parents that the state imposed on him. Sometimes one of us had to tell him to shut up.

Jack made a little room in a corner with a couple of extra.

"Hey, Lips. Get over here and don't say another word." Lips got up and went over to Jack and looked in the corner.

"Here is your bed. Two blankets and a brick for a pillow. If you want to fancy it up, I'll give you another brick, that's all the comfort we can give you." Jack smiled at our noisy new friend.

"Hey guys, thanks a lot."

"Now go with One Eye. He is the storekeeper."

One Eye grabbed him by the arm and led him to his

corner in the next room, Lips was so happy to have found a few new friends, he would have gone anywhere with us without question.

"Here take whatever you want. There are clothes, shoes, socks, and lots more, knock yourself out." Digging through the stack, Lips looked like a kid in a toy store.

"Man, you've got everything here, this is a big building. What do we do about wash up and using the bathroom?"

One Eye explain that the public library had a restroom by the entrance and that the employees didn't seem to care if we used it if we went in one by one.

"Go ahead and change after you find what you need. I'll wait on you in the next room." As he turned around to leave, One Eye remembered the most important rule.

"If you need something else, ask first. I'll get it, there's a lot of other kids out there that are in need. We take care of each other." We were all waiting when One Eye came and sat down with us.

"Is everybody comfortable with Lips?"

"Seems okay," Butterball answered.

Jack put his hand over his ears, but shook his head up and down, as Bill gave his approval.

"Well I guess he's in." came the verdict from Bill. After a minute of silence, I spoke up.

"Jack and I spent all our money for lunch."

"That's cool. I was planning to beg on the corner of Main ad Ruston Street," replied One Eye. With one eyeball out, woman have pity on me and give me more money that the men."

"I'll come with you to keep a lookout." Bill offered, "I heard that Rick is hanging out there," Jack jumped to his feet.

"Well, I need to go and teach that bully some manners." He started popping his knuckles and flexing his muscles.

"Hold on a moment, Jack, sit down. We don't need to

start a fight. Our life is complicated enough, let me talk to him." I said hoping to keep him out of trouble. Jack was about the strongest guy on the street and our protector, like a big brother, but his quick temper stirred up problems sometimes before troubles started.

"Alex, you're kidding. He beat you up and left you for dead, and you want to talk to that scum?' One Eye reminded me.

"That's why I should go." Said Jack in an angry voice,

"If he touches one hair on your head, he's blending with the pavement."

"Deal, but give me one chance to talk to him," as I laughed at Jack's shadow boxing his own self.

Lips appeared in the doorway standing in his new clothes with his old rags under his arm, "what do I do with these?"

Nobody answered him. We were all looking at him— sports shirt, slacks, and jean jacket made him totally presentable. Bill joked.

"Frame them for the memories,"

"No, we dump them." I said.

"Whatever. If you and Jack are going with One Eye, then I guess I'll head out to work." Bill turned around to leave for his job delivering groceries. It was low pay, but the owner's wife knew his situation and always gave him ripe fruits and packages of stuff about to expire to compensate. Besides, the tips were usually decent, and he got to clean up the store at night for extra change.

I got up to leave with One Eye a couple of minutes later when, Lips spoke up.

"What about me?"

"Right, I forgot. Come with us or crash here if you want, but if you go out alone, be sure that no one follows you. We don't need a city slicker investigating this building. It's too comfortable to lose it. And if you want to hang out with us, then you must stay away from drugs.

We already have enough ways to get killed or busted." I wanted to be sure that he understood the rule of the house.

"No problem. I saw to many space cadets in those homes, I don't want to be a druggie. I'll be careful when I live, for now I think I'll just hang on and sleep." Lips got the picture and obviously felt at home.

"See you later Lips". He had joined our family.

~~~

CHAPTER 8

One Eye and I left the building and walked across our bad section of town to an area with more people and money. It was finally starting to warm up, the sun was shining, and it took only about twenty minutes to reach Main and Ruston Street. The street was packed with swarms of people.

"To many folks," was my opinion. One Eye saw it differently.

"Leave it up to me. This corner is a money maker."

"Okay, I'll watch." I didn't want Rick sneaking up on me again, that was for sure, mostly I didn't see the point in one street kid getting beat up by another. Maybe he'd listen to reason.

It took me less than five second to spot Rick half a block down, soaking up the sun with two of his buddies. For me, there was only one thing to do, just walk right up to him with all the confidence in the world, shield myself with energy, and let go of all the anger and fear. Positive energy counters negative energy. (Where did that thought come from?) I wondered for a moment.

"Self, assurance always disconcerts the opposition," Was my last thought as I approached Rick and his buddies.

"Hey, Rick. Soaking the sun?"

"Now look who is here. Come after another fat lip?" Rick and his pals got to their feet and started trying to look tough. They all looked at me like my days were numbered.

"Take it easy," I said trying to keep my voice cool and confident.

"Why should I? I can whip you any day, so scram." Rick moved toward me and motioned to his friends who backed off a few steps.

"I just came to talk" I continued.

"Talk about what, rich kid? Why do you keep pretending you're having a hard life?" he snarled.

Had he beaten me up because he thought that I was rich "What do you mean, rich kid?"

"Cut the crap. You know what I'm talking about. I've been asking around, and so have your dad's company people." Rick caught me off guard with that last statement.

"Well if you've been asking around, you know I 'm from a small town, and I haven't gone back once since my dad kicked me out. I didn't need his rule anymore," I said, but I was wondering if my father had really been looking for me.

"Kicked you out? Bull! You're just spying, probably working for the cops or something." Rick sat down on an empty crate pushing his long dirty hair out of his face.

"Oh, yeah, I just love sleeping on cardboard, wearing dirty clothes, walking around with an empty stomach, and I especially like smelling like a wet dog all day and constantly looking over my shoulder for guys like you. Man, this is the rich kid's life, for sure," I sarcastically shot back.

"Yeah, yeah, you're a good man—good at faking it." This was harder that I thought it would be. This guy is sour on life. "Faking it? I can't look people in the eye, I'm so ashamed." It was hard telling this to a bully that I was ashamed, but it was true.

"That's crap!"

"My father kicked me you because I couldn't sleep at night and slept most of the day, he thought I was just a lazy, a bum." Maybe Rick could relate to getting kicked out.

"I heard about your wandering at night and that imaginary shadow that haunts you. Man, you are nuts or crazy. Just get lost, weirdo." He turned away.

"Fine. Have it your way," I said as I started to leave.

Rick called me back. "All right, so maybe you're not rich, maybe you're just a street bum like me. Why should we be friends?" For the first time he didn't sound so threatening.

Seizing the opportunity, I answered. "First of all, we all have enough problems in the street without creating more by fighting among ourselves. Second, I heard about you helping Peggy ward off an attacker as she came out of the shelter. I wanted to shake hands with a hero."

"You heard about that?" as his surprise spread across his face.

"Yeah, that's is the word in the street,"

"Well, she was getting mugged, and I just couldn't let it happen," he shrugged.

"That's what I mean. We have enough crap around us. That's why we need to take care of our own, and not waste time beating up each other. Street folks got to stick together, and you did great helping Peggy."

Rick smiled and flexed his chest like a proud peacock. He looked me right in the eyes and said, "She's the only real person around us. She cares, and half the kids would starve if it weren't for her." I extended my hand.

"So, let's shake," Would he do it, I wonder?

Rick put his hand in mine. All animosity was gone. He had a look of pride on his face and a twinkle in his eyes.

"So, you really heard? He questioned, still finding it hard to believe.

"Yes, we all think that you are a hero," I smiled and felt

truly relaxed for the first time.

"Stop. You'll make me blush." Rick glanced back to see if his friends could hear us.

How strange it was to see this side of the toughest guy on the street, "You are blushing? Get out of here Rick." I said leaning toward him so no one could hear.

"Well, this is the first time anyone thought I did something good."

Jack snuck up on us swaggering like a tough guy. I stepped between Jack and Rick seeing Jack's desire to help me and I said. "Everything's okay. We're just chatting about Rick helping Peggy last week."

Jack stammered. "Just checking on my pal. Let's go and see if One Eye has struck it rich."

I reached out and gave another street shake to Rick. "See you around, Buddy," Rick responded and smiled. I grinned back at him knowing that things were going to be better.

"Nine bucks in twenty minutes, I am on a roll," he laughed. One Eye had been lucky.

"Give me five, man. We'll go get the donuts." Jack was always as hungry as Lips was talkative.

"All right, Jack, but I'm saying. Like I said. I'm on a roll. Bring me a jelly."

"Jelly it is," Jack and I headed down the street.

~~~

CHAPTER 9

Every day in the street was a struggle. Most of the time it was hard, but it was never boring. In my next life I think I'll pick a better way to make it. Incredibly early one summer morning, just at the break of dawn, I came home from my nightly wanderings. I took off my shoes and t-shirt and got ready to lie down. Butterball and One Eye were sound asleep. It was then that the shadow appeared, more visible than ever, moving like crazy. I tried to dismiss it, but it gone more agitated. Hell, it got downright aggressive.

"What do you want? Go away. You don't scare me!" Again, it just vanished.

At that precise moment Lips walked into the room. We moved like he was in a trance and entered as silently as a cloud. He was shaking like a leaf on a tree in the strong wind. He tripped over Bill's blanket and almost lost his balance. He steadied himself and stood perfectly still, not uttering a sound.

I couldn't really see him clearly because It was still dark, I sensed that something was wrong. I started to panic inside. I felt a cold invading our room, as for Lips he just stood there, frozen in the dark

"What is going on?" Butterball asked while rubbing his eyes.

"Don't know." Said Bill, now awake also. "He tripped over me"

I jumped out of my bed like greased lightning, body hairs raised like a wild cat with the premonition of danger, I grabbed Lips by the shoulders. The panic was gaining on me. The shadow had just been an irritation or aggravation earlier. But now this?

"Talk to me, Lips. What is going on with you? You always talk. Talk now. Now, is not the time to keep it inside."

Suddenly I realized that I was shaking him as hard as I could, then I just grabbed him in my arms holding on to him. Everybody was up now and scared out of their wits. I took a deep breath. It was not the time to panic. Just stay calm. I grabbed Lips on each side of his head and looked him square in the eyes. They were empty, vacant, and distant. Tears slid down his cheeks, and his mouth was quivering.

"Talk to me Randy. What is going on with you? Snap out of it." By now the unknown was really overpowering me.

"Lips don't let go. Talk. You know we love you, but for god's sake, snap out of it."

Man, he was like a zombie. What had put him in such a state of shock? I had to snap him out of it. I took him into my arms. The shadow reappeared just behind Lips, it remains perfectly still, I began to feel an energy entering me—a peaceful strength—flowing through me and Lips.

The shadow slowly faded, but the room seemed filled with a soft light and a serene feeling.

First, Lips shook his head and just a whisper came out. Nobody could hear but me. His voice was incoherent at first, then after a few times the words came out clear enough to understand. They chilled me to the bone.

"He's dead, he's dead, he's dead, he's dead..." Lips kept repeating this phrase like a broken record, and now tears were pouring out of his eyes.

"Okay, Randy, calm down. Who's dead? I can't help

you if you don't tell me what's going on."

He looked at me like he was in a dream. "It's too late, Alex, he's dead."

"Who? Where? What happened? I don't understand. Say something." By now the terror was giving me cramps in my stomach. I couldn't swallow. The rest of the gang was panicked, to say the least.

"Out there behind the old bakery, he's lying there in blood."

"Who? Tell me."

"He's dead! Jack is dead!"

I didn't need to hear any more. I ran the four and a half blocks in record time. I ran around the corner behind the bakery, then jolted to a full stop. Tears were in my eyes. Jack was lying in Simon's arms.

"I called the ambulance." Said Ghost.

Jack was alive, barely. His eyes were glassy. I knelt beside him and told him to hang on. With all the strength left in him he lifted his arm and pulled my head to his lips. He whispered a word in me ear and died quietly in Simon arms.

In the background we could hear the siren from the ambulance getting closer. My anger was overwhelming.

"You did this! You used your influence and pushed him to steal cars and steal jewelry. Go away! Don't touch him!" I screamed.

Simon just looked at me. "Calm down. You're upset."

"Upset? You idiot, I said don't touch him!"

Simon eased Jack's body onto the pavement as the ambulance pulled up with its tires squealing. I didn't want to wait. I took off and left Simon to deal with the body and the barrage of questions that would follow.

Jack was dead. Dead. I was too shocked to register anything else in my mind. What Jack had whispered to me didn't make any sense. The word kept coming back to me, "Simon."

I know he died in his arms, but Simon? Was he the last guy he recognized or wanted to make right with or what? And why had he pulled me to his lips to say that word as his last?

"Simon." It didn't make any sense. I panicked. Just the night before Jack and I had talked and laughed, and now my life once again came to a screeching halt. Everyone reacted mostly with denial to the violence we saw and experienced.

I got mad. How could he be dead? We all got used to his coming and going, sometime disappearing for days at the time. At time he had been hiding, other times he had been in jail for petty theft or something minor. We could usually find out where he was through the other street kids.

I remember how we met. I was curled up in that AC shack above the print shop all beaten up. He never asked any questions; he had helped get me to safety and it was just his time to go. I didn't have the answers to all my questions. Nobody did.

~~~

CHAPTER 10

I was walking around in a daze. The night was cold, and it was raining. Nothing mattered anymore. I just lost it. It must have been two or three days since I had eaten or slept. My mind was scattered. I had lost all concept of time, it didn't matter. My stomach thought otherwise and brought me back to reality.

Where was I? The grayness made it hard to tell what time it was, and I had obviously just walked clear across the city. As a matter of fact, I was in a small suburb of the industrial part of the city.

I shook my head a couple of times. Boy, did it hurt. Having no food for so long made me dizzy. I was shaking like a hundred-year-old man. *This is humiliating. I've got to do something to get out of this funk. Swell, I was talking to myself. What's next? Hallucinations?*

It was this incident that got me off the street. I was slowly coming out of my altered state, and reality gaining a firm grip when I stumbled across a small fair. Lots of noise, strings of lights running around the outline of the Ferris wheel and carousel. Neon lights flashed "FUN" wherever l turned. Hawkers cried out the thrills promised on their ride was the best. People were smiling, children were laughing, couples were holding hands and carrying the stuffed animals won for their sweethearts. The weather was warm, and it seemed as if no one had a worry in the world. I guess these people had worked hard for this day of fun.

All the lights, music, crowd, kids laughing, and people shouting put me in a rejuvenated mood, I stood right in front of a cotton candy stand. A light breeze gently caressed my face. I was drunk with the smell of this mountain of 'sugar on a sick.' A good crowd can be the best remedy when you are down and out. I looked around me. If I picked someone's pocket? I was sure to get caught because I was too weak to run. I could already imagine two policemen running after me and hauling my butt off to jail. No time to risk something crazy.

As I dismissed that thought, I found myself in front of the bumper car ride, looking at the electrified grid of wires above the kids' head. The grid spit out fierce blue sparks. The cars were vivid in color and raced toward each other on the rubber floor, bumping into each other amidst explosions of laughter and screams. It was exhilarating to watch.

The boss lady was at the cash register selling tickets and briefing everyone on the rules, "No pushing, no bad language, keep your hands and arms in the car at all time. Don't get out of the car until you come to a complete stop and I say it's okay to get out."

All the kids nodded their heads. They understood. The line was long, but constantly ebbed and flowed as a new wave ran to jump into the recently vacated cars.

Her assistant was tall and slender, and sad looking. He would jump from car to car before the ride started to collect tickets. He was as agile as a cat, leaping from one car to another without touching the floor beneath him. In one fluid effort, he would grab the tickets and rip them in half. He didn't waste a single motion, not even to glance at the floor, his eyes were already on the next customer waving their ticket.

I was about to leave this show of acrobatic prowess when something strange happened. Maybe it was the hunger that made me see sharper, allowing me to see something just before it happened. In any case, just as I turned to leave, I had a premonition, and it nailed me to the ground. I couldn't move and had to watch. I knew something terrible was about to happen.

At this moment, the young attendant was jumping off the last car. All the tickets were in his hands, but as he jumped, his foot missed the wooden platform. At the same time, the boss, not realizing what had happened, turned on the juice. Sparks started flying, and the cars started moving and one ran over the young attendant's leg. It all occurred in a split second followed by a bloodcurdling scream.

The boss immediately turned off the power. People jumped onto the floor. The lady's husband made his way through the crowd. The attendant was moaning from the pain, his ankle dangling like a wet rag. He was in so much pain, there was only one thing for him to do—pass out.

The lady at the cash register grabbed the phone to call for help. One first aid person who wanted to help was already fighting his way through the crowd, but there was nothing he could do.

The ambulance arrived withing minutes. Two paramedics came through the crowd with their bag in hand. They knelt beside the young man and proceeded to wrap the young man's ankle to secure it. The other one checked his vital signs for shock.

The young man regained consciousness. He grimaced from the pain, as the police were asking questions about what had happen. The lady was closing the cash box, and the crowd was beginning to thin out. The paramedics lifted the poor guy after strapping him on a stretcher. The owner wasn't too happy.

"Honey," the cash register lady said to the ride operator, "What are we going to do?"

"I don't know. I guess I'll run the ride myself and take

tickets. I'll lose one turn for every four, but that's better than closing."

"All right I'll go open the register."

"You do that." He replied, returning to the main control.

"Hey, boss," I called as I waved my hand to get his attention.

He looked at me and turned his attention away from me. Guess he had experienced enough trouble to waste time on a bum-looking kid.

"It's bad, isn't it?" getting his attention again.

Not looking at me he answered, "Yes. Broken leg, but it could've been worst."

"Hey, six weeks in a cast and he'll be as good as new," I was trying to sound positive.

"Six weeks. Sure, but in five weeks the season will be over."

I tucked in my shirt and asked, "Do you have somebody to replace him?"

"No, but I'll do it myself in the meantime," He still hadn't looked at me closely.

"Listen. I watched your helper. It didn't look too hard to me. I can do the same, except break my leg, of course," I said.

For the first time he turned around and looked at me. I wasn't a great sight, I had a ten-day beard, I was dirty, I looked more like a hobo than street hood. Plus, I probably smelled ripe. When you live in an abandoned building you never look like a model on the cover of a magazine.

"Look, boss. A bar of soap and a razor blade will make me look human again, I promise, the name is Alex."

"Okay, Alex, I'll take you on a trial basis." He was giving me a chance. "Don't forget, in five week the season is over. You get $225 a week—plus room and board. Okay?"

"Great. I'll take it." (What a break, oops, I mean

opportunity,) I thought.

"Now look here, all you have to do is to collect the tickets as fast as you can. Take your time until you get the hang of it," he shook his head as he walked off.

I was tired, but happy, I had a job. I went right to it, jumping on those cars. Sometimes I did its right others went as smooth, the boss smiled the whole time. He signaled to his wife that everything was okay.

I lost track of time. I was overwhelmed by the lights, hunger, noise fatigue and hard physical work that was required. The next thing I remembered was the boss tapping me on the shoulder.

"Alex, put the hood over the cars while I close up. My wife is cooking our meal for the evening. We'll be done in fifteen minutes."

Boy, that was a long fifteen minutes. I could barely hang on. All the cars were lined up and had their hoods on.

"By the way, my name is Harold. Let's go inside. I'll introduce you to my wife, Jane."

I followed Harold inside the trailer, I observed it was spacious and decorated with taste, Harold went over and put his arm around his wife waist, "Jane, meet Alex."

"Nice to meet you, Alex. You look pretty worn out. Have a seat," she said smiling.

"Hi, Jane. Do you mind if I freshen up a bit?" I asked.

"Great idea, since it's going to be another forty-minutes before supper is ready. Harold goes into the closet. There are clean clothes in there that will fit Alex."

"Which closet?"

"You know, the one where you store your toolbox."

Harold proceeded to show me the spare bedroom with a double bed in it. It was more comfort that I had experienced in two years.

"Shower is next door," as he pulled out a shirt and a pair of pants out of the closet.

He'd barely stepped out the door before I was stripping off my clothes. There was a towel he must have laid out when I wasn't looking. I grabbed it and stepped out in the hallway. Jane was making noise with her pots and pans. While Harold was channel surfing with the remote control while sipping a cold beer.

I pulled the bathroom door closing it behind me. *Were these people for real?* I thought. There have been no questions about my appearance, and unless they had a major sinus problem, they had to have noticed my smell. Here I was in their home which was my realization as I turned on the water and soaked my body in the soothing warm water. I soaped my entire body and I rinsed off, wanting to laugh and cry at the same time. What a joy! A hot shower must be one of the great pleasures in life. I stayed a long time, running out of hot water made me jump out and I shaved quickly.

I dried my hair, and even slapped on a bit of aftershave. I went into my room and put on the clothes Harold had laid out for me. It was time for some serious business—food.

As I came out of the bedroom. Jane and Harold looked at my transformation in disbelief, and then laughed. Harold turned off the TV immediately.

Jane greeted me, "Come, Alex, have a seat any place at the table."

"No, right here at the head of the table. You did a great job today,"

"Yes, you did," echoed Jane, "Without you we would've had to close early. With no training you sure put on a show."

"Yeah, the way you looked; I didn't think you 'd last twenty minutes out there," Harold laughed.

"What do you want to drink?"

"Something fizzy," was all that I could utter overcome by her genuine kindness, although still a little suspicious.

She reached into the freezer and pulled out a few ice cubes. She put them in a glass and got a soda out of the fridge as I sat down at the head of the table. My emotions were overwhelming. I couldn't remember the last time I had sat in a home for a real meal.

"So, tell me, Alex, where are you from?" Harold asked.

"Here, there, everywhere," I replied, uneasy about answering questions.

Harold just took a long sip of beer. "Okay. If you don't want to tell me, I was just making conversation,"

"No, it's not that, I'm just..."

"It's all right. I am glad we found you, or you found us. Here has some soup,"

"Vegetable beef, homemade," said Jane.

"Have bread with it." Harold passed me a basket full of rolls.

I was in such a rush; I burned the roof of my mouth with the first sip of the soup and had to quickly take a swallow of the soda to ease the pain. Unable to remember when I had eaten last, my stomach reminded me to go slowly. So, I sipped the broth and added small bites of bread between each spoonful of soup. Later, Jane brought out a pot roast with potatoes, carrots., and plenty of gravy. I felt like I was on top of the world.

"It's wonderful," I said, breaking the silence.

"We're glad that you like it, by the way, today is Sunday, and tomorrow we are closed. That means I don't, which is just as well, because you are going to be sore tomorrow."

He kind of cocked his head, "After the physical labor you did today, I'd bet on it, and that was only a half day."

"I didn't think of it that way. It's been so long since the day of the week mattered," I verbalized.

"Well you just sleep in. Harold will be outside, and I'll be cleaning the house," Jane announced as she started to clean off the table.

"What time is it now?" I wondered out loud.

"One AM," they said in unison.

"You didn't eat much. Nothing wrong, I hope,"

"No. I'm just not used to such a feast and eating that much, but it was great."

She seemed to accept my response not knowing how I had understated my eating habits and asked, "Want a slice of cake?"

"Could I save it for tomorrow?" Realizing that she might need help, I took my plate to the sink.

"Sure. The fridge is right here if you get hungry in the middle of the night."

Rubbing my stomach, "Me? I don't think so."

"Well, Harold does it all the time,"

"Jane!" Harold tried to look shocked, he couldn't contain his laughter.

"What? Did you think that I didn't know?"

"All right, you caught me. I think I'll go and read my newspaper," Winking at me as he got up and headed for his recliner. "You do that," She touched his hand gently as he walked by her. Jane turned around to talk to me.

"Go to bed when you are ready. I'll have food prepared for you by the morning. We don't get up before noon."

"Mighty nice of you. I'm sure I won't either," I said. "Good night and thanks for everything."

"You too" Harold added as I passed him on my way to my room. He was already engrossed in an article.

I went to my room, took off my clothes, and slid between the fresh sheets. I pulled the cover over my head, and the next thing I knew sunshine was bathing my whole room. The sun was high in the sky. It took me a moment to remember where I was.

I had no dream, no voices, no confusing feeling. So many good things had happened in the last twenty-four hours. *It must be a dream,* I thought to myself.

~~~

CHAPTER 11

The first movement caused me to moan as I woke up. Oh, yeah, the bumper cars. My muscles were jumping and screaming in agony. This was not a dream.

Very slowly I extracted myself out of the bed. I wrapped a towel around my waist and headed into the bathroom for a shower. The hot shower brought me back. I dried my body and brushed my teeth with a toothbrush Jane had left for me. I went back to the room and put on the new clothes. Then I walked in the living room, the trailer was deserted, the TV was off, and there was a light in the kitchen with a note on the table.

"Help yourself," was all it said.

I decided to step out and smell the fresh air. I opened the door, and Jane was sitting just outside the door on the step knitting a sweater.

"For my husband, do you want me to fix you something to eat?"

"Not right now, thank you."

"How about a cup of coffee?"

"Yes, that sounds great. Where is Harold?" She laid the knitting down.

"I'll go make a pot. Harold would probably like a cup also. He's greasing the wheels, he does it every week."

"Maybe can help him," I said as I started toward the

cars.

She called back to me, "Tell him I'll bring him a fresh cup."

"Yes, ma'am."

"Alex, you don't want to make me feel old. Call me Jane, please."

I turned to salute her, "Jane it is."

"Can I help?" I found Harold who was sitting with grease up to his elbows. I stooped down balancing myself with the steel bar feeling the muscles in my legs tightening with pain.

"No, just ten more minutes and I'll be done. This is my last car. I've been at this for the past two hours." Harold added, "How'd you sleep?"

"Best night's sleep I've had in a long time. Jane is bringing us fresh coffee."

Harold put the wheel back on. He tightened up the nut bolts and dropped the jack. "Great. Just in time to wrap up and wash my hands." He wiped his hands on a towel before grabbing his tools and the pail of grease.

"How are the muscles, Alex?"

"Excruciating I must admit,"

"Told you." He smiled

"I am glad we're off today."

We walked to the shed, and I opened the door while he put the tools in their right places. Jane appeared with two cups of steaming coffee, she had brought a tray with cookies, cream, and sugar.

"I forgot the spoon; Harold takes it black. I didn't how you liked it."

"No need, Jane, I just take cream." We all sat down and chatted. The whole week had gone by so fast. The soreness in my body got better every day. I slept without dreaming. My appetite returned. I could eat two meals a day plus a snack from time to time. As expected, I got better and faster at jumping the cars, and now Jane and

Harold treated me like a son and called me "a vacuum with teeth." They put their beliefs and trust in me. It had been such a long time since that happened to me, and I was grateful for it.

I was constantly smiling. We got up every morning around eleven AM and drank coffee. Harold took this time to tell me his story. He told me where he stopped to put up his ride, where and how he met Jane, how long he'd been doing this job. The ride was a legacy from his father.

I appreciated his honesty and willingness to tell me his story, but I wasn't quite ready to tell mine. I was blocking the past for now, what little I remembered I needed more time before I could even think about all that happened. He knew I was a kid from the streets, but he was smart and respectful; and didn't ask questions.

Jane was always cooking or washing dishes, straightening the trailer, always busy. That was the most discreet woman I had ever met. There was a feeling of trust growing in me.

"Harold," I said one Sunday.

"Yes, Alex?"

Before I realized it, I was pouring out my story to him. I was relieved to have someone to talk to and surprised at how much I remembered. Maybe Jack's death shook something loose. I told him all that I could remember about Mom and Dad, Adam, the shadow, and the void. Then I really got wound up telling him about the street kids, especially Simon, One Eye, and Jack, and how we pulled together. It took me close to three in the morning to tell him, and he never interrupted. Every morning I picked up where I had left off the day before, and he would sip his coffee and listen.

In the afternoon, we would run the ride for the kids, it was truly another good week. No worries about anything, just working and living in the moment. During the second week I started to think about the other kids, but I needed more time to regain my energy.

The following weeks were spent getting to know all the folks operating the other rides. When I had a moment of slack time I walked around and everyone got to know me,

"Alex, come get a bag of roasted peanuts," or "come have one stick of cotton candy," Sometimes it was, "Come play the water pistol race, it's on me." I was the new kid there and became a new member of the family. It was a fairy tale life.

Every night when I returned to my room after a shower, watching TV and talking to Harold, I took the time to savor my good fortune. I felt safe in this room, the peace it emanated was enough to bring back a feeling I hadn't felt in a long time. Hope.

Every Sunday night like clockwork, Harold brought me my pay and said, "Thank you." It was me who should've been thanking him, but he genuinely felt good about my being in his home. Jane, on the other hand, had observed that I had a voracious appetite for chocolate brownies. She made sure that she never ran out of them. The whole five weeks we had brownies. A couple of nights I wept tears of joy and appreciation in my bed overwhelmed by their kindness and charity.

During the third week, Sam came back, still in the cast for his broken leg. He had gone to visit some of his family and had come by to visit his old boss. He stayed for the day, then he left.

The last days sneaked up on us faster than anyone expected. Harold, Jane, and I were all silent as we sipped our coffee. We all knew that was coming. Funny how you can get attached to someone so quickly. We spent the whole day disassembling equipment. We pilled the steel bars out of the ground and unbolted the steel panels from the floor. Next, we piled the panels onto the truck, followed by the cars on a trailer. The overhang mesh we rolled up and coiled up all the electric cord. Everyone associated with the carnival was breaking down their rides. The day went by so fast with little time to talk.

By evening, everything was on the truck and trailer. Harold made one last tour to see if anything was missing. Then we all went inside for supper. Jane prepared my favorite meal, beef noodle soup, chicken in brown gravy, rice, sweet peas, and of course, brownies. (*Who knew when I would eat like this again*, I thought.

During dinner we chatted about everything irrelevant. We were all too sad to look at each other in the eyes. Harold got up and came back with an envelope that he presented to me.

I opened it in silence. There was a note of thanks and five hundred dollars.

"What is this for?" I asked him.

"The $25 is for your last pay with an additional $275 as a bonus for a job well done."

"But..."

"Not a word," said Harold, "A simple thank you will suffice." Words failed me. I just nodded.

Our address is in there. If you come down south, you always have a room and friends who will be glad to see you.

"And brownies," added Jane.

"We come here every year, at this time," continued Harold, "So, come out to see us, if you can."

"You two are the best."

"There is also the name of a lumberyard. I have a distant cousin that I see every year when I am in town. Go to see him and say hello for me. I am quite sure that he will have work for you."

I knew exactly where the yard was located, and I felt proud that Harold would recommend me. "I'll go Thursday."

"Good, because you are going on Monday." Standing in

disbelief I stammered, "You mean I have a job already?" Harold had all the details written down on a paper.

"Yes, it's all arranged. You'll be in training for a few weeks learning the layout, doing some stocking at night. I told him what a hard worker you are."

"I don't know what to say, I'm truly touched."

"Say nothing, just go and he'll explain the whole job to you. I don't know what the pay will be, but he is fair."

"If he's as fair as you are, I'll be rich in three months."

Jane and Harold laughed. We were eating our brownies and enjoying the moment. After dinner, we went to the local diner to celebrate.

"My treat," I said, but they would have nothing to do with it. Harold picked up the tab.

Back in the trailer, I was in my room when I realized that this was the last time I was going to sleep here. On the bed were the clothes I had worn when I arrived, all washed, ironed, and folded in an opened suitcase. I went out and found Jane in the recliner.

"Harold is in the shower,"

"You know why I came out."

"Look, the suitcase is for you. Also, the clothes you wore while working for us. Just take it, it's the least we can do." I knew it wasn't a request, but an order. I walked over and said, "Thanks." Then I leaned over and gave her a kiss on the cheek, turned around and went into my room. There was nothing more I could say.

Nine AM. The smell of fresh coffee brewing woke me. I put on my clothes and wandered out in the living room. Jane was walking around the trailer.

"So, you slept well?" She said laughing.

"What is so funny?"

"Your hair is all which a way's."

"Oh, yeah, it does that." I said combing my fingers through my hair.

"That is better, come and get your coffee, want cereal

or toast and jam?"

"Toast thanks. Where is Harold?"

"Talking with the other owners. We're all leaving at eleven AM."

Just for a second, I wished I were going with them. Where to exactly?

"We all put our money together and bought land in Louisiana. We leave the equipment there during the winter months."

Harold came in around ten AM, "All the guys are ready." He said, "We'll be pulling out on time."

I went around one more time, shaking hands with everyone and gave a few hugs, especially to the girls close to my age.

At eleven AM I gave Jane a real hug, she had tears in her eyes. I shook hands with Harold, it was short and sweet. Harold helped Jane in the truck and went around the front and got in the cab. He started the engine, put it into gear, and the truck moved forward. He didn't look back.

It was better that way. I was standing in the middle of the fairground holding my suitcase. Paper littering the place, and the place felt empty after all the activity from the past five weeks, I had just experienced living with decent, caring human beings.

~~~

CHAPTER 12

I took the first bus going to the center of town. Wow, what an ordeal! I had never ridden a bus before, and I didn't realize that "Exact change" meant "exact change" I had to ask three people before I had the exact change so I could finally get on the bus. The driver had the personality of a barn door. I sat three rows behind him and asked.

"Is it extra to sit down?" He just rolled his eyes and kept driving.

We passed many gray buildings, company trucks, tractor trailers and parking lots with cars. I noticed a few small factories and oil field equipment piled up behind chain-link fences. This part of town had no character whatsoever, strictly industrial.

Slowly trees started to appear, along with nice suburbia houses with manicured lawns. Some had white picket fences, dogs, and all the extras. Then the traffic became heavy, and the bus got crowded, I gave up my seat to let a pregnant woman to sit down. She smiled, thanked me, and seemed to be surprised by my courtesy.

I looked at the people on the bus. There were all types, all ages, and races from different walks of life. Most were dosing off or daydreaming, but they all had a look of hopelessness on their faces. I got a cold chill down my back just looking at them.

The feeling was to scary. I decided right then and there

that I was going to get off the streets for good and do something with my life.

Jane, Harold, and everybody at the fairground were always smiling, singing, helping each other or just visiting. I had experienced the way that I wanted to live-like they did, with a happiness that was contagious. I had spent five weeks in a place where no questions were asked. You were accepted just as you were and genuinely welcome.

I suddenly realized that we were downtown. I got off the bus and looked for the connection to my part of town —slum city. I found it and gave the bus driver my transfer ticket. He was much nicer than the previous driver, the bus was almost empty. I went to the back of the bus and sat down.

I started to think about my future, I had worked for five weeks. No one had let me pay for anything, and room and board had been included. Harold had given mean extra week's pay, thus far, I had spent only ten dollars. I had $1,350 plus a job waiting for me, my goal was clear, I am going to get an apartment and start over.

Lips was the first one to see me when I walked into the abandoned building.

"Alex, where have you been? We've been worried sick."

"Working." Is all I said.

The rest of them jumped up and crowded around me. I had questions coming at me from everyone including two kids I'd never seen before.

"Whoa, whoa. Hold on guys. Let me walk in first," as I put my bag down.

"We had everyone on the street looking for you," Lips ignored me and kept talking as usual.

"Yeah," said One Eye. I looked around and nothing had changed.

"All right sit down and be quiet. What have you guys been up to?"

"You first," they all insisted.

"Well, what's with Butterball?" seeing him stretched out on the cardboard floor.

"I'm sick, Alex," he moaned.

I'll take care of you. Now, everyone sits down, and I'll tell you what happened.

I spent the next three hours telling them about the five weeks I spent away from them. They were hanging on my every word. I talked about the fair, the lights, Jane, and her brownies. I last told them how I would jump from car to bumper car collecting the tickets, I told about my warm bed, the fattening food, greasing the wheels each week, and the daily showers. I described Harold and his jovial outlook on life. I mentioned the fresh laundry, and the smiling crowds. I talked with so much passion, even Lips stayed quiet the whole time. Nobody noticed that it was dark by the time I finished.

We all went to see Maggie at the doughnut shop for a celebration.

"Hi, Maggie."

"Alex, where have you been? Everyone's been looking for you, even Rick."

"You don't say. Just got a job." I said casually. She had her hands on her hips.

"Peggy was worried sick, since you never went to the shelter for food or a shower."

"You see, I'm doing all right. Even put on a little weight," motioning to my waist.

"I must say, you're looking good," She said and added softly, "By the way, I was so sorry about Jack."

"Thanks, Maggie," Before I could say more, several people had come over to ask question about "the job." The curiosity and excitement were skyrocketing with everyone talking at once, I calmly assured them that I would give them all the detail later. Maggie stood there patiently waiting to take our order.

"Five cup of coffee, and two lemonades, and the bill is on me." I finally got to reply.

"Coming up." She was back in no time with drinks and a few donuts.

"The donuts are on me,' she added with a smile, she was so glad to see me again.

After we devoured the donuts, I turned around and asked, 'All right, Lips, who are these kids?

"The chubby one on your right is Andre. The other one with freckles is Ellis," he answered. "They were huddled together near our building about a week ago, and we kind of became big brothers to them."

I couldn't help but notice how young they were and remembered how bad it had been for me at first Lips continued.

"We've fed them and give them a safe place to sleep and kept the druggies and perverts away from them."

"Good enough." I excused Lips and myself from the group and found another table.

"Now tell me about Jack's death?"

"Everything we know is sketchy," Lips muttered without looking in my eyes.

Putting the cup down on the table I faced him and placed my hand on his, "I don't care, Lips, you were there with him that night, so don't beat around the bush. Tell me everything you remember."

"Well we were walking around,"

"No bull, Lips, it's me, Alex, you're talking to."

"As I said, we were walking when Jack spotted a man getting out of his car to go in a package store. You know the one where Martin works."

"Yeah, yeah, go on," I pushed.

He took a sip of coffee and continued, "Jack saw an opportunity and said 'See you at home' as he walked toward the idling car. The owner of the car wasn't even inside the store when he happened to look back and saw

Jack moving towards his car. He spun on his heels and with a running leap, jumped on Jack grabbing him by his jacket, Jack slid out of his jacket and took off like a rocket."

"Where was Simon all this time?" I interrupted again with a purpose.

"Let me see. Oh, yeah, the Ghost was just pulling in the parking lot."

What a coincidence, I thought to myself. "Then what?" I pressured on.

"Well, that's all. Jack ran like mad, the guy chased him for a hundred yards, gave up, and threw Jack's jacket and cursed at the night. He came back, turned his engine off and went inside."

"And?"

"Ghost and I went into the night to search for Jack and found him behind the bakery, flat on his back," He stopped and just stared at the cup.

"He must have tried to go up to the fire escape, but a few of the bolt were rusty and I guess they broke under his weight and fell back with the metal ladder on top of him."

"Anything else?"

"No," was all he said. Lips was swallowing hard and fighting back tears.

"What was Simon doing during this time?" I hated to push, but for some reason I really needed to know.

"Nothing. He helped me to pull the fire escape off Jack."

"That's it?" thinking to myself that there had to be more, *Was it just a freak accident?*

"Ghost looked at Jack and said, 'I think he's dead, go get the others.' Next thing you were shaking me like a prune tree."

We sat there for a few minutes and then returned to the group, and I told everyone, "I want all of you to stay away from Simon."

"Why do you want us to stay away from Simon?" asked Lips.

"He gives me the creeps, that's all. Just a premonition. Trust me."

I was silent for a while, trying to put my thoughts in order before I spoke again.

"I can't figure him out. He only appears at night, he pushes us to steal for him, and we don't know anything about him. He's evil, I'm telling you." I smiled back at Butterball and said, "Well, guys, you won't be living at the 'Ritz' much longer.

"What are you talking about?" they asked almost in unison. "You'll see."

~~~

CHAPTER 13

I needed to talk to Maggie, so I got her attention and after attending four more tables, she came over.

"Yes, Alex?"

"Listen. What are you doing tomorrow?"

"Why? You want a date?" She asked, leaning toward me.

The question caught me a little off guard, I gulped, "Tempting, but for now, I need your help."

"Name it," was her reply.

"I need your shower; I have a job interview tomorrow."

"Way to go," she answered with a thumb's up motion.

"I also need you to go with me to the office at your apartment, two bedrooms if they have one," I added.

At that moment Maggie's mouth fell open along with everyone else's

"Stop staring, Maggie, I know I'm not that good looking."

"Yes, you are, but don't let it go to your head."

"Oh, that's a come-on if I ever heard one," Said One Eye, smiling and jabbing me in the ribs.

"Knock it off," I started to blush.

"Red become you Lips." Laughed.

"Can't take the heat, pretty boy?" Butterballs join in.

"Help me out, Maggie."

"Keep me out of this. You can handle it."

She smiled and turned away to check on the other

tables. We all hung around for a while longer with each one taking a turn at telling me what they had been doing while I was gone. There was a festive, family feeling to our group. I asked One Eye.

"What do you know about the brothers?"

"Well, they're not really brothers. Like I said, they were together when we found them, so we called them the brothers. Besides, they go everywhere together. Both were bruised badly. Dirty, hungry, and we couldn't get them to tell us anything."

The two brothers were happily sitting in a booth, munching on another order of donuts. Each had sugar from the donuts on their faces. I handed the 'brothers' napkins and tried to get a little more information.

"Hey, brothers, what are your names again?"

"I'm Andre."

"I'm Ellis," said the freckled one.

"How old are you?"

"I'm nine," Andre answered.

"I'm ten, and I can count to one hundred," Ellis boasted.

"That's is great. I need to talk to butterball for a moment, I'll be right back."

Butterball and I moved to another booth, Maggie came over with refills and sat down for a few minutes. I told her about the job I had. She was so happy for me. A couple of customers came in, and she hopped up and went back to the grindstone.

"Alex, are you really getting an apartment?" Butterball was fading fast. He was white as a sheet.

"That is what I want to talk about. I'm going to get a two bedroom. I have the down payment, and I want to share it with you, Bill, Lips, and One Eye."

"Bill hasn't been around for the last ten days."

"He'll come back." I knew instinctively.

"Why me, Alex?" Butterball seemed like a little kid

asking this question.

"If you need to know, Jack asked me to take care of you, and to make sure nothing happened to you." It just came to me, and they couldn't argue with my reasoning.

"Now stop asking so many questions, and let's go."

"When are we moving in?" Grinning with pleasure, Butterball seemed to feel better immediately.

"I'm going to look tomorrow, but it may take about a week or so. Now let's go," Getting up to the register, I waited to complete the plans with Maggie for the following day.

She told me that she was off the next day, and I arranged to meet her at her apartment about noon so she could take me to the office.

Since Lips had taken the kids home, Butterball and I walked back in silence to our hideaway. The streets were deserted. When we arrived everyone was still talking, except for the brothers, who were fast asleep. They slept in the corner clutching each other.

"Well, I'm going for a stroll," realizing that I needed to walk and sort out my plans.

"Need company?" Lips stood right beside me asking if a needed his help.

"If you want to go that is fine, but I am not much for talking,"

"That's okay, it's just good to have you back."

Butterball was already lying down. Lips grabbed the extra blanket and draped it over him and said, "I won't need it"

~~~

CHAPTER 14

We left the building quietly and walked along the streets of this miserable neighborhood in silence. We had followed this same route a thousand times, and I never got used to it. The absurdity of life in the street was getting to me, Harold had made me realize that there was so much more to living, the brownies helped, of course, Man, they were good. Well tomorrow I'm getting an apartment. That's a first step, Lips snapped me out of my thoughtful state.

"Hey, look, Alex. There is Rick."

"Hey Rick, do any heroic acts lately?" I called him over to us. Rick was like everyone else anxious to hear my story, so we walked to the park.

"You put on the bacon," he observed checking me out.

"Three meals a day did it to me," I enjoyed telling him about the fair, brownies, and the good life.

He sniffed in my direction, "Jeez, you even smell good."

After listening patiently, Lips said, "By the way, Rick, we got two kids in our building. We call them the brothers. They're really young."

"Say no more, I'll come to pick them up tomorrow."

"Where are you taking them?" I asked.

"Peggy told me that the city started a program for kids under twelve." Lips and I both felt relieved and told him so with a high five.

"I'll get by your place first thing in the morning," he added with authority.

We spent the whole night talking. I told Rick what had happened and then about my plans. Lips never said a word for several hours. He was all ears for a change.

"Sounds great. Maybe I could get a job,"

"Now, how can we? It's impossible to find a regular shower, no place safe enough to sleep, and we're always worry about food," Lips jumped in with Rick shaking his head in agreement.

"I know, I know. But after I get an apartment, you know that you can come shower every day." Rick was a smart guy, and he had come a long way.

"Hey, that would be a good beginning."

"Well, it's getting light, and I've got to get a few hours' sleep before I go over to Maggie's."

He looked at me like he wanted to ask a question, but instead just said.

"Don't forget, I'm coming to get the brothers."

"Okay, tell Peggy I'll see her soon."

We walked back to our place. Lips was so tired that he almost fell on his face and was snoring the second he laid down. I wished I had it so easy. Usually I spent a fair amount of time chasing my demons. Besides, I had to go see Maggie in a couple of hours. It would be good to doze off for a few hours.

I was half asleep when Pick came to pick up the brothers. They were quiet as they left, so I rolled over and buried myself in my blanket.

When I woke up, the sun was way up in the sky. Shoot, I was already late getting to Maggie's. I jumped up and ran all the way to her apartment. I was out of breath when I knocked on the door and smiled sheepishly as she opened it.

"It's 1:15, where were you?" With both hands on her hips, she stood blocking the doorway.

"Give me a break. I don't have a watch." I could tell she wasn't mad but just giving me a hard time.

"You're going to need one if you are going to work," She was still blocking the door.

"I'll find one," I shuffled my feet noticing my sweat soaked my shirt.

"I have a spare that you can borrow for now. Let's go."

"Hey, can't I wash my face? I just ran ten blocks, and I look like hell."

"Come on in, I'll show where everything is."

"Nice place I looked around as she pulled out a towel and found me a clean t-shirt. I realized that it was the first time I had been to her place.

After freshening up she locked the door behind her, and we walked over to the office. In no time everything was taken care of since Maggie did most of the talking. She told them that I was from out of town, and she would vouch for me. Her recommendation went a long way and made everything go smoothly. I would have to wait a couples of days while they cleaned an apartment that had been recently vacated.

Afterward Maggie drove me to the lumberyard, where according to Harold, there was a supposedly job waiting for me. We arrived around three PM. She parked the car, and we walked over to the customer service counter.

"Hi, I came to speak to Big Joe,"

"No one here by that name," replied the girl at the counter.

(Bummer, there goes my luck,) I thought to myself. A tiny five-foot tall guy turned around, and looked at me, Alex?

"You bet."

"Harold phoned me. When can you start?"

It was that simple. I had the job based solely on Harold's recommendation. After telling him that I could start right then and there, he told me that the next day would be fine.

I introduced Maggie to Joe, and we talked a little about Jane. Then he told me that jeans and a t-shirt were satisfactory work clothes. I was still having trouble believing my good fortune when I heard my new boss say.

"Then I see you tomorrow at 5:30 PM. Oh, by the way, only Harold calls me Big Joe."

"Whatever you say boss. I'll be here."

Nice meeting you Maggie.

We walked out to the car. I was still stunned. Just a handshake, and I had the job. Harold really knew how to take care of things. We had barely reached the car when Joe ran up to us.

"Hey, Alex." I turned around surprised.

"Listen, We're short-handed around here. Do you know anybody willing to work?"

"Yes, I know someone."

"Bring him with you tomorrow. Same as you, in jean and a t-shirt at 5:30 PM. I'll explain the job tomorrow." He was already stepping on a forklift shuffling a pile of wood.

"Congratulations!" Maggie spoke for the first time, "Where to now?"

"Nothing to do until tomorrow night. Let's go to the park downtown, the one by City Hall," I took her hand.

She drove through the maze of streets. The closer we got to downtown the more the traffic we had to deal with. People were rushing everywhere like a bunch of ants. I was so overwhelmed. New job. A place to live. Riding in a car, chatting about sweet nothing with a girl I really liked. It was happening too quick for me. *Just take a deep breath and go with the flow, I reminded myself as I took it all in.*

"What are you thinking about, Alex?"

Oh, nothing. Except things are happening so fast. She teased me.

"Don't chicken out."

"Who me? I just held a job for five weeks. I didn't know anything about when I started, and I ended up doing a great job. Besides, I like what is happening to me and I've decided that I am not going back to the life I suffered, and I am going to help the gang the best I can, mark my words." She gave me a hug at the red traffic light

"That is the spirit, Alex, here is the park. Help me look for a parking space." We parked and locked the car. After walking for a while, I spotted an ice cream stand, and we shared a large ice cream in a giant cop. I don't think that I have eaten ice cream since I left home, it felt good wolfing it down, and sharing this delicacy. Maggie grabbed my hand, it startled me.

"Maggie, why are you holding my hand?"

She shook her head tossing her hair in the wind, "it felt good. Why else?"

It did feel good but a little uncomfortable at the same time, "Well, you're really pretty, but things are moving too quickly. I need time to absorb all of this."

"I'm just holding your hand."

"Yes, I just need for you to understand that for the time being, I can't get involved. I've got too many things to take care of."

"I never said 'Let's get involved.' I was just holding your hand," she said and pulled her hand away.

"I know I am overreacting, but I have personal stuff going on," I was not about to tell her that I didn't sleep at night due to freaky nightmares.

She casually commented that she had heard about my shadow and horrendous dreams causing me to scream out in my sleep.

Sounds like everybody on the street knows. I might as well write to the local paper and tell the whole city, but you must see how important it is for me to settle this part of my life, I pleaded hoping she would just let this conversation end.

"Yes, I do," taking my hand again. "By the way, I saw Simon after you left last night"

"He is a creep, and I don't trust him. What did he want anyway?"

"Just to say Hi and asked how you were dealing with Jack's death."

"I haven't seen him since he held Jack in his arms, and I don't care if I ever see him again. Please don't tell him anything about me. For now, let's just enjoy the park. I don't want to think about it anymore."

We walked in silence very conscious of each other's presence, acknowledging our pleasure with an occasional exchange of smiles. She was generous, as usual, when she broke the silence with, "By the way, if you would like, feel free to come by my apartment and shower before you go to work."

"Can I bring Tony, I mean One Eye, so he can clean up also?"

"Of course. He's welcomes too,"

"What time should we come over?"

"When we get home, I'll give you the extra key."

"Thanks."

We walked slowly while we finished our desert. It didn't bother me that she was holding my hand, I had been clear, and I felt better about it. We sat on the bench and talked about lots of unimportant things, just getting to know each other. When Maggie got tired, we drove back to our part of town, and I kissed her before leaving her at her door. It was special.

"Night Maggie."

"Goodnight, Alex. See you later."

~ ~ ~

CHAPTER 15

I went back to our shelter. I needed to tell One Eye about his coming to work with me at the lumberyard.

He was sitting in the middle of the room eating a sandwich when I walked in. Butterball was curled up in a corner. I asked him if he felt any better and if he had eaten. He told me that One Eye had already taken care of him. Friends are like that, I told One Eye about the job, and he was excited, I was so tired at that point, I stretched out and went to sleep.

The sun was high up in the sky when I woke up. One Eye was ready to go. "Alex, glad you're up." "Morning to you too. Let's go to the shelter and see Peggy and get some food." The word food always got his attention.

Peggy was ecstatic to see me. She understood how hard Jack's death had hit me and was glad that I was back. She looked great and was always as pleasant as she was supportive to all of us.

"Rick told me you have a job and are getting an apartment. Alex, I'm really happy for you," She said, "How about something to eat to mark the occasion?"

"Twist my arm, Peggy."

"Hey, Tony, feeling good today?"

"Real good, Peggy."

She never called us by our nicknames, it seemed to be her way of showing respect. She always had a kind word for everyone, never gave advice and never judged. Oh, she had her problems, also. She kept the shelter open late always giving more than she was paid for and made time to listen to all the hurt. On top of that, the city gave her hell for bending the rule and threatened to replace her. She would just shrug her shoulders and sigh in resignation. She was a real gem.

After a good meal that restored our strength, One Eye and I went to see Joe. We even arrived a little early. Joe was surprised.

"No one comes to work early."

"Hi, Joe. We're just eager to start."

"Who is your friend?"

"Tony, but we call him One Eye."

"Well, not at work you don't. Here we respect each other and what would the customer think if Sam said over the PA, 'One eye' customer assistance in aisle fifteen,' No way am I getting into this one."

"Got you, Joe. Tony it is."

Tony and I went to the office to fill out a fair amount of paperwork and became familiar with the place. We were assigned to a fellow named Karl, and we followed his every move to learn the tricks of the trade. It didn't take long to learn how to smile and be pleasant to the customers restock the shelves. After a week we were answering questions and were able to find just about everything. We still had much to learn but were free from following Karl around all the time.

Karl was a nice guy, but we didn't really relate to him, and he couldn't understand what we had been through. I wasn't about to explain. As for Tony, he still could not believe his good luck. He would follow me in the aisles, saying how It felt like he was living in a dream.

A few days after starting our job, we moved into the apartment with the Rick and Maggie's help. There was a lot of laughter and feeling of disbelieve and joy. I was so glad that we got an apartment on the far side of the complex. That way there were no complaints about the kids coming in and out taking showers, resting, and just hanging out, in a safe place. We had an electric stove, and everyone agreed that hot soup was better than cold. Life was great.

One day at work I heard over the PA.

"Alex Beard, please report to the office."

What do they want? I asked myself as I excused myself from a customer. I walked over to the office and went inside.

"Hi Janet, what is going on?"

She was sitting at the front desk and answered without even looking up from her work, "Joe is waiting on you."

"Okay." I knocked on the door and waited until I he told me to come in, I went in his office.

"Alex, have a seat."

I was always impressed with the neatness and cleanliness of Joe's office, "Hi, boss. What can I do?"

"Listen, I was going over your application. Are you related to the Beard of Beard Excavating and Foundations?"

"Yes, I am. He is my father."

He just sat there a second, then asked. "What are you doing here?"

"Long story," was all I felt like answering.

"Well, I won't ask, but you know his truck shows up here from time to time."

"I can't stop him, it's a free country." My discomfort was obvious as I squirmed in the chair.

"I know, but his men have been looking for you." He added.

Trying to hide my surprise, I smarted off, "Yeah, and I believe in Cinderella."

"Don't get smart with me young man, I don't deserve it," Joe fired back.

"Sorry, Joe. There are a lot of bad feelings. I cut all ties with him."

"Like I said, it's none of my business, but he is still looking for you, and he is a big businessman now." Joe was telling me something I didn't know.

"I would appreciate it if you don't tell him or any of his men that I'm working here."

"Okay. Now do you want to work more hours?"

"Whatever you can give me, I'll take it."

"What about night watchman? It's more hours, he offered.

"It sounds perfect to me. Hey, I don't sleep much at night. That would be great."

"Done. You can start next week, but first I need to find someone to replace you." Joe explained that he wanted someone to start as soon as possible so I could show them the ropes. It didn't take any time for me to think of Rick, so I told Joe that I was sure I could bring someone in the next day.

"By the way, your friend Tony is doing a great job. Thank you for bring him here."

"Glad that you like him."

"Now get back to work." Joe really cared about people for all his tough appearance.

I went back to my aisle. Great. I was promoted after two weeks. What more could I ask for? I needed to ask Rick if he wanted the job. I just assumed he would want the job, but I had better check with him after work. He was always hanging around Bobby's restaurant. I focused back on my work and the customers.

It was 10:30 when I left the lumberyard, but I had just missed Rick.

"Martin, where is Rick?"

"He went to the doughnut shop to see Maggie."

I took off and ran to the shop and found him standing on the corner begging for money to eat.

"Hey, Rick. Stop begging."

"You're buying?"

"No, you are. You've got a job at the yard." I couldn't hold my excitement any longer.

When he realized that he would be working with Tony and me, making good money on a job for the first time in his life, he grabbed me and gave me a bear hug, swinging me around off the ground. Suddenly sensing that it might look like we were dancing, he jumped back and said, "Great, man, when do I start?"

"Tomorrow night. You can sleep at my place tonight and then you can shower in the morning."

"Loan me five bucks, Alex, I'm buying."

"Good. Let's celebrate."

We went in and had a good time. Maggie finished at midnight and joined us until we left at two AM. We all piled up in Maggie's car and laughed all the way home.

~~~

CHAPTER 16

The next few months were relatively quiet. The apartment was like a revolving door for anybody who needed help and would follow the rules. We never locked the front door. I had not seen the shadow since Jack's death. I would hear about Simon from time to time, he would ask about me, but I told everyone to keep mum.

By then I was working as the night watchman as well as closing. Tony and Rick were still working the day shift, which made it easier to pay the bills. I still had my nightmares and the void overwhelmed me each time I closed my eyes, but I had reached a point where I could ignore it for the most part.

One evening as I was about to start my shift, an older gentleman walked up behind me and totally caught me off guard.

"Hi Alex, how are you doing all?"

I turned around and looked right at him, but I couldn't place him. He looked familiar; however, I got no name, no recall, no nothing when I saw him.

"You don't remember me, do you?" he said, smiling through his gray beard.

"Can't say I do," I confessed.

"Pat. Patrick McGill. I work with your father."

"Right, how is the wife?" I answered, faking it.

"What wife? I have no wife."

Oops! First mistake, "Sorry. I forgot."

So many things from the past had gotten erased. Sure, I know my name and where I 'm from, I even remember Adam and Dad as well as the pain that I would like to forget. It's all the details—the details that make the difference that make you whole. That was what was gone, the joy, laughter, friendship, and caring for each other.

"Listen. Your dad has been looking for you. Why don't you give him a call?"

"I didn't know," which was the truth.

"Come on. He misses you. I'll come over, and we'll barbecue like the old days." All I could say, was.

"Well, I will think about."

"Just call him. Now that your father is alone, I spend a lot of time at his place." He paused and then reluctantly added, "So I see his loneliness."

"I'll give it some thought, about calling dad, I mean it," I said

"You do that, Alex. Well, I got to get going. Take care."

"So long." Now that he was gone, I relaxed a little. It didn't take long, however, before my mind started to ask questions. *Did he really miss me? Can I forgive him? Do I want to go back? What is the big deal? Why bother? So many questions made the work much more difficult.* I couldn't concentrate with this new distraction, maybe what I should do is talk to him. I didn't know anymore.

Boy, Pat sure confused me. I didn't even remember him. My head felt like it was going to explode. I thought those events were behind me, but no, they were coming back with a vengeance.

I didn't even hear the customers question. Sam came by to ask if everything was all right. I brushed him off and said, "don't ask." He knew me well enough to know that I was not in a mood to be pushed for details. I was freaking out, plain and simple. What a lousy felling. I don't even remember closing or watching the yard. All I remember is Joe arriving to open the gates.

"Alex, you look like hell."

"Sorry, Joe. Can I go home?"

"Yes, see you tonight."

"Have a nice day," I muttered.

I walked home without paying attention. I couldn't have told you If the sun was shining. All I remember is trying to control the anxiety, without much success. I arrived at the apartment, took a shower, ate something, changed clothes, listened to people talking. It was so irrelevant.

"Hey, snap out of it." Rick was shaking my arm, and One Eye was behind him with a puzzled look on his face.

"Alex, have you seen a ghost or what?"

"Why?" barely hearing his voice.

"Cause you're as white as a sheet."

I shrugged, "Never mind."

"Never mind, my foot. It's been two and a half years of you snapping in and out of your funk. Well deal, with it, man." Rick was serious.

"It's my problem."

"No, it is not just your problem. It's affecting every one of us. So, take the bull by the horns and solve this dilemma or you are going to explode." Rick pushed on.

"Now is the time, no more postponing you hear?"

"All right. I'm going to take a few days off."

"Good. I'll take care of everything here while you're gone."

"Appreciate it, Rick."

"Don't mention it, by the way, Alex, if you need to be covered at the yard, I can arrange it with Joe. Now sit down and eat."

"Okay. But get off my back." They had gotten to me loud and clear. It was time.

Rick, Tony, and I sat down and ate a couple of chili dogs. Afterwards I went in my room to think things through. Maybe I ought to go home and see my father, talk things over.

At one time, if I remember correctly, he was a natural healer. He always said that the power of the universe can be shaped or tamed at will, and if your intentions are pure, anything can be accomplished.

Maybe I should take time on my next day off to go and see him. I could ask him about my nightmares, the shadow, and above all, my lack of feeling.

I tried to close my eyes and get some rest, but too many thoughts were spinning inside my head. It was late morning before I finally passed out.

Butterball came in to shake me at five PM. Just enough time to get in the shower and get to my shift in time. The evening dragged by. I couldn't wait until the morning, my day off was coming up. Now that I had made the decision, everything else seemed to fall into place. I would go home and face Zach and see what happens.

~~~

CHAPTER 17

Seven AM. I couldn't wait to get up. The evening before I phoned Maggie at work and asked if I could borrow her car. She was more than happy to accommodate me, and all I had to do was come pick it up at her workplace.

Allen came in to open the yard. My anxiety grew, and I left like a bolt of lightning.

"Bye, Allen."

"Where is the fire?"

"I'll tell you in a few days." I muttered as I left.

"Slow down, kiddo."

I was already turning the corner on my way to Maggie's place of work. The morning was already warm. It was going to be a real scorcher. I got to Maggie's restaurant in less than fifteen minutes, she was waiting for me.

"I took the rest of the morning off, so you can drive me home then you get the car," She invited me in as soon as we got to her apartment.

"You're my guest and I can take advantage of the time we have together."

Stepped into her place and she shut the door behind us. I kissed her cheek.

"This is for lending me the car."

"Any time, Alex. Now I am going to cook us a breakfast, it won't take long so sit and relax"

"I have to get going Maggie, another time if you don't

mine."

"You have just worked an entire night and haven't eaten anything, beside it's kind of tough with both of us working at night to see each other even as friends." She motioned for me to sit down.

It felt good to be in her kitchen. It reminded me of Jane and Harold's. Maggie was stirring something on the stove, and I even liked that she asked me to help,

"How about getting the apple juice out of the fridge, the glass is over the sink on the left."

I grabbed two glasses and the juice as she finished setting the table. Her place was so simple and neat, not like my place where all my destitute friends were constantly dropping it to sleep, shower, rest, grab a warm bite to eat and feel safe.

"Alex, are you listening? Bring the toast from the oven and turn it off, please."

"Turn what off?" Realizing that she meant the oven and I turn it off, "Right, sorry night shift."

We sat down and ate the egg and sausage casserole, toast, juice, and coffee that she had prepared, and I was right—it tasted as good as it smelled. When I told her so, she blushed and surprised me by jumping out and coming over and playfully punching my arm making me laugh which aggravated her more. As I grabbed her wrists to stop her, she pulled away causing both of us to tumble on the floor still laughing.

Suddenly I looked into her eyes and felt this overwhelming urge to hold her in my arms. It was a completely new experience to feel the warmth of another human being. In an instant, I was holding her, kissing her, and caressing her hair like I never had before.

Coming to my senses, I gently pushed her away, "Oh Maggie, I'm so sorry."

"What for?" she answered gently, "I care for you, Alex."

"But I don't know what came over me," I lamented.

"Maybe you just let yourself feel."

I stood up still shaken by the intensity of the moment. "I think I had better go." She handed me the keys leaning over and kissing me on the cheek, "Have a good day," was all she added.

As I stepped out in the sunlight and walked to the car, I had a special and beautiful feeling that we would be together forever.

I started the car and rolled out of the parking lot with caution. For some reason, the day seemed brighter, maybe it was the closeness I had experienced with Maggie that gave me a new outlook on life, whatever the cause I was excited about going to see my father. After two hours in the mainstream of traffic on the Interstate, I turned south and headed out in the country via a scenic four-lane road. With my memory on hold, it would be a lot of fun to find my way home after so many years. I vaguely remembered the road and a few landmarks, but mostly I found myself driving through open field with fences covered with honeysuckle. Nothing so far gave me a clue.

Not long after turning right, the road narrowed to two lanes, and after a few miles I saw a small stone church— only one small town to go through.

I was really starting to have butterflies in my belly signaling a little anxiety, now I was too close to turn back.

On the other side of the second town I could see a small lake and recognized immediately the location where the tragedy had happened. Caught up in my memories I drove right into town and pass the house without recognizing it. Well, so much for concentration. Turning the car around, I drove slowly, and there on my right I saw our house. The landscape had changed, the bushes and trees were much larger, and several flower beds had been added.

After parking the car in the driveway, I walked to the

front door and rang the bell. My hand was shaking, and I suddenly realized how dried my throat was. *Why worry? After all, it's no big deal. It has been nearly three years, but after all, he is my dad.* When no one came to the door, I rang again, but still no answer. Might as well try the back door, it was open.

Entering the house, I was unexpectedly overwhelmed by emotion. It had been so long, I walked in unprepared for my response to the smells, the sight of the furniture still arranged exactly the same way as the day I left, an ashtray full to the brim on the coffee table, the remote and magazine on top of the television, books everywhere.

Nothing had changed except for the missing laughter of my brother Adam and myself. Wandering through the house I decided on an impulse to go downstairs to the basement while waiting for my father to return.

I opened the door, turned on the light and went down the stairs. Mostly boxes, so I started snooping around, mostly junk and records from Dad's business, tools, more boxes with china and crystal wrapped in old newspaper, clothes, boots, toys, and old pictures, nothing had been thrown away. I sat there looking through pictures of us playing baseball, the company barbecues, the three of us in front of the old church, an old photograph of my mother. She was such a beautiful woman. More photographs of Adam and I in the pickup truck, playing on the swing and fishing on the pier, but none of these pictures made sense.

I saw myself in the pictures and recognized Dad, Adam, and Mom, I could not remember how It felt to be a part of the activities. Even the toys didn't have any special meaning *Well, guess I might as well wait upstairs.*

Reaching the top of the stairs, I was conscious of the smell of the house and had a fleeting memory but couldn't make heads or tails of it. As I walked through the living room one more time everything was familiar, still It seemed too far away to trigger my memory, I went into the kitchen, I think that we had a lady who worked for the us three or four days a week, but for the life of me, I couldn't think of her name. I opened the fridge *Let me see* I whispered; a drumstick seemed inviting. So, I grabbed it, took a bite, and savored the flavor and taste slowly as I walked on my father's study. The rays from the sun were seeping through the sheers flooding the room with soft light as I walked in his office. Father's desk was cluttered with papers including blueprints, bills, notes, a framed photograph of Mother and another of Father, Adam and me holding soccer balls.

~~~`

CHAPTER 18

As I opened the drawer looking for anything that might help me to put all these clues in context with the last three years, I hear a car pulling in the driveway. Good, it must be Father. Returning to the living room, I saw him coming through the side door. Since he was not expecting anyone, let alone his son, he was visibly startled by my presence.

"Alex?"

"Yes, Father, It's me."

He just stood there obviously too emotional to say a word or move, so I decided to go to him. My heart is pounding, what do you say after almost three years.

"Help me, Father, this is not easy."

As I crossed the room toward him, he started toward me with his arms open wide.

"Welcome home, son, let me look at you," as he stepped back looking me over.

"It feels strange to be back home after all this time." I noticed that he looked older, when I left, he had seemed so tall, and now we stood shoulder to shoulder.

"Well, Alex, it will take you a little time to adjust. Are you staying long?" he asked, and quickly added "You know that you can stay here for as long as you want. This is your home."

"Not really, I work in the city, and I have an apartment. I just came to try to straighten things out."

We spent most of the day just talking, catching up, but somehow, I felt too ashamed to reveal the details of my time on the street. It was easier to talk about my working on the bumper cars, the lumberyard, I even kept those detail vague. He told me about going back to work after my departure just to fill the time rather that spent it going mad from pain. He expanded the company.

"Let me ask you something, Father. Why did you kick me out?" We looked shocked, "Me, kick you out, never? You were wondering around all night, sleeping all day, like a typical teenager. If I questioned you or asked for the reasons of your sadness, you just ignored me. No answer, no response, it was as I didn't exist."

"So, I was a teenager. So what? That was your reason for dumping me?"

"You're not doing anything didn't bother me. It was the fits of rage, the outburst of anger without any provocation or reason that were hard to deal with."

"I was hurting."

"We were all hurting, Alex." The sadness of the memory was genuine as he turned his face away as tears streamed down his face.

"Yes, but the void was driving me crazy."Good, I said it,. "I had a void, and It is still there increasing, feeling as it is eating me alive."

"Void, what void?" He turned around to face me, visibly concerned.

"What are you talking about? You've got to describe this void!"

"The void, Dad, the void in my head, in my head destroying my memories and..."

"Slow down, Son, take a deep breath... slowly, talk to me."

Taking a deep breath... Slowly I told him all about the nightmares increasing the terror, the loss of feeling, memories vanishing every night while I slept, vanishing into the void never to come back. I told him about going through the pictures in the basement, and none of them making any sense.

"Are you telling me that you have no feeling whatsoever?"

I was pacing as I spoke, "Nothing, no love, tenderness, my body is always numb, constantly asking myself why everything is so screwed up around me."

"From what you are describing, Alex, I believe I know what is happening. Sit down. Prepare yourself for what I am about to say."

"Tell me. I can take anything you have to help me understand what is happening to me for the last three years.

"Alex, I am afraid that someone has stolen your soul."

"That is craze! What do you mean stolen my soul? That can't be possible."

"Yes, it is possible by a powerful energy force," Sadly he shook his head.

I was struck by fear, the blood was exploding in my temples, inexorably the reality still escaping me. I was trying to fight this terrifying thought that someone had the power to yank my soul without my knowing or even suspecting this calamity.

"Who could have done this to me, Zach?" Shouting, not realizing that I have called my dad for the first time by his given name.

"I have no idea, but we will find out. There are people with this power, but no one has the right to take someone's soul. It is sacred. When did it happened if you could remember?"

"I don't know other than it started in the middle of the night, soon after Adam's death, when you had a gathering here at the house."

"I remember, I had a few guests over to show them my appreciation for their support after the funeral" Zach sat quietly, "are you absolutely sure that it was that night."

"Yes, it was the same night, it felt as a powerful vacuum cleaner attached itself to the middle of my head and poof it gave me a giant headache. I felt disoriented and I could not stand up as everything was spinning in the room. I've had the nightmares nearly every night since then."

Father started to write down names, "All right, let's start from there. Who was here that night? There was Pat, my foreman, Mr. Belvos, my client, Sam his accountant, and there was another guy, he was a financial advisor for my client, what was his name...?

"Never mind his name, who else," I impatiently queried.

"Mr. and Mrs. Roundo, their secretary, the treasurer of the company and his fiancé, and the corporate attorney, Winston..."

"Maybe there's is no connection." My hopes dropped.

"Perhaps you're right, it was a long shot. Wait John Languish was the tall man's name. I had never met him before that night," he was still trying to remember, rubbing his temples as he paced around the room.

"What tall man are you referring to?"

"Hmm... the financial advisor. I remember he had a mole on his chin, on the right side and strange eyes."

It hit me like a slap in the face, I ran to the front door and made it to the front porch, bent over the rail and I vomited violently. The thought alone had just ripped me apart. It was "Ghost." That low life had my soul. Zach had followed me and came up behind me with a towel in his hand.

"What is it, Alex, tell me," he pleaded.

Grabbing the towel out of his hand I wiped my face, tears of rage running down my face, trembling like a leaf in a high wind, saliva drowning my chin. After a while I came down a little.

"Simon, that man is Simon. John Languish is Simon."

"Do you know this man?"

"Of course, but why was he here?"

Father told me that he was introduced as an advisor to Mr. Belvos and wasn't on the guest list.

"This man is evil. Why didn't you stop him?"

"Son, you're not rational. How could I have known? I had no idea." Looking at my father I suddenly knew.

"I have to stop this evil man."

I could feel the rage mounting. My own father does not understand, he cannot grasp the magnitude of the horror I have gone through. My knuckles are white from clinching my fist, my jaw is sore from grinding my teeth, I am filled with anger and pain.

"Please, Alex, calm down."

"Calm down, how can you tell me to calm down? You have no idea what it is like to lose all feeling, not only about the past, but not to be able to feel the sun on your skin, the rain on your face, love in your heart, you don't hear the birds singing with joy, no taste in your mouth makes you feel good EVER. Do you understand? Father." Rage is blinding me.

I haven't felt anything but fear and pain, do you hear me, nothing I could hold on to in three years... Just the avoid. I can't distinguish the seasons, I haven't heard a cricket singing, I don't recall admiring the moon. I see people smiling and children laughing, and don' t understand; in fact, it actually irritates me. The nightmares occur night after night, relentlessly, causing me to toss and turn asking the same question... Why, why, why? Like a broken record.

"Maybe I can help." Zach responded and tried to calm me down.

"Dad, you don't get it. What I had to endure, and it is still happening." I was screaming inside for feeling cheated. I had been robbed of three years of my life, three years gone forever, and no hope for the future.

"No, I can't comprehend, but. Let me help you." Dad gently guided me by the shoulders back to the living room, shut the front door, stopped in the kitchen to get a glass of juice, grabbed a couple of pills, and brought them back to me.

"Alex, take these, they will help. We need to talk."

"What are those pills?"

"It will calm you down a little," his voice soothing me." Stay a few days and rest."

"Thank you." I drank the juice to help me swallowing the tablets "I can't. I've got to find him."

"No. Not tonight, you don't. Why is it that you won't listen? You don't know what you are up against."

I jumped out of my chair, ran toward the front door, across the porch, got into Maggie's car, and frantically turning on the ignition.

"Alex don't go!" he shouted from the porch.

"I have to... You have never understood."

He said a few more words that I chose not to hear. I couldn't hear anything for the anger in my head. I threw the car in reverse, spinning the wheels without looking behind me, pulled out of the driveway almost hitting Zach's car, slammed the car into first gear and spun the wheels for at least a half block. I was blinded by the anger driving like a crazy man down a small country road.

The shadow appeared silently but bigger than it had ever been, appearing very agitated, moving erratically from one side of the back seat to the other.

"What are you doing here?" I screamed.

An eerie feeling ran down my back as it continued to dance around the car. It didn't seem threatening, and strangely I was getting accustomed to this whatever it is. Besides nobody or nothing is going to dictate my life.

"Hey, you, whatever you are, tell me what you are and what do you want or just go away, scram, vanish, fade away, dissolve. You're a nuisance, get out of my life."

It swirled around for twenty or thirty seconds, and "poof" it was gone as quickly and silently as it had appeared.

I shivered and tried to brush the uneasy feeling away from me.

"What is it, and what does it want from me?" I thought, but now with it gone I concentrated on just getting back to the city more confused than ever. I had no idea what time it was vaguely remembering the sun having set on the horizon as I left the house.

Figuring Maggie would still be at work, I dropped the car in the parking lot at her apartment deciding to avoid a conversation with anyone until I had a chance to sort the events of the previous hours.

Getting out of the car without consciousness I started running as though my very life depended on it.

~~~

CHAPTER 19

An enormously powerful spasm almost yanked me out of the bathtub. Now I remembered what had happened. The realization of having been shortchanged by life itself released the anger again, and I had trouble remembering how or when I got in the bathtub. Looking at my wrinkled skin as I sat in the stone-cold water, I surmised that I must have been there a long time and had gradually recalled the last three years. Now my direction was clear... I must find Simon.

Slowly extracting my numb, shivering body out of the tub. I grabbed a towel, superficially dried myself and opened the bathroom door. Everyone was there in the living room waiting. Butterball, Rick, One Eye, Lips, and a couple of other kids just staring at me as I emerged through the door.

"What happened to you?" As usual, Lips spoke first.

Rick came to my rescue and restored order, "Come on, guys, law of the streets 'Never ask questions'."

"Thanks Rick."

"We were all worried."

They in turn told me how I had arrived at the apartment, tearing off my shirt and staggering into the bathroom, slamming the door, and emerging hours later. I gave them a pitiful grin.

"I am all right."

"If we can help, just ask." Lips and the rest of the gang

gave me a sad smile, the concern all over their faces.

"I know, but this one is too big for all of you. Cheer up, I will manage."

"Promise that you will ask when you need help." There was a hopeless tone in his voice.

"I will, Lips, don't worry." I couldn't give them details; however, I did explain that there was something that I to do on my own for a few days.

"Listen, Guys, I got to talk to Maggie now so don't wait up for me." Everyone nodded in agreement.

By the way, have any of you seen Ghost lately? No one had seen him for over a month.

"If you see him, tell me immediately every detail... Where, what time, what kind of car he drives and were he goes, everything you hear on the street about him."

They were curious and started to ask questions, I stopped them. "Just do it, and I don't want him to know anything about this, so be discreet. Understand?"

"Will do."

"And don't get too close to him. Keep your distance, he is bad news," I said my goodbyes and headed over to Maggie's hoping that she would be there. I knocked at the door.

"Alex, is that you?" Her voice dampened by the closed door.

"Yes, open up please," I asked while pacing in the hallway.

She unlocked and pulled me in her arms, "Alex, I was so worried."

Guiding her gently over to the kitchen table, "Listen, Maggie, you know how fond I am of you, and I need to ask you to trust me since I can't give you any detail right now,"

"Alex, you must know that I trust you. What can I do?"

"Don't ask any questions. Just know that my whole future depends on your help. Lend me your car for a few days."

I knew that I was asking a lot. She would have to go to work on foot or by the bus.

She tried to make me think that she needed the exercise to lose weight. Didn't she know how perfect she was to me?

"The car is yours for as long as you need it," she pulled me to her sensing that I needed to be held. Her kisses made me feel safe and forget the previous twenty-four hours. Relaxing for the first time I must have fallen asleep since I was awakened the next morning by the sun streaming through the window. Time had obviously become irrelevant.

Maggie came in carrying a stack of hamburgers, "I thought you might be hungry."

"Indeed I am." The drumstick at Zach's was the last time that I had eaten, and that didn't stay with me long.

We ate sitting on the floor, picnic style, laughing and playing like kids.

It felt so wonderful to just be in the moment even though Simon was always in the back of my mind. I didn't know what to do, but I knew that I would do whatever was necessary to regain control of my life. He was not going to get away with this so easily.

"Maggie, you have been so wonderful, however I have to go. You are so special."

"Go. I understand. Here are the keys."

"I'll call you later or come by to see you at work. By the way, do you know Simon?" I obviously needed all the help I could get.

"Simon? I didn't think so,"

I described him the I said, "The tall, dark guy we call Ghost,"

"That creep. Yes, I know him." wrinkling her forehead as she answered with concern reflected in her eyes.

"When you see him again, I need you to tell me as soon

as possible. It's extremely important, be careful and don't let him know that I am looking for him."

"Don't worry, I never talk to him anyway. He's a real looser and never leaves a tip," She lightened the mood.

"It would help to know what kind of car he drives and his license plate number. Just trust me, I'll tell you more when I can.

"I'll see what I can find out. I can feel how important this is to you."

As I kissed her goodbye it felt good to be so close to someone. The power of human touch and kindness was amazing.

With no plan at this point I took off in the car crisscrossing the whole town wandering through streets I had never even heard of before. I knew that the chance of finding him this way was near none, but my determination was no lessened, in fact, I felt my strength increasing with the task at hand, plus just knowing what had created the void gave me new hope.

I had to be patient. This search could take quite a while. The lumberyard came to mind. Better go by and decide. As nice as they were, I wouldn't blame them if they sacked me. Don't want to break the trust we have developed. First thing in the morning I'll go by and talk to Joe. Simon and Zach were still spinning in my head and driving all over town was getting me nowhere, I needed to get organized, check out each street one at the time. I decided to go back and start over with a viable plan.

~~~

CHAPTER 20

Time for a caffeine and sugar fix, I drove to the dinner where Maggie worked, walking in on two taxi drivers having a heated argument trying to get Theresa involved as she effectively ignored them.

"Hi, Alex, what's happening?" She greeted me. The place was packed.

"Not much." I asked where Maggie was and found out it was her day off, and Rick, Lips and One Eye were looking for me. They were sitting in the back booth.

"Thanks Theresa." I walked toward the back. She was mobbed with customers but still winked as I passed.

The boys stood up as I walked toward them "Alex, we've been looking for you, we put out the word to everyone."

"I told you to be discreet."

"We just said that we had a lot of hot merchandise and needed help getting rid of it fast," Lips reassured me.

"That's all? Okay, it just might work, you guys, good plan."

Rick hadn't said a word obviously, absorbed in his thoughts.

"Talk to me, Rick."

"Alex, I contacted all of my buddies, and you know I have a lot of them. Nobody knows where he lives. So, I was thinking that we ought to go to talk to Peggy in the morning. She may have some information or ideas."

"Good thinking"

Lips came up with another thought, "Hey guys, has anyone searched around the old building where we use to live in?"

"Don't think so, it is worth a try."

"I heard that there's several new kids who live there, I know one of them" Rick pointed out.

"Let's go see him, I have the car" We all jumped into the car and drove to the neighborhood. Since Lips and I didn't know this guy we just let Rich lead us around until he spotted him.

"Garry, come over here!" Rick got his attention, yelling at the guy walking across the park.

He looked at us suspiciously especially at the car then came over when he recognized Rick.

"Rick, I see you are moving up in the world. Got yourself a car."

"Don't be stupid. It's not mine, but I do need to ask you a couple of questions, actually, Alex here need to ask you." As he patted my shoulder.

"Who are these guys and why should I answer anything?"

"Alex and Lips, they are legit." He then opened the door. "You don't want to make me get out of the car, get my drift."

Garry immediately remembered, he turned around to Lips, "I heard about you. What a kisser you've got, and they say you never shut up." Lips smiled and fired back, "You're not doing too bad yourself."

"Can it you two! Don't make me get out of the car." Rick interrupted, "You'll regret it."

"Okay, but tell him to shut up," Garry had to save face, motioning at Lips to back off.

"Lips, put a sock in it, this is important," I chimed in.

Garry lowered his head. He hadn't known that this was no time to joke, I got right to the point, "do you know

Simon, alias the Ghost?"

"Vaguely, he comes by here once in a while."

This was difficult. He kept looking over his shoulder. I realized that he was nervous talking to a guy in a car, so I got out and walked over to him away from the car. He loosened up and told me that Ghost came by every week or two but avoided talking to him if he could help it.

"I met him about one year ago by the fountain in the park where all the rich kids hang out by City Hall and figured he was bad news, just creepy, you know?"

"Exactly." Now I knew where he got his tips to give to Jack to do kids dirty work.

Garry added, "That's about all I know, but hey listen, there's this wacko kid in the old abandoned building behind the print shop. He knows the Ghost." Rick and Lips had walked over to us.

"You mean the yellow brick building? We used to live in there. What's the kid's name." I continued.

"Bill, but be careful, He is crazy."

I looked at Lips and Rick puzzled. None of us had seen Bill in months.

"We know him. Let's go find out what's going on." Rick echoed my thoughts.

"Forget it. At night he goes where there's light, and people as well as activity like a bus terminal."

"Why?" Rick kept asking. A chill engulfed me as a suspicious reality got a hold on me.

"How should I know. We've seen him going in the building in the morning talking to himself. Look, nobody talks to him. He's strange or something...doesn't wash and stinks. Moaning and screaming until it gets dark then constantly on the move like he is running away from something." Garry finished and backed off. "That's all I know."

"What got into him?" Wondered Rick, "He knew the streets better than anybody, it's just not like him." By then

I knew for certainty what was going on with Bill, I kept quiet.

"Yeah, he was the first one to help me and taught me the laws of survival on the streets." I remembered as we got back to the car. "He must be in a heap of trouble. We've got to find him, and fast."

"Like Garry said, 'not tonight'," Lips was in the back seat of the car with his simple wisdom.

"What did you say, Lips?"

"Not tonight, Alex, this is a big town."

We headed home... all talking at the same time, elaborating on theories, developing conclusions, just trying to figure out what could have happened to Bill. We were all shaken.

When we arrived at the apartment, I jumped in the shower to try to calm down. So much had happened in such a short period of time. No sense in going to bed. I was too hyper to sleep, and I could hear Lips still talking about the events of the evening, so I joined them, and we talked to dawn.

"I've got to get a few hours of snooze; I am working tonight."

"Take my room. Rick." Staggering to his feet, Rick wobbled toward the bedroom and asked, "What about you?"

"I've got to go see Joe to arrange for a few days off, and then I'm going to find Bill."

"Great, I'm going to lie down." Rick left us at dawn.

~~~

CHAPTER 21

That same morning, I jumped in the car and headed to the lumberyard to speak with Joe and smooth out things. He was in the office and greeted me.

"Alex, what are you doing here so early?"

"Hi, boss, I'm in trouble and need a couple of weeks off."

"Nothing bad, I hope. Can I do anything?"

"No, just personal stuff," I answered hoping that he wouldn't ask for more information.

"Here is my home phone number in case you need it. Put it in your wallet," he instructed.

"Right now, sir. Thanks for your understanding. You'll hear from me soon."

Now I had to take care of Bill, he was in trouble there was no doubt about it, and it was my turn to repay all his kindnesses. Pulling in the deteriorating neighborhood I went directly to the yellow brick building that we called "The Ritz." What a dive!

I pulled a couple of boards off and slid in sideways suddenly having a bad premonition. I wasn't prepared for what I was about to see.

Walking through the building was an experience, at one time this was my home and now just a few months later I wondered how any of us could have stood it. Now was not the time to reminisce about the past, I was out of it.

"Bill! Hey, Bill! Are you here?" Nothing but dead silence hovered around me.

"Bill, where are you? It's me your pal, Alex, talk to me. I'm here to help you." Luckily, I had brought a flashlight that I found in the glove compartment. I continued to call out his name in a nonthreatening, reassuring way as possible since I had been warned of his strange, frightening behavior.

"Bill come out and talk to me. It's me Alex, remember we've been friends for a long time," calling his name again. The cardboard were still lying all over the floor like it was yesterday. Moving slowly, searching in the dark, I heard a small whimper in the next room where One Eye kept his inventory. There was a stench coming out of this room that was almost unbearable as I approached. It literally made me retch, holding a handkerchief over my nose I proceeded very slowly letting my eyes adjust to the darkness.

"Bill, it is me, Alex." I heard something dragging across the floor. "Bill please answer me. I'm here to help."

The ray of my flashlight caught him in the face. The sights instantly turned my stomach, taking all my strength to not turn and run. There was this unrecognizable form in a corner shivering while holding a two by four ready to strike anything that moved toward him, He was tall, painfully thin, and filthy from ling in his own waste. What a pitiful sight.

Very slowly I extend my hand, I cried walking toward him, the horror affected me, I had to get a hold of myself.

"Come, Bill, we are going home." He just stared at me while lowering the board.

"It's me Alex. You know me. Hold my hand, man, I love you." I spoke as softly as possible. He remains suspicious.

I uttered the last words with all my conviction, but he still just stood there moaning and shaking his head. "Bill, let me help you."

"Don't come near me!"

"Sure. Whatever you say."

"I mean it, stay away," as he raised the board again.

"I am not going to hurt you."

"They all say that." While leaning against the wall and lowering the board.

"Yes, but you know me, and I came to take you home."

"No, I can't get out of here."

By now I was so close to him I could almost reach out and touch him, so I decided to wait and lowered the beam of light hoping he would recognize me.

"You're one of them."

"No, Bill, it's just me, Alex. Trust me please,"

"Why should I trust you?" He raised his two by four again.

"No reason, just give me your hand." I stood completely still not wanting to scare him away and felt that he wanted to trust me. Suddenly he collapsed on the floor overcome by hunger and day after day not being able to sleep. It all became clear to me as he started babbling incoherently.

"Bill, it's the voices, isn't it? Tell me."

"Yes. Help me." My suspicions became reality.

"You're coming with me." Grabbing him gently by the waist, I pulled his arm over my shoulder and dragged him out of this hell hole through the board and into the car. He immediately shivered in a fetal position closing his eyes.

I drove in silence gently stroking his head. I went directly to Maggie's apartment and knocked on the door.

Not surprisingly when Maggie opened the door, she couldn't suppress her horror and let out a scared moan when she saw the inhuman form in front of her. I held the door with my foot and lifted Bill from his waist into the room.

"Alex, my god, what happened?"

"Close the door. Now!"

She closed the door and grabbed Bill by his other arm and helped me carry him in the bathroom. We removed the filthy rags from his body as he just stood in the middle of the bathroom shivering. Then I guided him into the shower, gently soaping him down and quietly reassuring that everything was going to be okay.

"I can manage from here, Maggie."

"I'll get him something to eat."

"Just broth, his stomach is too week."

"I'll be right back."

She left the bathroom. Bill was like a rag doll unable to stand unsupported, so I eased him down in the bathtub letting the warm water calm him. He allowed me to shampoo his hair and only stared vacantly in the nothingness babbling on about the demons of the night.

Returning withing a few minutes, Maggie helped me dry and wrap him in a robe that she had brought. We supported him enough to get him to the table where he sat and slurped a half a dozen spoonfuls of broth. Looking at us with empty eyes he began whimpering. Maggie took him gently in her arms, rocking him like a child. We got him to her room and laid him down covering him with several blankets.

We took turns holding his hand and talking softly to him all night as he struggled with the fear and voices withing him, I quietly explained to Maggie what was happening to Bill, but I purposely omitted telling her about my experiences and my search for Simon. I knew that it was not the time to alarm her when there was nothing she could do.

"Don't hurt me," he screamed sitting straight up in the bed scaring the wits out of us and then just as collapsing back on the pillow.

"Man, that scared me," she whispered.

"Me, too." We were both startled by his sudden outburst from within his own private nightmare.

"I'm going to make a pot of coffee Want any?"

"Yes, that sounds good." I watched as she left the room, then focused my attention back on Bill."

She stuck her head back in to say. "I thought I would warm up a little broth for us also."

"I'll be there in just a minute."

She walked out of the room as I wipe the sweat off Bill's forehead and then I joined her in the kitchen.

"I cracked an egg in it," smiling as she handed me the steaming bowl of broth.

"Poor Bill," came out of my mouth as I also thought of myself. No one deserved the hell he was experiencing.

"Will he be all right?" she asked, sitting the bowl of soup on the table.

"I hope so," was all I could say.

We sat in silence eating our broth and enjoyed the warmth of each other's company. She returned to Bill's side as I rested for one hour so I could relieve her. There was no way I was about to leave not knowing if he would freak out. After about four hours of desperately needed sleep he was terrified when he woke up not knowing where he was. I calmed him down talking to him gently until he looked at me clearly and said,

"Hold me, Alex."

I took him in my arms and said, "Welcome home."

Maggie walked in the room. "Food is on the table." I've to go to work."

"Bill, are you hungry?"

"Yes, who was that? Am I safe here?" He whispered. He had curled up like a trapped animal would have when she had walked in.

"Yes, nobody knows that you are here but Maggie and I." I assured him. "You'll get to know her, she's great."

"Good."

"Now let's eat."

Bill was very weak, so I helped him to the dining table where sandwiches and hot soup were waiting. After I warned him to eat slowly and chew small bites, he was able to eat a little and then wanted to go back to bed where he slept for six hours with no nightmares. Still weak but feeling much better, he could walk on his own and was looking in the refrigerator when I heard him stirring.

"I must have dozed off."

"Hi, Alex, can I...?"

"Sure, go ahead."

He took the rest of the sandwich asking, "Want some of it?" It sounded good, so we sat down eating in silence. I finished quickly and cleaned up the kitchen then I sat back down with Bill.

"Tell me Bill, what do you know about Simon?" He turned white and started shaking.

"It's okay. He won't come here. I believe that I know what you are going through. It's like a void in your head every time you close your eyes." He acknowledged with just a nod of his head.

"It's like you have no memory of feeling, except for the terror of the nightmares and voices always spinning in your head."

"How would you know?" He looked at me wondering how I could know so much.

So, I continued, "Remember when we first met how I would sleep all day and disappear at night?"

"Yeah, how did you make it?"

"Well, I don't know about that, but I'm able to cope." I paused. "Any more than that, I really can't remember how I made it."

"So, tell me what's this all about?"

I really didn't have an answer so I told him to stay put and that Maggie would take care of him. He wanted to know where I was going and all I could answer was, "Out to find Simon."

"Can I help?" he asked.

"Right now, you are too weak. I want you to rest and build your strength, because I will need you later," I assured him.

Bill went back to the bedroom crashing on the bed and smiled at me for the first time, "I'm glad that you came looking for me."

"You would have done the same for me. Now rest."

~~~

CHAPTER 22

It was late afternoon and time for me to hit the streets in search of that low life scum Simon. At least I had more information and a place to start. The fountain.

Arriving downtown everything appeared calm, just several kids playing ball, a few couples sitting on blankets near the bushes, several yuppies jogging, mothers with their children, people coming out of the surrounding buildings with briefcases. As the sun started to set on the horizon, the crowd began to thin out and soon there was only the homeless wandering around, and a half dozen kids that had nothing better to do.

I stayed for over five hours and no sign of Simon. Well, I struck out this time so I decided to head back to Maggie's place, she would be home soon, and maybe Bill would be strong enough to answer a few of my questions.

Driving toward home along the deserted downtown street I spotted Simon coming out of an alley adjusting his jacket and tie. He walked over to a car with someone waiting inside and took off. I was so surprised that by the time I turned around to follow him, it was too late.

I could see the car, but a traffic light turned red, and with a police officer sitting having a cup of coffee in his car at the intersection, I decided that it was best to stop.

I drove down a few more blocks looking to the right and to the left at every intersection, but they had disappeared, so I decided to go back to the alley and street where I first saw them.

Inside the alley was an entrance to a witchcraft store. It was obviously closed, but I knocked anyway. After a few moments I heard the latch click and the door was opened by a distinguished looking, older man with white hair. He looked around the alley without a word. Grabbed me by the arm, yanked me inside closing the door behind me, took me over to the light and examined me more closely.

"Young man," he said then paused, "what I am about to tell you must never leave this room. Understand?"

"Yes, sir."

"And you were never here."

"Absolutely, whatever you say. *(Is this guy for real or what?*

"What is your name?"

"Alex, sir."

"I thought so. My name is Clayton, but people call me Clay. Come upstairs with me. We need to talk."

I followed him up the narrow stairwell as I was told and led into a large room with high ceilings. It was filled with candles, crystals, and various artifacts I didn't understand. I could smell the heavy presence of incense burning.

"Sit down," he ordered me as he pointed to a chair and a large round table with only a crystal and a deck of cards on top of it.

Sitting down I said to myself, *what am I doing here?*

He sat close to me, shut his eyes while putting his two index fingers to his forehead. Lowered his hand he opens his eyes and looks straight at me, then he spoke in a deep, quiet, and soothing voice.

"Alex, brother of Adam, son of Zachary and Sarah Beard, unfortunately defunct on the day of your birth. You have been going through a horrendous time for the past three years, the suffering you are experiencing is but the removal of your soul by Simon against your will. It is vital that you get it back, but you cannot do it alone. He lives in a big mansion in a wooden area out of from town not too far from your apartment complex.

I slumped in the chair just having had the wind knocked out of me. He told me of my troubled, I was trying to understand for the last three years in one revealing sentence, I was speechless as he continued.

"You will need help, but do not worry, I will come to you when the time is right. From now on you must believe in yourself." Another pause, and he dismissed me with.

"Go now, young man, we will meet again soon. Goodbye." He made an arm gesture toward the door.

I got up out of the chair like a zombie, walked to the stairs, and proceeded down the steps with Clay silently following behind me.

He opened the door letting me out and locked it behind me. I was standing in the alley in shock, my mouth open, drained of my energy *What and who was he?* I asked myself. *How did he know so much?*

Feeling like I was still in a trance, I got in the car and drove away in disbelief of the whole incident.

~~~

CHAPTER 23

When I walked in my apartment, I got a more pleasant shock, there appeared to be a party going on with the room filled with familiar and unfamiliar faces. Lips jumped up from the other side of the room attempting to get to me through the crowd.

"Hey, Alex, over here."

As I crossed the room, I took a quick inventory of the faces, I noticed Rick, James, One Eye, Mary, Jeff, Louise, Eddy—all laughing and having a great time. Butterball was chatting with two new girls I didn't recognized. It was a zoo of smiles. Lips made it across to me, "Alex, how do you like it?"

"What is going on?" I questioned.

"We've never had a party, and it's Peggy's birthday. So, we got a few bags of chips and dip as well as a cake and invited everyone. Yeah, just put the word out in the streets, *Et voila*. Isn't it great?"

"Yes, I'm glad that you did it." Boy these guys had come a long way.

"Alex, are you all right."

"I'm just too emotional to talk." I guess I must have looked a little or maybe a lot out of it. I was not going to screw up this wonderful moment.

"Since it's Peggy's birthday, we all went together and got her a card and roses."

"You did good," unable to say more.

"By the way I signed it for you,"

"Thanks, I owe you."

He looked at me directly and added, "You will never know how much you mean to all us. We all love you." With that he went back to the party having a good time which I was just as well since I was speechless.

I rotated on my heels walking straight toward Peggy and Maggie feeling the love and hope in the air. Peggy was trying to get to her feet when I stopped her with a gesture and got on my knees to embrace her.

"Happy Birthday, Sweetheart."

"Thank you, Alex."

"You are more that welcome, but it is all of us who are saying thank you. I wonder how many of wouldn't have made it this far without your help."

"I am fifty years old today. Quite a milestone wouldn't you say?"

"You don't look a day over thirty to me, plus your age is not important to us who love you."

She looked as she was about to cry, "In all those years this is the first surprise party given just for me."

"Peggy, you deserve it, and there are many more to come."

"Birthdays."

"Sure, as well as other parties and celebrations, you are invited to all of them."

With that she burst out crying, "Sorry, I am so happy."

" Don't worry." I said, "It's just raining in your head and flooding your face."

Laughing as she wiped away the tears, she reached over and gave me a kiss on the cheek, and another thank you with her eyes.

"Quiet everyone" a voice shouted from the kitchen door. I must have been the only one to hear it with all the laughter and chatter going on, so I voiced in. "Quiet everyone!"

The whole gang was there by the kitchen door—Rick, Lips, Bill, One Eye, Big Joe, Butterball—holding a cake with five red candles burning, and the whole room started singing.

"Happy Birthday to you, Happy Birthday to you, Happy Birthday to you Dear Peggy... Happy Birthday to you." There was a round of applause as they placed the cake on the coffee table in front of Peggy.

Silence, silence. Alex wants to make a speech. I could have killed Big Joe for putting me on the spot.

"Speech, speech, speech," Rang from the room. There was no getting out of this one, so I raised my hand to quiet the crowd.

"Peggy, I want to thank you, and I believe that everyone in this room share my feelings. You have inspired us and given us hope, fed us to keep up our strength and above all we regard you as a loving mother. Peggy, we love you."

By then the small children were pinching at the cake with their fingers leaving messages of enough talk, let's eat.

"Champagne for everyone," Lips announced as he came out the kitchen followed by three other guys carrying half-filled plastic goblets on a tray. As they weaved through the group handing out the glasses to everyone, Lips smiled and whispered to me, "Ginger ale." I caught him off-guard with a friendly jab in the ribs as he moved on.

With all the celebration and everyone trying to talk to Peggy. I grabbed Maggie's hand and led her outside.

"How's Bill?"

"Better. As you can see." Bill was laughing at something Peggy had said.

"I am glad you brought him."

"I didn't want to leave him alone."

"Good thinking." I barely completed my comment

when she embraced me giving me a kiss that made my head spin. "Is it hot in here?" stepping back from her and fanning myself.

She smiled back and whispered, "Get back to the party you soft-heated tough guy," Slapping me on the backside as I went back inside.

Peggy left early graciously escorted to her car by Big Joe, leaving the rest of us to party all night. The younger kids slept on the floor, and I noticed that Bill had some color back in his cheeks and was enjoying in just like the old days. As the hours passed by, I sat with Maggie and her friend Theresa talking and sipping our make-believe champagne.

Bill approached us and sat on the corner of the coffee table.

"I just want to tell you how much I appreciate all you have done. All three of you have made me feel alive again."

Theresa jumped in, "Come on, Bill, forget it. We all need help from time to time."

"There's another piece of cake just waiting for you, Bill." Maggie commented.

"No more for me, I'm stuffed."

"Good, Bill, matter closed. Right?" Theresa had moved over to make room for Bill to sit down next to her.

"Sure, Theresa, whatever you say."

"In fact, why don't you come with me to the restaurant tomorrow? We need a dishwasher."

"Yes, Theresa," he moaned in a tone of voice that made us all laugh.

It was close to five AM when everyone called it a night.

~~~

CHAPTER 24

I got up late in the afternoon still puzzled by the turn of events in the last twenty-four hours. The party had distracted my thoughts enough to have a great evening and a good night's sleep. Took a shower, brushed my teeth, gave up on my hair which seems to have a mind of its own these days going in every direction, dressed, and walked out trying not to disturb anyone.

It was getting dark, so I headed out to search for Simon as I for the following four nights with no luck coming home early in the morning only to eat, shower and sleep a few hours and hit the streets again. Wandering down every street, ally and surrounding wooded area, asking questions even checking out the pawn shops, I had found nothing.

The discouragement was starting to weigh heavily on my shoulders. So, I decided to make more trips around the old print shop, looped by the yellow "Ritz" building but still nothing.

"I know that I will find him, there is no other way out," I muttered to myself and decided that it was time for me to regroup, so I went by the restaurant to see Maggie.

"Theresa, is Maggie here?"

"She just left."

"How about a ham sandwich and a cup of coffee?" I asked.

"No sweat. Have a seat."

I found a seat by the entrance in the last empty booth. The place was packed as usual, so I closed my eyes and listen to the soft music while waiting for my order. Theresa startled me as she placed my coffee cup on the table.

Leaning over as she poured my cup of Joe she whispered,

"Alex, check out the last booth on the left."

"I can't see anything, what is going on?" Cutting her eyes toward the back.

"He's back there, the man you are looking for, you know that Simon character."

"Thanks, Theresa, make me a coffee and a sandwich to go if you will."

"What are you going to do?"

I was trembling inside as I spoke, "Wait in the car and follow him."

"Be careful."

Her concern touched me. "Don't Worry."

"I'll get your order to go."

Waiting for Theresa to return I couldn't believe that I was sitting here looking at the back of Simon's head and neck, as well as the man he was talking to. The other man was wearing expensive looking clothes and gold-rimmed glasses. He had gray hair and a well-groomed beard—not a local guy. His most peculiar feature was the look in his eyes—dark, piercing, ice cold, almost inhuman. He made my skin crawl.

Here's your sandwich, she startled me out of my thoughts.

"Theresa, please, go snoop around Simon's table and try to catch the name of the man with him."

"He has an accent, definitely not American. Could be German or Dutch."

"Thanks, I am going to wait in the car."

"I'll try to get more information. Alex, I did notice that Simon drove up in a black car with a silver roof."

"Good Job, Theresa, I owe you."

"Just pay me back by being careful."

"You've got it."

I grabbed my sandwich and coffee, went to the car, and pulled out of the lot and waited a half block away in the dark.

I could see the car in front of the restaurant, so I started to sip my coffee and nibble on my sandwich when I notice that Theresa had put a brownie in the bottom of the bag. What a doll!

I listened to a great radio station playing alternative music, drumming the beat on the dashboard, and singing along with my terrific voice. Suddenly I jumped with fright bumping my head on the roof when I saw that shadow sitting right beside me in the passenger seat.

"What are you doing back? What do you want from me? I can't believe I'm talking to this entity like I expect to get an answer. Go on get out of here."

Well he could hear me since it moved to the hood of the car. Great, I've got a comic shadow. I must be losing my mind, not only do I have a shadow following me, but now I'm talking to myself. Maybe I should ask this thing if it wants to play cards while we are waiting. At least I've kept my sense of humor.

"Hey, get out of my car and start polishing it!" Just as I said these words the mirage changed its position and disappeared.

Well, I guess it wasn't into hard work, I thought to myself. *You just can't find good help these days.* As I was smiling to myself over the comical interlude, Simon and his companion came out of the restaurant, stood on the sidewalk, and exchanged a few words, shook hands and after helping the gentleman in his car, Simon got in his car.

I cranked the car and engaged the first gear ready to follow as he was pulling away from the curb. Now I just had to follow him without him noticing me, so I stayed back as far as possible turning off the radio so that I could concentrate. It was exiting never having done anything like this before, I had no idea what I was doing. Guess I'll just have to improvise as I go along.

We traveled on a busy highway for about twenty miles. Then we turned right and continued for a mile to a wooded area. The road twisted and turned as I moved closer—I wasn't going to lose him now. When I saw the light of his car pull into a side road, I drove on past for fear that he would notice my car, then I parked the car about five hundred feet down the road.

As I hiked back to the entrance to the property I mused, *Wow, what a mansion!* Eight posts on the front porch, a four-car garage, windows, and gables everywhere, a solarium on the right I noticed, as I could see the plants when I got close. None of this fit—Simon selling hot cars, jewelry, a crook at best, living in this luxury.

I circled around the back There was a deck across the entire back side of the house with a built-in hot tub, and a grill. No wonder he didn't tell anyone where he lived, especially not us street kids.

A light came on in a room upstairs on the second floor as I sneaked up the stairs to the giant deck.

I could see his shadow upstairs as I approached the French doors noticing that the door was open three or four inches with a doorstop holding it place, probably to air out the room. *How convenient,* I thought as I quietly entered a large study. A massive desk dominated the room so cluttered with books that there was room for only a desk phone and a writing pad on the center.

Four bay windows graced this beautiful room filled with exquisite antique furniture, paintings, sculptures, and tapestries. As I moved toward the door across the room, I heard the water running from a shower upstairs, and I felt safe to open the door that led to a great showcase foyer with an enormous chandelier.

A double French door stood open to the dining room revealing an elaborately carved, mahogany table with ample room for the twelve chairs surrounding it.

Sweat was dripping off my face as I took several steps toward another double door thinking to myself that it must be over eighty degrees in this house. Pushing the door open revealed the elaborate sunken living room.

"Alex, so glad you could join me." I froze in my tracks. *Where was he and how did get downstairs so fast and quietly?*

~~~

CHAPTER 25

I slowly turned my head toward the sofa, and there he sat with the head of a snake resting on his lap. I couldn't take my eyes off this humongous snake; it must have been fifteen feet long and bigger around than my waist.

"How do you like my friend?" Simon was stroking the snake's shiny body.

"A perfect friend for you," I snapped back regaining my wits while keeping an eye on this freaky, threatening reptile.

"Oh, come on, he is beautiful. He is so gentle," he added as he placed his hand on his menacing head.

"Well, glad you like him. It can be your bed partner for all I care." I must have insulted him. This sleaze who has tormented my soul for the past three years.

"So, you are not found of snakes?" His eyes closed halfway.

"What was your first clue? By the way, what do you call this jungle beauty?" I asked, trying to keep him talking.

"Slider." I started laughing uncontrollably.

"On top of being sinister and evil, you have a sense of humor. Slider, why not Slime Ball?" I could say no more as an invisible force was chocking me, bringing tears to my eyes, and cutting off my air supply.

The pain was unbearable as it literally slammed me in a nearby chair and two invisible straps pinned my arms to the arms of the chair. The grip on my neck tightened, I couldn't breathe and could barely hear his words although the sound was louder.

"Listen you punk, it's one thing for you to follow me to my home and break in, but I won't take insults from someone as insignificant as you. You're nothing."

A white veil came over my eyes as I started to lose consciousness. He must have eased off his invisible chocking grasp around my throat because suddenly I was coughing and gasping for air.

All I could mutter, was "Then kill me, if you must."

"I'll think about. Why are you here?"

"I want my soul back."

"Not possible. Yours is special, and I need it."

"How do you mean special?"

"For some reason your soul regenerates itself, my congregation and I have not found a rational answer so in the meantime you are mine. No one knows where you are."

"I hate to be a nuisance, but tell me something, if you are so powerful and wise. How come you deal in drugs, petty theft, carjacking and other trivial illegal activities."

"Alex, Alex I am over tree hundred years old. First do you think that I didn't know that you were following me from the restaurant, I even know that Theresa gave you a sandwich, and I felt the joy when you discovered the brownie as you were sitting in your car. Next, I do the activity outside the law, simply out of boredom, and finally all the people I have working for me I mainly use for practicing reading and manipulating souls.

"I don't mean to insult you. So as far as I am concerned you are a freak." Boy wrong sentence I figured out when I immediately felt the chocking sensation tightening again. This guy has no appreciation for quality sarcasm. "Sorry," was all I could say.

The grip loosened. I better lay off the insults and

concentrate on how I am going to get out of this place. Be smart, keep him talking, came into my mind.

"Can I ask you a question?"

"What for since I know what you are always thinking, like right now. You're wandered how you are going to get out of this situation and in the same time, you wonder if I took Jack's soul, no way out for the first one, and of course for the second, you see Jack's soul was a bonus. So, go ahead we find you entertaining for the moment," he continues to stroke Slider.

"What do you mean 'them'? How many do you have under your control?"

"Right now, only four. But I have had countless in my exceptionally long and prosperous life."

"Are you really over three hundred and fifty years old? You don't look old." Got to keep him talking, appeal to his insanity or ego, or whatever.

"I mean it you don't look over forty-five,"

He laughed, caressed the snake, and started talking to him.

"Do you hear that, Slider, forty-five? You've got to like this kid."

Turning around, he focused his attention on me. His expression had changed, his face had become cruel, the eyes glared with a sinister, ice cold stare.

"There is no arm in telling you my story knowing that you are going to cease to exist afterward."

I was stunned for a moment and asked a dumb question,

"Then you are going to kill me?"

"Such an ugly word, Alex."

"Are you scared to call a spade a spade?"

"Nothing scares me. Nothing. Everyone must meet his master at some point in his life, and you have met yours. I am three hundred and fifty-seven years old and have the power of taming time."

Man, this wacko could make a fortune marketing his beauty cream, but I thought better of saying it since I wanted to keep breathing.

"How can you be so old?"""

"The souls I gather keep me young. Let me explain it simply. The mind and spirit control the body, right?" I shook my head feebly and he continued.

"When people say, 'mind over body,' they have no idea how close they are to the reality they are. And a few believe it. I draw energy from maybe one soul at a time, just a little at a time.

"You mean like a spider keeping its prey alive so it can feed whenever it wants. "

"That is what I like about you, Alex you are so clever and get the overall picture immediately without a lengthy explanation."

"Do you have any concept of the cruelty of your act? You destroy the very essence of life leaving only a void and a shell of a body. There is no joy, no emotion left but fear. No way to describe the pain and misery it's creates.

"So, what is your point?" My words seemed useless as I tried to understand his insanity,

"How can you have no feeling when you're draining other people of their lives, their self-confidence, their memories at the end their very soul?"

"Isn't it obvious, Alex. The power lies in not caring. No one matters but me, my life, my needs, my existence,"

Wow. Simon really believes all that.

"Why me?" I tried not to sound pitiful.

"Why not you? Also, you have a power, an energy source greater than you know or can imagine, an energy you have not discovered yet, and not had the time to develop. So, it was necessary to neutralize you."

"What power are you talking about?" I was getting confused.

"Never mind. Now that I have your soul, it really

doesn't matter."

"Man, you are really pathetic," again he gets offended and tightened the invisible grip around my arms and neck, I continued with difficulty,

"So, what scared you about my power?"

"Nothing. We just decided it would be wise to disable you." It took a second to sink in.

"Who is this 'we'?"

"That is of no concern of yours."

"The older man I saw with you tonight, does he have anything to do with you?"

Simon was obviously enjoying this opportunity to boast and toy with his pray, happening to be me right now, and I didn't relish that feeling.

"So, you know him?"

"No. I don't even know who you are. My father called you John Languish, but everyone knows you as Simon."

"Changing one's identity is necessary when you are as old as I am. Besides, it makes it more difficult to be traced."

"How can you change your identification?"

"Don't concern yourself. I've had a great deal of practice and with the papers in my strong box, it's simple." He motioned toward the study as he spoke.

"How did you get by my father? Did you trick him?"

"No. It was easy. He was weakened by months of grieving and anger, so he didn't even suspect."

"Who else have you got?"

"No one you would know, except Jack."

My blood turned cold in my veins. I had spent days trying to figure out what Jack was telling me. It was so clear now; he was warning me about Simon. "Why Jack?"

"Just a bonus, as it happened."

"And me?"

"You were and still are a nothing, insignificant zero as you are. Young, weak, angry, unaware of your potential powers. It was so easy to take you then... plus by taking your soul we weakened your father's powers also. All of which helped me to achieve a higher rank in the organization."

"What organization?"

"You don't think that I am alone? Seriously, Alex, you're smarter than that."

"How many of you are there?" This was getting scarier by each moment passing by.

"Not too many, but our numbers are increasing, and we are well placed through the world. With the use of drugs increasing, our feeding grounds are vast. The individuals are unimportant, but with so many available weakened souls our energy and power grow."

As he was flapping his jaw so full of himself, silently the shadow appeared with lightning speed and hovered above the ugly snake. Simon had not noticed.

"What are you going to do to me?"

"Dispose of you. You are only a body now, no soul, no feeling, no purpose. You are expendable."

The snake twisted and turned, recoiling itself on the sofa and looking up toward the ceiling. Before Simon could react, the snake seemed to be propelled off the sofa, as if it were thrown, hitting the coffee table on his way to the floor.

"Slider, what is going on?" Simon asked as he pursued the erratic movement of the snake destroying everything in his path.

Simon's guard got weakened as he temporarily forgot about me. The restrictions on my arms and the pressure around my neck lessened, and then we were gone. I bolted from the chair and ran for my life through the foyer and study, across the desk, jumping down the stairs, picking up speed when I got to the yard. Not daring to look back, I made it to the road and then in the car, fumbled with my keys, panicking a second trying to get the key in the ignition, started and drove like a maniac.

He is insane, he must be. How could any of this be real? But what if...I've got to get back to my apartment, I must find them and stop them, I must fight for...

~~~

CHAPTER 26

Floating is a fantastic sensation; I feel like I am floating on a cloud I'm so light. There's such a clean smell all around me, and the peace and quiet together with this weightlessness is exhilarating, I can see a blurry, bright light off in the distance getting dimmer as it drifts away and vanishes in the darkness. At times it seems to be within my reach. A voice in the background flows in and out of my consciousness just like the light disappearing into nothingness.

The light is slowly getting brighter, the voice stronger, my vision clearer. I feel so good, maybe this is heaven. I try to shift my body, but it is too heavy, and my arm has a sharp pain when I try to move. The room is spinning, the voices vanish and come right back.

The room stopped spinning. I could see a form coming between me and the light, a white blouse, the good smell returns, and I'm floating again. Nothing seems real.

"He is regaining consciousness. Get the doctor. Stat."

What's is going on? Where am I? It smells so good, and the spinning has stopped. Footsteps on all sides, something on top of me moving my arm, someone grabbing it, white blouses are back, my mouth is dry. I don't understand, my arm still hurts, tears in my eyes, I feel light-headed.

"Alex, do you hear me?"

I can't speak. The white blouse gets more distinct, a

woman, she smiles. I blink my eyes. The light hurts now. I try to talk, but no sound comes out. Someone moistens my mouth.

"He can hear," said a voice.

"Give him a couple of drops of water."

"Right away." More water is coming in wetting my mouth.

"Alex, can you hear me?" Same question again. I'm not deaf.

A person puts his fingers near my eyes. *Don't you pick my nose,* I think, but it's still just a voice inside.

"How many fingers, Alex?"

I'm looking, it's blurry. I blink my eyes trying to focus.

"Two." *Did they hear me?*

"More IV, we're losing him."

My arm hurts again. Two fingers dangling over my head. Now I can see them clearly, the light is bright. "Two, two, two, two." I am babbling.

"Just leave me alone, who are you..."

"Nurse he is coherent, wipe his face and slow down the IV."

"Where am I?"

"You've been in a coma, Alex."

I fall in a gentle sleep. What happened? My mind is awake. I open my eyes, the light it still here, things are clear, the room is still. Someone is looking at me smiling. A man, a tall man, a nurse. The other man approaches and look at me.

"Alex, it's your dad, Zach."

"Where is this?"

"You are in a hospital. You have been in a coma."

My arm still hurt and I'm hot. "Who are you?" My jaw hurts, it's hard to focus, my head spins.

"I'm your father, Zach," the man answered.

"Dad, what happened?"

"You were in an accident. You've been in a coma for

seven months."

The words slowly sank in. Seven months, out cold, I don't remember anything. Just the floating and the emptiness. I feel weak again and just want to sleep, "go away," I muttered as I closed my eyes.

"I'll be back tomorrow." Said the man as he leaned over and kissed me on the forehead before he left. I am so exhausted. I just want to be left alone. I am confused. *Coma? Hospital? Seven months? What accident?* I must stop all these questions and sleep.

The nurses are back lifting me up, changing the sheets on the bed, and then putting me back in the bed and tucking me in. I feel much better. My mind is getting clearer. The nurses are talking now. I must have been hurt, but when? Where? Someone comes in. It is that man.

"Hi, Alex." I just look at him. "you are looking better today; you are going to need a lot of rest.

"Please tell me how I got here?" To utter that question was excruciating.

"Slow down, Alex. I am here to explain." He turned around and grab a chair, pulled it close to the bed, sat down, poured himself a glass of water and said gently.

"I will start at the beginning."

I just nodded my head in agreement.

"Seven months ago, late at night, I got a phone call from the hospital telling me that you were in a serious car accident, and that your chances of making it were slim."

"How did they know?" I struggled to form the words.

"They checked you for an ID, but all they found was a phone number. So, they called, and it was your boss from the yard. He told them that you were my son, they immediately contacted me for permission to operate. I got here after they had taken you in the operating room. They worked on you for fourteen hours and really didn't give me much hope that you would live." He paused and breathed deeply, fighting the wet eyes.

"After the operation I stayed here with you by your bed for a week, then the doctor told me that it could be weeks or months before you would regain consciousness—if then. We've all come to be with you. Joe come often. Maggie every chance she gets. Rick, One Eye, Lips, Butterball, everyone comes from time to time."

"Maggie, how is she?"

"Better than you, but she is worried about you."

"What about her car? Did I wreck it."

"She has a new one."

"You mean you...?"

"Yes, her car couldn't be repaired plus she seems fond of you, so I took care of it. Your apartment rent has been paid for the year, and an account set up to pay the gas, water, electricity, and phone. Lips is in charge."

"We don't have a phone."

"Well now you do, and Rick supervises everything. Lips is the accountant, and they manage very well."

"How can you be so nice after all the horrible things I said?"

"I was hurt just like you, Son. We had a disagreement, let's just leave it at that for now. We can talk about all that later. Know that I never quit loving you."

"Okay."

"You woke up a month ago but only for a few minutes, then out again. Five days ago, you seem to come to. But you were incoherent and too weak to grasp what was happening and passed out again, the doctor seems to think that you are back this time for good. It will take quite a while with care and rest to get you back on your feet again."

As my father was telling me all the details, I thought to myself that the lights, the spinning room, floating on clouds had been a dream, but I was wrong.

"Alex, I'm going to go for now so you can get a little

rest."

"Bye," is all I could say as I faded fast. I didn't see him get up and leave. I was already sinking in a dreamless sleep.

I awakened a couple of times during the night when the nurse came to check on my IV, overall, I slept peacefully until the hospital aide came with my food in the morning. Well, I wouldn't call it food exactly, mostly liquids. It had been so long since I had anything to eat even the liquids made sick to my stomach, fortunately my nurse was patient.

"Take your time."

"What is your name?"

"Heather," she had a bright smile

"Thanks, Heater, why does nothing taste right?"

"You must get use to food again, give it a chance."

"Okay, give me another bite, what is it anyway?"

"Vitamins, and the rest you don't want to know."

I ate making faces which made her laugh. Afterwards she gave me a bath which really embarrassed me. She said that I was blushing, I felt my head started to smoke from embarrassment.

Next, they came to change the bed, two big guys moved me gently over to a stretcher while the housekeeper stripped and remade the bed. Then they put me back in.

Boy, I had nothing for almost three years, and now I have my own room, a television, and private care. I dozed off still too weak to concentrate on the TV program.

Maggie walked in all dressed up looking even more beautiful than I remembered. She was all smiles, behind her Theresa with flowers, then Rick, Joe, and my father. Maggie sat next to me and planted kisses all over my face. Someone was quick with their sense of humor,

"Slow down, you're going to choke him," "Don't worry. I'll be gentle." She giggled.

What a surprise, Rick and Lips were all dressed up. Everyone started talking at the same time.

"Slow down. I'm too weak to listen to all of you at once."

Then minutes later the doctor walked in the room and called my father out for a private talk. They both looked at me a couple of times then Zach came to my bed and said.

"Sorry, Son, but you are still too weak for all this excitement. We are going to let you get some rest."

Maggie got up kissed me and gave me a sad smile, then she left the room with the gang. Father left after everyone.

"Young man, you will have no more visitors for at least a week."

Therapy every second day took it out of me, I tired easily, so I took a lot of cat naps. Almost three months since I woke up from the coma, had a grueling therapy session, I closed my eyes as soon as I returned from the pool.

When I opened them again, that annoying shadow was dangling over my head. I had forgotten about that silly ball of mist.

"Go away. I am depressed enough."

It did trigger my memory of that last night with Simon which had been suppressed. I wasn't ready to deal with that silly game yet. It took all my strength to lift my arm to chase it away, so it just went to the other side of the bed. I watched it for a while then I closed my eyes.

Who cares? I thought as I drifted off.

~~~

CHAPTER 27

One day after they returned me to my freshly made bed and fed me a good meal, I felt strong enough to conquer the world, or at least stay awake and watch a little television. Father and a man came into my room.

"Hi, Alex. I brought a visitor."

An older gentleman walked in behind him. He was dressed in a classic suit and turtleneck which called attention to his strong chest. He had white hair like fresh snow in a field but walked with a stride uncommon for a man of his advance years.

"Hi, Alex, we've met before."

I could not place him although his face was vaguely familiar. I had also noticed when they walked in the room a feeling of great serenity about him.

"Sorry, I don't remember you."

"That is irrelevant. My name is Clayton, but if you prefer Clay will do fine."

The name rang the bell, still nothing returned in my head. My father was walking around the room waving his arms in a gentle and orderly pattern and said.

"We are ready now."

"What is going on?"

The man with the white hair grabbed a chair and sat down, pushed one chair toward father and instructed.

"Sit down, Zach, we have a lot to do."

I don't remember anyone commanding my father to do

anything. He was gentle, but no one ever gave him orders. With him everything was to be discussed and to be ordered around made him mad, his philosophy was that everyone was equal and had the right to express themselves and to make their own decision, so I was shocked when he obeyed.

"We came to ask you about Simon." Clay started.

"What do you want to know? My memory comes and goes. I hardly have any recollections."

"Everything you can remember, and I'm here to help you."

I observed that my dad had just sat, listened, and didn't say a single word during the entire conversation. The stranger was in control as he continued.

"Don't be afraid Alex, I know what has happened to your soul, and we must get your soul back."

"How are going to do that?"

"I 'm not sure yet, but we will find a way."

Maybe it is too late. He has had my soul for over three years now. It must be fading by now. I didn't know where those thoughts came from.

"Your soul cannot fade away; you have special powers which I will explain later."

"So, what do you need to know?" I wanted to cooperate the best I could.

"Anything you can remember."

I spent the entire morning trying to remember anything I could about this despicable character, but for the life of me I just drew a blank.

I was on the verge of telling him to fly a kite and to get out of my face when Dad interrupted

"Alex, this is very important."

"I just can't remember. Do you think that I'm trying to protect him?"

"No," Clay replied, that man as well as his organization, must be stopped."

"I keep telling you that my past keeps slipping away. I wake up every morning not knowing what will erase itself, only the most traumatic moment of my life remains, all other evaporate into thin air."

"I understand, Alex, still you must keep trying in order ..."

Clay jumped up; the chair flew violently against the wall behind him. Father and I watched in total chock as the shadow was right in front of Clay, growing stronger and more distinct. Clay was paralyzed, his face disfigured by the terror. Neither Zach nor I felt threatened.

A faint blue light surrounded the shadow, and it emitted a feeling of tranquility. Clay's face returned to normal as he started to look in admiration, he kept nodding his head saying.

"Yes, I will tell them... I will ask... Don't worry... I'd be delight to do that..."

It seems that he was having a conversation with the ceiling as if someone just walked by.

We didn't move as Clay continued to talk and respond for what seemed like a long time. Finally, Clay relaxed and turned around, picked up the chair and put it by the bed where t had been previously and sat down. We had waited patiently and watched the shadow fade away.

"Okay, tell us what is going on," Zach insisted.

Clay was smiling, his voice trembled, and you could feel the joy and happiness he was reflecting from the turn of events.

"It may surprise both of you, but I just had a fascinating conversation with your son and your brother Adam."

"What?" We both spoke at the same time.

"Let me explain. The shadow right here, right now in this room is the spirit of Adam, and he had been protecting Alex all along."

Now I understood what had been going on. My brother

was my guardian angel. Whenever there was danger, when Rick was still a bully and had beaten me up, when we heard the news about Jack, the rescue from Simon and the snake, it all his doing. The realization just blew me away, and you should have seen my father's face filled with laughter and tears. There were no words to describe the emotions at that moment.

"What do we do next?" Zach wanted to know.

Clay closed his eyes for a moment, listened to something we could not hear and in a very shaking tone of voice conveyed.

"Adam said that he would like to go inside Alex's body if it is alright."

"Sure, it's okay with me, but can he do it?"

"He said he could with your permission." I asked

"How can you hear him?"

"Telepathy. I have the ability and training, but if you let him inside of you, you will be able to communicate with him." He made it seem so matter of fact and simple, like it was done every day.

There was an excitement in the air, I needed answers.

"How so?"

"Well, your lips will not move. It will all be inside your mind."

"I don't understand" I was not sure that I was ready for this change of events.

"You don't have a soul right now; you have a void. So, he will come inside you. And don't forget you will still be yourself." Clay answered.

It sounds logical and sensible, and I was ready. "What do I do?"

"You do nothing. Adam will do all the work. He said it is painless, just relax and let it happen."

Zach remained silent finding it hard to believe what he was about to witness, overcome with emotion. He was smiling, shaking his head, and stretching his arms in the air silently.

"What are we waiting for?" I asked, Clayton approach the bed.

"Lie still and relax."

I relax although I am feeling a little worried looking at the shadow still finding it hard to believe it is my brother, no matter how I analyze it. It makes no sense and yet there he is moving over me. He comes closer and wraps himself around me like a blanket. The next feeling, I experience are the wave of feeling—love, peace, serenity, hope, forgiveness, humor, compassion, joy. It is all exhilarating, then the voice started speaking and I could not control it, the words came out of my mouth.

"Hi, Dad, it is us, Adam, and Alex. Come here and give us a hug." Dads got up like a zombie and came to embrace us. "Dad, we love you, but for now Alex is exhausted so you and Clay must go."

"I'll be back tomorrow."

"No. Not tomorrow. Alex and I have a lot to discuss, and I will spent a lot of energy to make his body stronger, buy the time you come back he will feel and look like another man, so run along, You Clay must return with father." Adam is talking through me. "Right now, we need each other."

I gently close my eyes as Father and Clay leave the room, and I fall into a beautiful sleep with no dreams, no nightmares, no panic, Just peace.

When I awakened the next morning, I have a feeling of well-being that I had not experienced in years, also I feel being truly rested as well as rejuvenated.

"Good morning, Alex. Sleep well?"

"Morning, Adam." Boy, it feels strange having Adam in my head. I can talk to him without uttering a single word. Just think it *ET voila*. Even more amazing is that I can hear him loud and clear like in a normal conversation.

"It feels so good, really good, Adam."

"I feel pretty good myself."

"What do you mean?"

"Well, it has been a long time since I had a body around me. Somehow I feel a little more protected and solid."

I tried to imagine what the people would think if I told them that dead brother was talking to me. They would probably lock me up.

"Listen, Alex, I am so glad to be with you."

"Why didn't you come before?"

"The accident in the lake occurred too suddenly, and when I drowned my spirit was too young."

It was so easy to communicate. "To young for what?"

"To do what I can do now. I was just a kid when I died, and I have learned a lot since. I've gotten stronger since and so will you. Hey brother, we're together and talking. That's quite a step."

I could hear, no I could feel a happiness in his manner of expression.

"What's next?" I asked silently on my head.

First, we must keep building your physical strength. After that we will have a lot to do together.

"Yes, it was dumb, you just left me in that boat facing the music with Father, it took a while for us to get over it," thinking how much I had missed having Adam with me. Now feeling his presence, things were getting better.

I heard, "Sorry," in a whisper.

"Sorry, my foot. Do you know what we went through?" Could he ever understand? It didn't really matter now. "Not at first, but when I came back, I found you running in the streets."

"Oh, that was you pushing me through the night."

"Who else could it have been?"

"Something is puzzling me, Adam"

"I already know what you want to ask."

"I didn't ask yet."

"Yeah, but remember I am in your mind now. When you think, I already hear it." *Hay, that's not fair was my first thought. My second thought was, Well, what was my question?*

"You are wondering why your memory came back as you asked the question?"

Adam knew exactly what I was questioning in my mind, so I waited for the answer.

"It's easy, right now I have your whole childhood memory transferred to you. In addition, I was constantly with you in the street so since I saw and heard everything that you saw and heard, I have your memories as well as mine."

"Keep going."

"Not right now. It would be too much information for you to absorb all at once, so I will tell you a little at a time."

"Fair enough."

"Beside your breakfast is just outside the door. Heather is taking the tray out of the wagon and putting the orange juice on the tray."

"Hey, how do you know that?" Thinking that he was a magician.

"You'd be surprised at all the tricks I've learned like going through walls and being here in your body."

"Da, da, da, da... my brother's a spook."

"Watch what you are saying."

"Spook, spook, spook." "Bing," something pinched me inside the head. "Stop it. That hurt." A great laughter started inside my head. Adam was just as playful as ever.

"You are still a spook, but I am glad you're here.

~~~

CHAPTER 28

"How is my favorite patient this morning?" Heather asked, pushing the door with her foot with a tray full of food in her hands.

"You wouldn't believe if I told you," I laughed.

"Well you are in good spirits."

Man, I just lost it, I started laughing out of control and since she had no idea that what she had said was so funny, I answered with the only reply that came to me. "Yes. I am, and I can eat for two?"

"You're mighty energetic today. What got into you?"

That made me laugh even more. "Heather you are so funny. Come here and give me a big hug."

"Let me put the food on the service tray first." She let the tray down and came to give me a hug. She was so happy to see me so jovial.

"This is absolute the best I have felt since the accident."

"What is going on, Alex?"

"I had a spiritual experience." Exploding in hysterical laughter,

Boy, was I witty today? When I calmed down Heater was staring at me in shock. "Are you sure you are all right?"

"Never felt better. Now let's get breakfast on the road." She lifted the head of my bed into a sitting position cutting her eyes at me. I was smiling.

"Take it easy," said Adam, "You're going to give her a heart attack."

"Okay, but admit it was funny."

"Yes, it was, now get a hold of yourself."

Heather brought the tray of food and tucked the napkin under my chin. It was a wonderful moment when the first bite touched my palate, I could feel the texture of the eggs, rolling on my tong as I chewed slowly. It was so good to feel, taste, appreciate, dissect the flavor and textures. It was such an awesome feeling, I had to share this joy, so I just grabbed Heater and kissed her on the forehead.

"Thank you, God," I said aloud with tears running down my cheeks.

"Are you sure you are all right?" She asked surprised to see me weep. "Heather, these are tears of joy. I'm just so glad to feel alive."

"But you've always been alive."

"No, it's hard to explain, but I can actually feel the blood running in my veins."

"I guess, we all take little things for granted."

"You're right. That's why we all need to be more thankful and forgive rather than judge and complain."

She just hugged me. She had no reply.

I ate the whole breakfast and felt like a new man. When Eddy and Gary came to pick me up for rehab, I literally jumped out of bed and when they eased me in the water, I couldn't believe how wonderful it felt. Eddy knew immediately that something had changed. He didn't have to make me move or hold me or even to support me. He simply asked.

"Your aura is pure gold. How did it happen?"

"One of the visitors I had last night was my brother."

"You seem so happy. You should ask him to visit you more often," he suggested.

"Believe me, he will. You don't seem shaken by my

statement."

"Why should I? If you listen with your heart, the one you love never leaves you." Good old Eddy always had the right words, no questions, just resolutions.

"Eddy, I admire you. You are always so calm, joyful, and easy going. What is your secret?"

Without hesitation, he answered, "I just got tired of fighting everybody, judging them, trying to control or be controlled by others. So, one day I said to myself, 'I got to change.' And I did."

"And what did you do?"

"Accept, just accept."

Could it be that simple? I thought as he elaborated. "Accept who you are and accept who they are—no more judging or criticizing, no more pointing the finger, no more feeling sorry for yourself or others. Simply feel good to just to be you."

"Maybe I should try it."

"It can't hurt."

We looked at each other and smiled. I was so happy to be able to talk and feel the passion of being alive and remembering each word during that hour of exercise. It went so fast that it surprised me when my two chauffeurs came to pick me up and rolled me back to my room. I was babbling at a hundred miles an hour. I was noticing everything around me, things that were there before, but hadn't noticed.

They put me in bed, tucked me in and wished me a great day. They left and I started whistling.

"Earth to Alex," I stopped whistling and looked around.

"In your head, it's me, your brother, remember?"

"Right I'm not use to someone talking to me from the inside of my brain. So, cut me a little slack."

"Okay. Now pay attention, Alex. Tomorrow Clay and Dad will be back, so I am going to feed you information as well as part of your memory back."

"How long will it take?"

"A few days total. I'll go slowly, you are still too weak to get all of it all at once."

He spent an hour or so feeding me accounts of different events in my life, as well as some of his observations. He was right, it was very tiresome, but he knew when it was time to stop and let me rest for a while. He woke me up just before lunch.

When Heater came in, I could tell that she was still a little worried about the craze display this morning. She had no food.

"It will be a few minutes. They want to do a few tests first."

"Oh, Yeah I forgot the Tuesday blood test. Do your job master." The lab nurse came in and laughed at the statement I made while Heater got me ready, the little nurse took out her instruments of torture and was through playing vampire in a few minutes

"I'll be right back with lunch," Heater left behind with the nurse.

She returned in less than two minutes with a loaded tray of food. It smelled so good, I devoured it faster than usual. After lunch Adam came back to give me more information and then my needed rest.

Around five o'clock in the evening the nurse and the doctor walked in, He pulled up a chair and sat down.

"Alex, how do you feel?"

"Great."

"That is good to hear. We just wanted to check since the result from your tests are way out of proportion."

"Is that bad?"

"Not in your case, but the improvement from last week is amazing." He was obviously pleased as he continued.

"Nothing about your recovery has been predictable or rationally explainable. Let me just say that your results are favorable."

"My spirit has been uplifted." Another brilliant quip on my part I thought.

"Just keep doing whatever what it is you're doing cause it's working. I'll see you next Tuesday," he turned around and left with the nurse.

"Alex to Adam. Alex to Adam. Come in. Did you have anything to do with this speedy recovery?"

"Who me?" I heard Adam's answer.

"Don't give me that. Did you or did you not affect the tests?"

"Yes and no." His personality hadn't changed a bit. He was still as playful, and sometime exasperating as ever.

"What kind of answer is that?"

"Well, for you to get better, you needed to believe in yourself, and now you believe, Don't you? So, what do you think happened?"

"I get it you infused a lot of your own strength inside of me. Well thank you for your push."

"You're welcome brother."

I spent the rest of the evening dozing off and on, when the morning arrived, I had experienced another peaceful night.

Waiting for the morning chores to be done as I call them were not difficult as I was full of energy, and I was impatient for Zach to arrive. The morning crept by slowly and after lunch when they arrived, I was more than ready to get the show on the road. We greeted each other and immediately started talking about the information that Adam had given me which took about three hours. Clayton asked questions, and Dad took notes. This time I had no problem remembering every detail.

I learned that the older man with Simon went by the name of Lazlo, and that he was high in the organization and had to be stopped. They emphasized that it was not my concern for the moment. They knew that Lazlo came in town a couple of times a month to work with Simon. Adam had been investigating their movements on his own and found out that they always met at the same hotel every time.

After I had given them all the information, Dad and Clay left. I was mentally drained and spent the next two days returning to my old schedule of eating, resting, and exercising. Adam had warned me that it would be hard on me, so he left me to recuperate.

During those stressful time, Maggie was the only visitor, and was just what the doctor ordered.

The next month I improved so fast that all the doctors came to visit me like I was guinea pig, they had no answers for the remarkable increase in my strength, stamina, and vitality. Finally, my doctor gave me a clean bill of health while kidding me and saying.

"We are sending you home, because you are eating us out of our profits."

The day before my release Father, Maggie, Theresa, Rick, Lips, and Butterball came bringing me new clothes with the tag still on them. They were so happy and proud; everyone was talking at the same time including Adam inside my head. To say I was confused was an understatement.

"Whoa, Whoa, Whoa, you guys," I said" My ears are buzzing, calm down."

Everyone quieted down except Lips who kept flapping his jaw wanting to be the center of attention. Theresa made a great suggestion.

"Put a sock in it, Lips."

"Like who died and put you in charge?" Lips, snapped back, but he knew that he was wrong at the instant he finished his sentence. Theresa give him the evil look

"Words are like bullets once they leave the barrel you cannot bring them back."

"Now," I got their attention "What do you want me to

try on first?"

Maggie handed me what she had selected.

"Okay, Girls, turn around." Rick took charge.

Maggie whined making all the guys giggle for her remark. "Do we have to?"

We were turning the hospital into a circus, and it only took a few minutes for Heater to come in and ask us to quieten down. We solved that problem by asking her to join us.

She accepted and Maggie told her that the girls were supposed to turn around while I changed.

"Why should I? I've been bathing him every day or months."

"Lucky you." Both girls laughed making me blush.

I modeled the whole wardrobe even though I needed only one outfit the wear home. My father graciously offered to take the rest of the outfits home. The afternoon went fast, but when the gang left, it was hard for me to settle down and wait for morning.

Adam cheered me up by telling me about my days on the street restoring memories of sleeping on the top of the printing shop, some of the stunts Bill pulled to keep me fed, unbeknownst by me and working on the bumper cars at the fair. He even reminded me of the perfect brownies that Jane made that I liked so much. Just thinking about them made me instantly hungry. I finally fell asleep.

~~~

CHAPTER 29

"It's morning. No therapy today, I went to the pool to shake hands with Garry and to thank him for his hard work, patience, and wisdom. On the way back to my room Eddie was there to help when I got tired.

After lunch, my father came to pick me up. I had been dressed and ready to go for hours. Eddie arrived pushing a wheelchair, loaded me in it and rolled me out to the car while father grabbed my belongings. The whole scene was quite emotional.

Half of the staff was at the exit lined up to say their goodbyes. I voiced my thanks again and crawled in the car. Zach drove away, and I saw the hospital disappearing behind us, my thoughts were still with them.

"It may sound strange, but I am going to miss that place, especially the people. It is a wonderful place of healing," I realized.

"You're so right. I get a deep sense of pride every time I'm there."

What do you mean, Dad?

"My construction company built it, and I am on the board."

"You're kidding."

"With both of you and Adam gone I went back to work at my company. It's done very well."

We drove along the four-lane highway for the entire trip in silence both of us lost in our thoughts. When the first double iron gate with the carved silhouette appeared, then the second and third shortly after, my excitement grew remembering that I grew up in this area. But it was only when we pulled pass the massive main gate with the same carving in front of the awesome pink stone mansion that my memories kicked in. It was as beautiful and timeless as ever. What a landmark. It felt so strange and emotional to drive back in town after so long. I couldn't help but recall how full of anger and fear I was the last time I passed those gates.

"Dad, I want to apologize for my behavior the last time I was here."

"It was not your fault. Neither one of us knew the force we were dealing with. We were still reacting to our sorrow and guilt."

"What about me?" chimed Adam in my head. "I had a monumental reaction and was hurt also watching you two fight like cats and dogs."

"We'll try not to let it happen again," I answered for both of us.

"Adam, what if we forget about the heated discussion, and Dad and I concentrate on getting to know each other and appreciate who we really are?" I realized for the first time that I really knew nothing about who my father really is.

"Suits me just fine," Adam responded in my head.

I told dad about our conversation and agreement, and he was pleased.

Adam interrupted as we entered our hometown.

"Hey, look at the carillon park with the four bells. Remember. Alex after that ball game you and Cindy making out? First French kiss under the bells."

"Thank you, I do remember Adam."

"What are you thinking about, son."

"Adam and I are just reminiscing about the tower."

"How do you feel?" Dad continued sounding like a

parent.

"A little tired."

"Do you want to stop?"

"No, let's just go home. I'll feel better after I rest for an hour or two.

"Janice has been working on the house for weeks looking forward to your coming home. Everything 's spotless with new sheets and curtains in your room. She wanted it perfect for her baby boy. Guess you'll have to adjust to her spoiling you again."

I had forgotten all about Janice, our nanny. She took such good care of us, just like a mother and she is a great cook, if I remembered correctly.

"I'm so glad that she is still with you, she must be getting up in years."

"Almost seventy, but as spry as ever. You'll see for yourself when we get there."

It took only a few minutes to arrive at our house. I sat for a moment looking at the dark two-story house with gingerbread trim and five posts encircling the half-moon porch. The three wrought iron doors with the tall evergreen tree near the entrance and the contrast of the gray color of the house painted a homey picture.

"Home sweet home." I said with a smile.

"I am glad you're here, Son."

Janice came rushing out the door, running down the stairs and came to open the door. She was already crying and couldn't wait for me to get out of the car so she could hug me.

"Alex, my little one. It's been such a long time. Welcome home."

I held her in my arms and felt the realness and sincerity of the love between us, I must be in paradise. She smelled like the bread she had probably been baking, and when I looked in her misty, blue eyes I could sense a strength and the resolve to watch over and protect her love ones—like typical grandmothers of the world.

"Let's get him inside. He had a big day and needs to rest."

They helped me up the stairs into the house, Dad had moved his desk and a few things out of his study and into the living room and created a bedroom on the main floor for me. I was overwhelmed by the feeling of the familiar surroundings. This time I was truly home. I suddenly felt so weak I didn't know if I would be able to take another step when I felt Adam's strength surge through my body coming to my rescue.

Safely tucked in bed I feel asleep overpowered by the mixture of the activities and the emotions of the day.

I spent the next two weeks building my strength. I started walking a little each day increasing the distance as I felt up to it and resting when I was tired. Just paying attention to my body. I had remembered correctly about Janice's cooking. My appetite increased twofold just looking forward to her cooked meals.

I could feel Adam's presence, but he made the decision to let me adjust and not add to my memory for a while. So, most days it was just Janice and me at the house since Dad made frequent trips to the city. I moved to my old room. Adam and I were sharing it again. The healing was coming along.

~~~

CHAPTER 30

About a week after I left the hospital, Clay showed up for the first time. He was amazed to see father and myself out back playing basketball.

"Hey, guys, who's is winning?"

"Dad, but not for long," I answered.

"I better enjoy my victories, at the rate you're going I'll be a has-been by next week," Dad admitted.

I had come a long way. I was walking with a mixture of jogging between two and three miles a day, jumping rope, lifting weights, and playing basketball with Dad whenever he had the time.

"I see you are ready to face the world," Clay observed. "By the way have you practiced the exercises I taught you. "

"Every day without fail."

We all went inside for iced tea, sitting at the dining room table while Janice buzzed around serving cookies and cake.

"What brings you here?" Zach already impatience was visible.

"We are all going to the big town to a baseball game."

"Great," I responded, "when?"

"This Saturday. Now let me explain," Clay continued. "Zach remember that donation you made to the city?"

"Of course."

"Well, I had your office call and request tickets to the

game figuring that they would send VIP tickets, and sure enough we have tickets in the private box with the senator."

"What's this all about?" Adam interrupted telepathically in my head.

Clay heard him and turned around to me, but spoke directly to Adam through transference, I will definitely need your help. Adam replied immediately. He spoke with so much emotions that, Zach picked up on the vibrations and heard it also.

"I've been ready for a long time."

Clay and Adam avoided out questions and suggested that we just forget about it for now, and to enjoy the day. Just to get our minds off the obvious tension, Dad got out a deck of playing cards and the three of us played gin rummy until dinner. Clay enjoyed Janice's pot roast and left to drive to the city without answering our concern.

Dad and I tried to pry Adam after Clay left, he wouldn't budge. "The matter is close for now, beside if I tell it is going to unsettle Alex and he needs as much rest as possible."

Saturday morning, Father and I got dressed for the occasion, found our old baseball caps, and loaded in the car. It was a great day, not a cloud in the sky, not too hot or humid, just a perfect day for our favorite team to annihilate their opponent.

When we arrived, the stadium was already packed. Thanks, goodness, for the VIP parking card the office had sent with the tickets. You could feel the excitement in the air. Everyone swarmed into the stadium like ants in a massive hill stopping only to get their food and liquid refreshments. The blimp circled above with two small planes pulling some commercial banner that I couldn't read.

The gate was packed with baseball fans young and old with banners in their hands ready to cheer their team, it had an almost circus atmosphere with fans wearing hats, wigs, painted faces and signs on their bodies, carrying hot-dogs, popcorn, drinks and cotton candy. For a moment I flashed to the fair and the bumper cars as well as Harold and Jane. What a nice time in my life, hope they're doing well.

I hadn't kept up with any sports for years, but after Clay came by, I checked the newspaper and found out that this was the first winning season in many years, like with their season for our hometown way back in 1977. Dad found an usher who was trying to help several dads with their impatient kids to find their gate.

When we presented our passes, he took us directly to a special entrance for the home team locker room. Several players as well as the manager knew Dad and were thanking him for something. I was impressed. We stayed only for a few minutes.

"Come on Son, let's go up. Good luck, Coach."

We took the door behind us back out in the exited crowd to an elevator which took us to the IP floor. There were some security men waiting to check us out when the elevator doors opened. After all the senator was going to be present. We were checked again before we could enter the box.

There are six or seven people already enjoying the buffet and drinks from the bar, seats for about twenty-five to thirty people. Situated at the top of the stadium over the home team dugout, we had a perfect view of the playing field with little closed-circuit televisions so we could hear the commentary. The team had moved in the new stadium in 1994 so everyone was commenting on the new facilities.

It was quite thrilling even for Adam who was impressed, "Is this fantastic or what?" he whispered to me. Before I could agree with him several people walked in the door and immediately Adam whispered to me.

"From now on I can't talk to you, and please don't try to talk to me. You'll understand soon."

One of the men entering was Lazlo with his cold penetrating eyes. A chill ran down my back. *What is going on here?* was my immediate thought, that and being totally freaked out. Fortunately, being in the streets for three years helped me to regain my control instantly.

"Hey, Dad."

"What son?"

"This man is Lazlo." Speaking with as much control as I could muster at that moment.

"You don't say." He didn't seem surprised.

"Do you know what this is all about?"

"No, but I 'm sure that it will be all made clear when Clay arrives."

Keeping my voice low, I couldn't take my eyes off Lazlo and admitted, "Zach, I'm worried."

The old gentleman sat down in a chair removed from the other twenty or so other chairs available. I wondered to myself why would someone sit in the very back of the box when there were seats closer to the front to watch the game. Maybe he didn't come to watch the game crossed my mind.

"Has Adam said anything to you," Whispered father.

"Not a word."

A dozen individuals came in, mostly officials including the mayor, greeting each other, and shaking hands with the rest. Dad knew all of them.

"Zach, glad to have you with us."

"Good afternoon, Mr. Mayor." Dad answered.

"Thank you again for your generous donation. I'm sure you know how much it means to the city," the mayor continued.

He introduced father to several visitors, then Dad presented me to everyone. Lazlo got up and mingled with the group. He seemed to know all of them, a real diplomat.

Down in the ballpark the fever was mounting with the roar of the crowd penetrating even our enclosure. Vendors going up and down the aisles selling popcorn, peanuts, drinks, team memorabilia. Fans still trying to find their sears, and across in the press box technicians were making last minute adjustments, commentators shuffling papers, talking on the phones for last minute instructions.

The door opened with a loud slam, and everyone turned around toward the back room. The senator entered.

"Mr. Mayor, how are you?" His hand extended ready to shake.

"Senator, glad you could make it."

"Wouldn't have missed it for the world. Our team's going to make the whole state proud today." Spoken like a true politician.

The mayor introduced everyone including Dad, Lazlo, and myself. Then he picked up the phone telling an official that the senator had arrived. Taking his arm, he escorted him to the front of the window where the two of them stood and waived to the crowd while the loudspeaker announced his presence and displayed it in the big screen.

Clay had slipped in the room unnoticed during all the cheering, and Dad walked over to shake his hand.

"Zach, I see you made it," Clay held his hand.

"Of course, I made it, I was beginning to wonder about you."

I walked over to the two of them, "Alex, are enjoying yourself?"

"Very much, Clay, but what is going on?"

"I'll tell you later. Now, let's go watch the game."

They announced the national anthem, and we all moved closer to the window looking down on the players standing in the middle of the field with their hats over their heart singing along with the crowd. Me, woman, children, all creeds and colors, all walks of life joined in unison with "Oh, say can you see...."

With the last note the announcer added, "God bless America," and the crowd went wild, the stadium filled with energy. The umpire yelled,

"Play Ball!"

The multitude exploded when the first ball was struck by the bat. Hit high, high up in the air, it looked like a homerun but sailed to the left just out of bounds as it came down. What a rush! The fans settled down a little, and we all finally took our seats. The visitors have a one run lead at the end of the first inning, but our team has plenty of time. We all settle down to a scoreless second and third inning.

Then in the fourth inning we have the base loaded, and the pitcher steps up to the plate. Great, bases loaded, two outs, and the pitcher is up, but on the second pitch, wonder of wonders happened, he knocked the ball out of the ballpark. The fans are ecstatic, jumping up and down, kissing and hugging perfect strangers on their right and left. Our group was not so physical, but visible exited.

We had them on the run, so to speak, leading four to one through the fifth and sixth innings.

Then during the seventh inning they got a rally going and scored three runs, tying the game at four to four. The box got noticeably quieter, and several people got up to get drinks or a sandwich.

I noticed that Lazlo had moved over near the Senator standing about four feet behind him with no one noticing.

Clay casually eased over to Dad, whispered something in his ear, and Zach signaled me with his hand to move over to the left. Our team was at bat having just struck out straight batters at the plate. Three up and three on—things were looking good for the home team.

The pitcher got the signal, wound up and released a fast ball right down the middle. Contact! There was a knowing in the sound that tells the crowd that the ball was long gone.

Everyone in the stadium was on their feet. The mayor, the senator, and everyone in the room were standing and cheering. The energy was incredible.

Lazlo raised his arms, and at the exact time Clay raised his arms and said, "NOW!"

~~~

CHAPTER 31

Zach raised his arms and at the same moment Adam spoke to me, "Raise your arms in Lazlo's direction and pull the energy. I will do the rest."

I felt an immense rush of forceful energy going through my body pulling with inconceivable strength. The crowd screams, the Senator screams, everyone cheers. Lazlo screams as he turns around and we all have our arms raised. Five shadows ripped out of his body, he contorted in hideous pain, his body shriveling into a pile of dust.

Clay grabbed his clothes and threw them in under the refreshment table. No more than nine or ten seconds had passed, just long enough for a homerun to be scored. I am visibly shaken. Adam speaks to me.

"Snap out of it, Alex."

"What did we do?" Was all I could think.

"We released five souls." Adam answered with no emotion.

I was shaking all over, "You guys are nuts."

"How do you think we will get yours?" Adam's presence calmed me a little.

"Some kind of warning would be appreciated."

"Sorry, but it might have jeopardized the plan. It had to be spontaneous, and at just the right moment Even Clay and I had no idea until Lazlo made his move for the Senator. That was the perfect moment. His energy was directed toward the senator, and he had no defense against us."

"I am traumatized and all you can say is 'Sorry'."

"If you want, I'll send you a letter of apology."

"Good make it soon so I can frame it." Our dialogues were just like the ones we had when we were kids, Adam always wanting to have the last word. "Now, Alex, got to' leave you and take care of these five souls with Clay. They have got to be more scared that you."

"Don't let me stop you."

He blocked me out so I could not hear him, but I saw the shadows calming down, listening, and eventually following Clay and Adam out of the room.

"Dad, did you know what was going to happen?" He shook his head.

"I just knew to be ready."

"This is all crazy."

"Listen, Son, these people must be stopped."

"Yes, but..."

"But, what. Do you think they ask permission when they yank the soul out of people? Do you think they give them a warning or decision in the matter?" Dad had a point.

Clay came back in the room and walked over to me "Sorry, I didn't have a chance to warn you, I just had to play it by ear."

"Next time I'll be on my guard." I had calmed down enough to respond.

"And well you should, Alex. Good job."

The game had started again. We were leading by four and amazingly no one noticed a thing, people cheering, getting food and drinks. The Senator came over to look and grabbed a drink. As for me, I was getting over my initial shock. Life went on as usual.

"Lazlo will not be missed," Dad said, kind of reading my thoughts and put his arm on my shoulder.

How about some refreshments, Alex?

"Why not?"

I asked father what would happen to the souls, and he just said that we would talk about it later. I took a sip of my soda, while the Senator and his entourage were about to leave, possibly to beat the rush.

Stepping over the window I watched the last pitch of the game in a daze. The home team was triumphant, and the fan were streaming on to the field in celebration. There were lots of hands shaking and patting on the back going on in the room as everyone was leaving.

Clay, Dad, and I were the only ones left in the box. There seemed no reason to get in the crowd as they all rushed toward the exits holding children or loved one. In their place they left paper, cups, all sort of trash, and boxes for the cleanup crew to dispose of. In fact, the crew were already starting in their work in the nosebleed section with their blowers pushing all the debris down to the lower levels to be picked up.

Clay had been speaking to Dad when he turned and spoke to me "Alex, we hope that we didn't shock you too badly."

"As a matter of fact, you did, but I'll recover." Smiling as I spoke.

"It is the first time we have attempted a task of this magnitude, so it was necessary that we be able to improvise and use the elements of surprise to our advantage."

"Well, you sure surprised me," I admitted. "How did you know what to do?"

"The basics I found in an ancient book. "I'm glad it worked." Clay explained.

"So are we. Simply said we just took all the positive energy,"

"Why don't people use the positive energy for themselves?"

"They forget. It's easier to feel sorry for themselves than to seek out the positive and fight."

"What was my part?" I asked.

"Lazlo was incredibly old and knowledgeable in the negative force, so we needed as much positive energy as possible. You and Adam possess more positive energy than you can imagine. You'll learn as time passes; I'll see to that. Just be patient and trust for now."

"Why did he disintegrate?"

"His body was over four hundred years old," he answered nonchalantly.

"That is not possible." Realizing as I replied that I was slowly learning that anything is possible.

"Yes, it was possible for him. He had mastered removing the soul from innocent, unsuspecting people without their awareness. He would use up their energy, their life force, released it and get another." Clay hesitated. "Imagine how many innocent bystanders he had personally destroyed over his four hundred years lifespan. These people must be stopped!"

"There is more," Adam's voice had manifested itself in my head loud enough for all three of us to hear him telepathically. We waited for his thoughts.

"Three of the souls were very deteriorated, so I let them go to their well-deserved rest, but the other two were puzzling."

For the first time Zach spoke up and asked, "Adam, don't keep us hanging."

"Well, one is a high-ranking officer in the military, the other a successful businessman in a large corporation."

"Where are you going with this?" Clay interrupted.

"Well, we took them back into their own physical bodies after they had both told me about being manipulated." Adam had carefully picked his last word." Manipulated how?" Zach asked.

"After their souls were removed, they were asked, or

rather instructed to perform tasks or reveal certain information or they would never feel their souls again."

Zach blurted out. "That is blackmail."

"You've got it, and you can ask Alex how it felt to have no feeling with nightmares every night. And since they had total control, there is no way to rebel."

"No way to fight." I added.

"No, when your soul has been removed without your knowledge, it is too late to fight." Adam concluded.

I suddenly realized that with my soul gone for so long in Simon's control there could be nothing left, or it could be in a bad shape, so I asked, 'Could it be too late for my soul?

"No, Alex, you were born with a gift. For unknown reasons your soul cannot be destroyed." Dad quickly tried to erase that fear from my thoughts.

"Simon's must be keeping it for an especially evil moment in his life," Clay added.

"Charming," came to my mind.

"Don't worry, we'll get yours next,"

"Don't worry you say, the last time I saw him he nearly crushed my windpipe."

"I know. I was there. I was the one who had to toss his snake, and I don't like to touch snakes, even with my soul."

More anxious than ever, I pushed, "So how are we going to do this?"

"The element of surprise. You need to rest for a couple of weeks first. You're still pretty weak," Adam interjected.

"Two weeks. No more. I have you guys as my witnesses," motioning Zach and Clay for support as I spoke.

"Give a day or two," Adam tried to hedge.

"No. Two weeks, no more."

"Yeah, yeah, yeah." Again, he played me like a fiddle.

We all laughed. We got up from our chairs and headed

out. Lazlo's clothes were left, he wouldn't need them. The ballpark was deserted, even the ushers and security had left. Only the vendors and janitors still busied themselves. The parking lot was also empty. We walked Clay to his car and sent him on his way. Zach and I climbed in the company truck and drove home. What a game! What a day!

~~~

CHAPTER 32

Riding home was fun. We talked about our accomplishments and winning the ball game, we passed the white brick church. From there I knew we were only five or six miles from home. Dusk was falling rapidly. I was exhausted from the events of the day.

Alex are you okay?

"Just tired, Dad."

"Hang on, we'll be home in a jiffy."

"I'll be all right."

Zach grabbed the cellular phone, dialed a number, and waited for the party to answer.

"Janice, Zach here. Listen, prepare something to eat. Alex and I will be home in five minutes. Thanks," he turned the phone off and sped up all at the same time to get us home faster. Janice was waiting for us on the porch, and we had barely gotten out of the car before she started asking questions. "So, we must have won?"

"Yeah, by four runs. Didn't you watch the game?"

"I didn't have the time."

"Who told you that we won?"

"It's written all over your faces."

"I had no reply. I just followed her to the dining room, where a tray of sandwiches was waiting for us. I had a voracious appetite and dove right in; Janice came in with a steaming bowl of soup for each one of us.

"What kind of soup is it, Janice?" Dad asked.

"Navy beans and sausage, Mr. Beard, and save room for fresh peach cobbled. One of the local farmers left a basket of peaches on the back porch this morning."

"I'm going to enjoy it."

"Me two I haven't got peach cobbler as well as homemade made soup in years." I sounded funny, but it was true.

We paid homage to this well-prepared meal, and I was stuffed by the time we left the dining room. I went straight to the bathroom and took a shower while father went to the study. After my shower I barely made to the bed. I was exhausted by all the events of the day.

The coma had really whipped me out, and it had taken so long to gain my strength again. Now I was well enough to know that I wanted everything right in my life, and patience was not in my vocabulary.

The sun woke me up since I had forgotten to pull down the shades. I laid in bed wondering what today was going to bring, when there was a knock on my door, and I came out of my daydreaming.

"Come in."

Dad walked in and sat on the bed. "Sleep well?"

I looked at him still half asleep. "Yeah, Dad."

"Good. Get ready, we have a long day ahead of us."

No matter what I asked, all he would answer was that it was a surprise. I gave up and asked, "Okay, when are we leaving?"

"After you freshen up."

"Why so early?"

"Early? It is five to ten, you lazy bum." He added that he was willing to bodily throw me in the shower by force.

"Well, I learned from the best."

He grabbed me, and we wrestled a few minutes before he let me go, I let him win, of course. His ego must be handled gently. I told him right after we stopped.

"I could have hurt you. I let you win, cause you're my

Dad."

He just looked at me from the corner of his eye, and we both laughed.

He left and I thought about the friends who helped me to survive in the streets, and it is because of them that I can now wake up and wrestle with my father. None of this would have been possible without them, I shook away my memories and jumped in the shower, went downstairs, and asked surprised.

"No breakfast?"

"No, we are going to the restaurant."

"Which one?"

"The buffet, all you can eat downtown." Boy, he Knew how to get me moving.

Grabbing the keys as I headed for the door, "Let's go Dad.

We drove across town. It was always quiet on Sundays, but we could hardly drive on any Saturday when it seemed like everyone in the county came in town.

We found a spot right in front of the restaurant, locked the car, and walked in. Since it was early, it was seat yourself. We located a table in the nonsmoking section and ordered our drinks. I got up to walk over to look at the airplane the restaurant had on display. It was made of bent rosewood, but the most amazing thing about this plane was that it could take off vertically. The inventor developed his design from passages he had found in the bible. The story was remarkable.

"Dad, did it really fly." He got up and joined me.

"Not this one, it's a replica. But the original one flew one year before the one in Kitty Hawk,"

"How come no one knew about this one?" Remembering how Adam and I loved to sit and look at this plane as kids.

"The inventor was bringing it to the 1904 World's Fair, but it was blown off the train. It hadn't been strapped down properly." My question got answered.

"Neat machinery," I observed.

It took twelve years to rebuild, and the second time out crashed on takeoff.'

My mind wondered to the plans that Adam and I had made to build our own airplane. We must have been about ten years old.

"I wish I had the knowledge to build a machine of this quality."

"Me, two, Alex, but let's eat now. We have an appointment,"

We sat down and were served by the most charming waitress; it was her first day at work and felt very inadequate. We left just in time, as customers were pouring in from every direction. I got in the car; my stomach was full. I asked Zach, "Were to next?"

"Surprise."

Again?

"No, this is the big surprise."

We headed out of town towards the interstate. Adam decided to pop in and made himself known, Hi, Dad. Hi, Alex. The telepathy still spooked me some, I guess I'll have to get used to it until I get my own soul back and the sooner the better.

"Hey, Son."

"Where have you been?"

"Just in another dimension."

"What do you mean?" I pressed for more information.

"Now that you are used to me inside if you, I can come and go without your noticing."

"But I don't have the void anymore."

"Yep, I know. I filled it with our memories, hope, peace, and love, so I'm free to get on with my work without you freaking out."

"What work?" I couldn't let it go.

"Are you two ever going to stop discussing everything

to its minute detail?"

"No, Dad" we both answered together, which made me smile, but didn't distract me from getting an answer.

"What work?" I asked again.

"Listen, Alex," Adam has things he must do by himself. We can't help him; we can only trust him."

"I'm just trying to learn to deal with this energy stuff, and how to cope with being a spirit," Adam finally replied.

By now we had arrived at the interstate. Dad pulled into the interstate, put on the cruise control, and headed west. We talked about the game for a moment, then our conversation drifted to our childhood.

"Remember when I took you two to the pony ride for your fifth birthday?" It struck me that Dad must have really been lonely with both of us gone.

"I remember. It was so much fun riding the ponies. Adam's pony was gray, and mine was brown with a white tail. We insisted on giving them names before mounting them."

Neither one of us could recall what their names were, but it didn't seem important. We were sharing memories —that's all that mattered to me.

"Remember, Dad, how sick we got?"

"Of course. Both of you ate and drank too much."

"Yes, we got sick in the car, and you got upset." I blessed being able to remember.

"I cleaned the car for two days. It still smelled for a month." Adam added.

"It's your fault, you let us eat so much."

Dad made the hundred mile plus in less than two hours and was heading toward the old neighborhood. My stomach was getting to feel like butterflies. Obviously, we weren't going to the apartment but toward the deserted yellow brick building. I felt anxious, I had so many nightmares there.

I had found Bill there in a state of filth and totally out

of his mind. Remember Lips coming in to tell us about Jack. I wondered why we were going there but was afraid to ask. Perhaps I was getting a cold chill because I had recently experienced the cleanliness of the hospital, and the coziness of my home. I dreaded facing the reality of the miserable life I had lived in that neighborhood.

"Alex, do you remember yesterday when the mayor thanked me for the donation?"

"Yes."

"Well, Son, I said I would explain."

"I remember."

"How about when Rick, Theresa, and all the others talked about how much work they had coming up?"

"What are you trying to tell me?"

~~~

CHAPTER 33

When Zach turned at the next corner, Maggie was standing on the sidewalk waving at us. She was wearing a new yellow dress with a purple belt and matching shoes. She looked like a model with her hair flowing in the breeze waving at us wildly the minute that she saw our car.

Dad stopped the car. Maggie came over and opened the door. She leaned and gave me a kiss on the cheek. She got in beside me and Dad took off. She handed me a box that was wrapped with a bow tied around it. She also had an envelope, which she handed me.

"Open them." She asked softly.

I opened the envelop attached to the card, it read, "We all missed you, but I missed you most of all, Maggie." And the card was signed by all my friends.

"Open the box, open the box," She was getting impatient. I ripped off the paper and opened the cardboard box. Inside was a yellow t-shirt matching her dress. I lifted the t-shirt to look at it more closely. In bold print the letters spelled, "Glimmer of Hope."

"What does it mean?" I asked Dad.

He turned the car solely to the left into the narrow street. Everyone was there in yellow t-shirts jumping up and down and screaming.

"Surprise."

Maggie was hugging me. Lips, One Eye, Garry, and

Theresa were mobbing the car. Everyone was shouting, laughing, clapping. I was more than surprised, I couldn't speak. Bill opened the door and pulled me out after helping Maggie out.

He was about to shake my hand. "How do you like it?"

My knees went weak. I took a few steps forward. Zach raised his arms, and everyone got quiet. The crowd split in the middle and standing there were all the important people in my life—Peggy, Big Joe, Harold, and Jane with a box of brownies in her hand. Even Garry, my therapist, and Heather, my nurse, and Janice was there. Wow!

I didn't know what to do. I turned around to ask my father what it all meant. He was just behind me smiling and holding a purple velvet pillow with a symbolic pair of golden scissors in his hands. He leaned over and whispered.

"Welcome home, Son."

The emotions were overwhelming. I blushed; my eyes exploded as tears streamed down my face.

Truly I didn't know what to do next. Maggie came to my rescue and gently reached for my shoulders and turned me around. Dad came to my left still holding the purple pillow.

"You are supposed to cut the ribbon," Maggie lead me on smiling.

I took the scissor like a zombie, while all my special friends stepped aside and unrolled a red ribbon. It was blocking a new door to the entrance of the building that I formerly called "the Ritz." It had been totally renovated and looked elegant. I cut the ribbon feeling as if I were in a dream, and at any moment would wake up. But everyone applauded and yelled, "Hip, hip, hurrah!"

Peggy came forward with a piece of paper in her hand. She had prepared a speech. Everyone quieted down.

"Alex<" she began, "when your father found out about your accident, he started to investigate, Big Joe helped him. When they found out about the conditions you and all the other kids had lived in, he was touched. What really impressed him was how you found jobs for so many of the older kids." She turned the page.

"He was also impressed with your getting yourself an apartment and letting everyone come to rest and shower. He hears how you clothed the little kids, too. He decides to go to the mayor and arranged to buy this city block and renovate it. He bought it outright and hired me to manage it. So today, everyone is here to thank you for giving us hope and helping us believe in ourselves again. This building is equipped with a kitchen, dining room, rec room with sleeping quarters and shower on every floor. I've said enough, so come inside and see for yourself."

There was no stopping the tears at this point, this was surely a dream, it was too good to be true. I stepped inside the front door. There was nothing left of the building I remembered. Gone was the dark, moldy, smelly cardboard laying all over the floor. Instead a bright, airy, and clean floor that had been waxed until it gleamed. There were flowerpots and plants along the side of the walls. I could smell fresh paint. Walls had been knocked down to create the dining room. The kitchen was completely equipped with pots and pans, an industrial refrigerator, and a double sink for washing dishes. Upstairs the bedroom was bright and had two bed per room. All the bed had fresh linen and soft pillow. All the windows had curtains, and beside each bed was a table and lamp with a desk as well.

I was so emotionally touched by this transformation that I had to lean against the wall, my head was spinning. This was a dream come true.

"How do you like it." Maggie asked, taking the opportunity for us to be alone as we walked through the building.

"It's fantastic! And you never told me a thing about it

during all those months."

"You were too busy loafing in the hospital."

"I had an accident." Stammering like a kid even thought I knew that she was teasing. "Nobody asked you to have an accident. So, we didn't ask your permission to start this project."

"Boy, this is more than a surprise."

"Don't you forget to thank your dad. It couldn't have happened without him."

"I assure you, I won't." How could I ever really thank him? I thought as Maggie guided me through the hallways.

Each hallway had a bright ceiling light, and every floor was painted a different color. All the doors were solid wood, not that flimsy particle board, and had a brass doorknob.

"Maggie, how did you come up with 'Glimmer of Hope'? That's what you call this place, right?"

"Yes. We had some brainstorming sessions, and one night that's the name that stuck."

"I like the name." *It really fit with the only thing that kept us going when it was cold, no food, and no help in sight for all those years,* I thought.

"So, do we. Lips actually came up with it."

"Lips? It must have made him feel pretty proud."

"You bet, but what really makes him proud is that he's in charge of maintenance around here."

"How so?" I was intrigued.

"In order to give everybody a vested interest, each person has a job around here. There's bookkeeping, laundry, kitchen, and the nursery duty. Then there's our information program, and security, this gives everyone a chance to contribute and feel needed."

"I'm so impressed."

"We're self-sufficient for seventy-five percent of our expenses, the rest we find outside," she went on.

"Like what, for example?"

"School, kindergarten, plumbing, garbage pickup, accounting, and legal stuff. The main structure is taken care of by Zach."

"What about money?"

"The city provided a little, and Theresa oversees fundraising, and again Zach pays for the difference."

"By the way, where is everybody?"

"Downstairs having a great party to celebrate your return. After all, this is the grand opening. We better go down and join them."

" Yes, ma'am," I answered and added, "I'll follow you anywhere."

She laughed. She was so proud of this place. She was glowing. It seemed as she was floating on air. I couldn't resist and took her in my arms, kissed her, and said. "I love you Maggie."

"Hey, hey, hey, behave yourself," Adam was talking in my head.

Meanwhile Maggie was blushing and hugging me around my neck.

"Alex, we were so worried about you when we found out about the accident. The first time I saw you in the coma, I cried. To see you here, I won't ever let go of you again."

Adam quietly gave me his opinion, "You are hooked, brother."

"Don't get jealous, Adam or I'll block you out. Do you hear?"

"Don't waste time talking to me, kiss her again," was his answer.

I took his advice, put my arm around her waist, and we walked down to the dining room.

The party was going on strong. Everybody was having a good time. The radio was blaring, but thankfully in this neck of the woods we weren't about to disturb anybody. Most of this neighborhood had been deserted for the past ten years. It looked like we might be bringing some new blood in the area.

Maggie and I joined the crowd. I met Big Joe's wife, who was almost a foot taller than him,

"Alex, I want you to meet my wife, Alice."

"Please to meet you, ma'am."

"Me, too. I heard you worked for Harold and Jane. They are dear friends of mine."

"Yes, ma'am. I had a wonderful time with them. They gave me the will to fight and live again."

"They are pretty found of you, too."

I kept mingling. Each person wanted to know how I was or to thank me. Dad was also getting his share of appreciation and hero worship, which was well-deserved. I needed to have a serious talk with him once everything was over.

Lips came to thank me. "How does it feel to be a hero to everyone?"

"Great." I became uncomfortable to be classified as a hero, so I changed the subject rapidly.

"I hear congratulations are in order, Lips. You are overseeing keeping the place clean."

"Yes, Sir, and clean I will keep it."

"How many do you have working with you?"

"There are four of us. We clean the hallways, bathrooms, and kitchen. Everyone does their own bedroom. We sweep the sidewalks every morning, empty the garbage, and clean the rec room."

"Enough, enough. I understand," I laugh.

"Is he bothering you?" Bill had sneaked up behind me and put his hand on my shoulder.

"Bill, what are you up to these days?"

"Not much. I still have the nightmares, and the fear, but I have complete confidence that it's going to get better with all of you around me."

"Now that I am better, I can help you more often."

"Appreciate it, man. I see you're doing fine," Bill had come a long way.

"Never better." What a wonderful feeling being back with my friends.

"Maggie is a fine girl. You better take good care of her and treat her right, or I'll come after you," Max said laughingly while squinting his eyes to look threatening.

"Beat me up, right."

"Something like that."

"So, tell me, what is your task in the building?" I asked Max.

He told me that he mainly worked outside of the shelter going from business to business asking if they had any jobs available, the he would take the kids over to fill out applications and help them get started.

"What kind of response do you get?"

"Great, I must say. The whole city has heard of your dad's donation and people don't want to get left out, so they give us a chance."

"You do this alone?"

"No James helps me. He's a little older, but I do most of the talking." Pausing to get his breath he rushed on, "We make a good team, he get us in the door and I tell them about life on the streets and how crime will decrease with people getting work, by the way, did you hear about One Eye?"

"No, what happened? Perhaps showing a little concern in my question.

There was pride in Max's voice as he talked about himself and One Eye, "Don't be alarmed. Remember Thomas, the old man who owned the print shop?"

"You mean where all of us lived above the shop in the air conditioner structure?"

"That's is the one. Well he retired not too long ago

since there wasn't enough work. Zach came and bought the shop and cleaned it up. He added some new machines as well and asked Thomas to reopen the print shop and teach us a trade. One Eye is chief editor."

"You're kidding."

"No, Thomas gave him an old leather visor that reads 'editor' across it. It's old and worn out, but One Eye wears it every morning. He gets to the shop before old man Thomas to set up the machines. Then at nine AM they start working."

"What do they print?"

"All sorts of great stuff." Max continued, "Pamphlets on how survive in the street, where to get help, how not to get pregnant, how to get your GED, just to name a few. We also print information on diseases, drug prevention, who to call if you're abused, where to find food and shelter, how to apply for jobs, and a lot of other things. We even have a little book of hope and self-esteem, and it's all for free."

"Man, this great."

"Yes, but the thing I like the best is the fact that 'Glimmer of Hope' is never closed. We have a room on the main floor where you can shower regardless of who you are or what time it is."

These guys had thought of everything. Max was on a roll and proceeded to tell me about the "clothes while you wait service". House coats were available until the clothes they wore in were washed and dried.

"What a great idea!" I was impressed and asked, "Who thought of that?" Bill snuck up on us.

"Theresa. She's really committed to this place," Bill showed his pride as he mentioned her name.

"How is she doing?"

"Great. She works outside, plus some at the shelter."

"I heard you two are going out together."

"Yeah, we've been dating for the last four months."

"She has such poor taste." I said as I slapped him on the back.

"What can I say? Love makes you blind."

"I'm glad you two are happy."

"Let me introduce you to Thomas. He's wanted to meet you, and I see him near the door."

We walked over to an older gentleman with thinning gray hair. He had red cheeks and big ink-stained hands, probably from all those years working the printing press.

"Thomas, I want you to meet someone."

He turned around and said with a twinkle in his eyes, "Bill, it's good to see you." Then asked, "Are you having a good time?"

"Just great, Thomas. I wanted to introduce you to Alex."

I extended my arm and shook the hand of this gentleman; it is amazing me that I had never actually seen this man all those years.

"Please to meet you, Sir."

"Me, too. Please call me Thomas."

"Mighty nice of you to come out of retirement and teach us how to operate all the printing machines."

"Oh, it's good for me, too. I was getting bored with staying home all the time. I've heard about you, young man." Thomas had a peacefulness about him as we spoke.

I felt comfortable with the man, "You probably know now that we used your roof for a home."

"Yes, but I still don't understand why you didn't ask me for help."

"We street kids don't like to ask. Kinda' tired of hearing no, and most of us have been deceived or disappointed by parents or grow-ups. We learn to quit trusting and are actually afraid of adults," I tried to explain.

He looked puzzled. "How could we scare you?"

"We don't want to be deceived repeatedly. Plus, we see

a lot of adults say one thing and do another." I sensed he understood what I was trying to say.

"I understand. I grew up during the war," he added.

"Then you understand why we were confused, but also why it's so vital that for us to learn to trust each other again." And I thought to myself, *it was like a war in the streets*.

"That is the reason I came back to the print shop. I wanted to make a difference, even if it was a small one."

"How is One Eye doing?"

"He's a very good student, he never misses a day, he's always punctual, and I have to kick him out at the end of the day, or he'd stay and work all night."

One thing I'll say about him is that he'll never let you down.'

Maggie walked up to us. "Excuse me Alex, Peggy wants to talk to you."

"Coming Maggie. Nice to have met you, Thomas."

"Likewise, Alex." We shook hands as I turned to leave.

"Thanks to you and your dad, maybe we can change things for the better." He had the right idea.

We walked our way over to Peggy, but not without getting stopped a few times to say hello to folks. There were so many happy people, Big Joe, and Harold together with Garry had started a barbecue place. Sausage, chicken, and hotdogs were piled high on the table. On another table girls were preparing a giant salad, and Jane brought the pastries. She'll make us all fat, as I sized up the brownies.

Rick had returned in a van that had "Glimmer of Hope" logo printed in gold letters across the side and back. He opened the side door and lifted out a tasty looking cake. Two kids ran over to help him, everyone wanted a piece before the main course.

Peggy was moving toward me, "Alex, how do you like this?"

"Absolutely unbelievable."

We stood arm-in-arm in silence watching the festivities.

"Your father came one day after he bought the building and asked me if I wanted to oversee the center. He really caught me off guard and I told him no at first."

I couldn't believe it. "Why? You are perfect for it and I know you've worked for years to help get us kids off the streets."

She was caught off-guard with her answer, "I didn't think I could do it."

"Peggy, you can do anything. You told me so yourself." I reminder her.

"I realized that with the help of the youngsters, and your father wouldn't take no for an answer. We're doing all right as you can see, and I couldn't be happier."

"How can I help you, Peggy?"

"I have a couple of kids from one of the gangs who want to get out, but they're scared of the leader."

"I'll talk to my dad about it and see what I can do."

"They just need another street kid to talk to them and help them to feel strong."

"We'll talk more when I come back in a couple of days."

"We also have a room here for you. It's there for you anytime."

"Peggy, you're the best." There was a thank you in the hug I gave her.

~~~

CHAPTER 34

"**B**ARBECUE'S READY! COME AND GET IT!" shouted Garry. He was as jovial as usual with an oversize fork on his hand, waving it in the air as he spoke.

The rush was on. Folks grabbed the paper plates, plastic forks, and zoomed in on food. Hunger was evident, the children were all over the place, while the older folks waited patiently until the stampede calmed down a bit.

"Alex, your brother is back in your head," I heard Adam say, while laughing at the same time.

"I'm not speaking to you. You never told me about this wonderful project."

"And ruin this surprise? You've got to be kidding!"

"To be honest, I'm glad you and Dad surprised me," I admitted.

"Zach had a lot to do with it."

"It looks that he had everything to do with it."

"You did most of it by believing in yourself. Then you took it one step further by letting others at your place and helping them find jobs and restore their dignity."

Zach walked up next to me, "Talking to your brother, are you now, Alex?"

"How much have you invested in this project?"

"Irrelevant, isn't?" That was a typical answer coming from Dad.

"Of course, but do you have enough to pay for all of this?"

He looked a bit uncomfortable talking about money, "I have enough to do a lot of good, and then some."

"But we live in a small town in a small house."

"Well, Alex, the roof doesn't leak, and there is always hot food on the table. Isn't that enough?" His logic was perfect.

"I guess so. I'm just surprised."

"Do you want me to put an ad in the paper and tell the whole world our financial status?"

"Stop joking."

"Well, I decided long time ago that you and Adam should grow up simply and not have to worry about anything. I did the best that I could, and we still had our problems. Now I have the resources to help other kids, and so I feel privileged to be able to be of assistance. You actually got all of this started, all I did was to give it a little push and financial backing."

"I never realized how much you love us, Dad."

"I know I didn't show it all the time. I was busy and distracted more than I realized at the time, or maybe my priorities were out of balance."

"Well, you've done good," I said as I hugged him. "Now, let's eat a slice of cake."

Dad and I joined the rest of the crowd, and the remainder of the afternoon was a total success. I didn't have a worry in the world. The reality of the street was forgotten, and for a few brief hours everyone relaxed and acted like loving human beings, just being themselves.

Maggie was sitting at one of the tables in her yellow outfit and smiled when she saw me. Lips had a group listening to his stories, and Rick was singing along with the radio. Bill and Teresa joined in. None of them could carry a tune to save their lives, but it didn't matter. Harold was sipping a cup of coffee, and I grabbed the opportunity to go and talk to him, since I hadn't had a chance to say a word to him and Jane.

"Harold, you made most of this possible."

"Alex, you did it yourself." We hugged with a mutual love and respect.

"I must have looked scruffy when you first saw me."

"No kidding, but your smile seemed sincere."

We walked over to a couple of empty chairs. "How is the bumper car business these days?"

"Don't know."

"What do you mean?"

"I got diagnosed with cancer, nothing terminal, but I thought, 'Why not take a break? Now I devote my time to Jane and living every day to its fullest. "

"She must be glad, and good for both of you."

"Well, no one will take care of me but myself. Even lost a few pounds."

"So now you just travel around?"

"Yes. We bought a small RV and got a cell number so my family can contact me. The rest of the time we are going where it's warm in the winter and cool in the summer. We found this place in the north country for the summertime. It's in this incredible forest, and I do a lot of trout fishing." I saw the pleasure in his statement.

"You've got it all figured out."

"I spent thirty-one years in the bumper ride business. Don't you think Jane deserves my undivided attention for a while?"

"Hey. Go for it and make her happy. Looks like it agrees with both of you."

We reminisce about the five weeks we spent satisfying all the customers. I asked about the other ride owners, and how they were doing. He insisted that I take his number and to call if I ever needed any help. I said I would call even if I didn't need his help, I wanted to stay in contact with him and Jane.

They were the turning point for me, and I'll never forget them, I wanted to keep them in my life, even if they didn't live here.

Dusk was falling. All the children had been taken inside, and the volunteers were helping them get ready for bed.

We started folding the chairs and taking down the tables. Others put away the food and cleaned up the remaining paper plates and trash. Butterball got a broom, Lips followed behind with a trash bag. In less than an hour the place was spic and span again.

People sitting in groups, talking about the day and how much fun they had. I sat down on an ice cooler, and Big Joe came over.

"I gave your job away."

"No sweat, I'm still not in shape to get back to work."

"The yards are expanding, so I asked Rick to bring a few young lads to apply. I am promoting him as a supervisor. He's going to oversee hardware, he'll be restocking, cutting chains, finding the right screw or bolt. He really likes the challenge."

"I hope he liked the advancement."

Big Joe laughed. "Well, he's been hounding me for the last two months."

"Alex, we need to leave." Father had walked up.

"Be right with you, Dad."

"How are you doing, Zach."

"Joe, can't complain, and you?"

"Great! We don't see you around much anymore, Missy would like to have you both to the house for dinner."

"Call me, and we'll set a date."

"I'll do it next week."

"Come on, Alex it's getting late."

We said our goodbyes to everyone before heading back home. We were back on to the highway leading to our town.

~~~

CHAPTER 35

As we turned into our driveway, I recalled an important subject, "Dad Peggy approached me about two street gang members that want to get out of the gang. It's just that they afraid of the consequences if they do."

"When do you want to take care of it?"

"You don't mind?"

"No, not as long as you take someone with you. And I don't mean Adam. I mean someone physical."

"You're making a joke."

"Yes, but I mean take someone with you."

"Who do you suggest?"

"If you do it in the next couple of days, Pat or I will come with you."

"Pat?"

"Pat McGill, you know, he used to come to the house all the time."

"Don't remember."

"You saw him at the yard. He's the one who told me you were working there."

"Now I recall. Why don't we do it toward the end of the week?"

Back in town. The large brick house on the main street was all lighted up. They must have been having a celebration of some sort. It looked nice with eight brick columns, four on each side of the entry way decorated with tiny lights encircling each column. They had built two balconies that covered the front porch. People were coming in and out of the porch door as well as the other side entrance.

Gentlemen in black ties held their glasses raised for a toast, and ladies in long elegant gowns stood by chatting. The balconies were visible due to spotlight pointing upward, and the window's walk was decorated with more tiny white lights giving the house a castle effect. It looked so elegant.

We turned and drove by the park and then past the gazebo with the duck on top of downtown. We were both pleasantly exhausted as we arrived home after stopping for milk for breakfast.

A knock at my door brought me out of my daydreaming.

"Come in."

"Alex, could you come out and meet me in the study? I have a lot of work to do and could use your help."

"Be right there, Zach."

I slipped out of my robe to put on a pair of jeans and a light shirt.

I walked downstairs in the study, where Dad was sitting at his desk. It was almost completely cleared off, except for a couple of frames with picture of Adam and me. The telephone was off to the side. I looked around the rest of the room, it was almost empty as well. Gone were the stack of papers, books, and magazines.

"Sit down, Alex. There are quite a few things that I need to be cleared up."

I sat quietly in the recliner, while Dad seemed to gather his thoughts. He sighed and seemed anxious as well.

"There's a lot I have to tell you, but feel free to interrupt and ask questions."

"Before we start, where is Adam." I asked.

"Adam's soul is inside you, but the essence of his spirit

can come and go. You have your own life to lead, and he doesn't want to intrude all the time."

"So, he's here right now."

"No. He left you enough of his soul to fill the void in your heart... .He replaced feeling, memory, love, forgiveness, and if he thinks you need him or you are in danger, he will automatically return."

"I been wondering about that, sometimes we can talk, and other times he just disappears. Now it makes more sense."

"Let's go back to the beginning. For a long time, even before I met your mother, I had been involved in the consciousness movement. It focused on loving everyone without judgment, helping each other, self-awareness, directing the energy of the universe to the betterment of others and oneself, I met your mother Sarah at one of those meetings.

We began seeing each other, and as our love grew, we made plans to spend the rest of our lives together.

After a pause he continued, "Later I found out that your mother had special powers, more powerful than anything I had ever encountered. She rarely talked about it, but she was always made sure she surrounded herself with a shield of energy. When it was up and around her, she was calm and serene, but when she got sick and couldn't keep the shield up, she was nervous and anxious. No, even more than that, she was downright scared." We stared at each other.

"So, one day I asked what it was all about. What she told me came as an avalanche and left me dumbfounded for a long time. She had been part of an organization of people with interests like hers that were developing or researching ways to control weaker spirits without the person realizing what was happening. The person would just suddenly start experiencing fear and not much else. These people could take a soul either by being with the person or over the phone using hypnosis. Your mother was a part of this, but eventually she couldn't cope with the way they were using their power and questioning their subjects. One day she decided to leave, knowing it wouldn't be easy and that they would never stop hunting until they would find her."

"To protect herself, she put up a shield of energy, and by doing so she was safe, and no one could find her. Your mother and I share twelve special years. During that time, I met Clayton, he became a good friend. He also became my mentor, and I learned a whole lot from him about metaphysics, Slowly I let my guard down and told him about the secret organization. Turned out that Clay had heard of them, but no one ever knew where they were or how they operated. With time, Clay and I forgot amount, or let's say we put it on the back of our minds. However, your mother never let up her vigilance, I guess Clay and I just couldn't grasp the magnitude of their power to destroy people's lives." Father got up to get himself a drink and came right back.

"One day your mother came home with the second most beautiful news in the world. She told me that she was pregnant."

"Zach, what was the best news in the world?"

"It was a few second later when she told me that we were going to have twins."

Now that made me smile. No matter how serious Dad was, he always had a way to bring a smile or laugh in the flow of the conversation. "I felt so proud about the good news, I immediately took off one week, we flew to a private resort and celebrated. Upon our return, I decided to become less of a workaholic. I would take off two days a week to spend quality time with her."

"I can't tell you what or when the changes happen, because I'm not sure myself, she must have let her guard down. That part still puzzles me, how it was that they got a hold of her. In any case, she started to experience the fear again. She never let it interfere with our life. All she would say was that no matter what happened, her love would always be with me. I still feel it today as strong as the day she said, 'I do'." He whipped his face and blew his nose.

"On the day you and Adam were born, your mom was in the middle of labor. We had just moved her to the delivery room. Her contractions were continuous. She was close to giving birth, she delivered Adam, and you followed minutes later. We were so happy, but your mother was quite drained." Zach face changed at the painful memory.

"An intern appeared, and moved his arms, I didn't know it, however he drained her of her last energy. Your mother suddenly turned white, clutched my hand, and drew me down close to her."

"She looked at me with sad eyes. The life was draining out of her, and it scared me like never. At that moment she musters all the energy she could and sent all of it toward Alex, as he received the entire dose of life force, she then whispered the words, 'Take care of the children. You know I will love you forever.' And she was gone just like that."

~~~

CHAPTER 36

"The heart monitor went off, and I was screaming. Everyone was trying to bring her back. The intern slipped out the door, he looked back one more time, and I caught his eye. I will never forget what he looked like, and I spent years keeping my eyes open for him. When you were in the hospital and were describing the eyes of the man sitting with Simon, I knew it was the same man. Lazlo had drained the life out of my Sarah."

I was in the recliner shaking. A cold sweat was running down my back. That no good animal had killed my mother, depriving us of her forever. The anger was mounting.

"Alex, snap out of it!"

"How did you find this Lazlo character again?" Father hesitated.

"I didn't. It was Adam who spotted him while he was protecting you."

"So, he knew who that man was."

"Not really. Adam came when I was with Clayton and communicated with him. So, when you were following Simon, we were already after Lazlo. Your impatience almost blew everything by going to see him by yourself. Luckily, Adam was watching over you."

"I guess so."

"Now you understand why we were not remorseful about terminating Lazlo at the ballpark."

"You told me that he was powerful, yet he put up no resistance."

"He was concentrating his energy elsewhere, so we got him by surprise."

"What happened to the five souls you released?"

"There were eight, but three of them were so consumed that they faded upon release. Three of the other ones were battered beyond repair, and Adam took them. He showed them the way to the other dimension, where they will receive a well-deserved rest. The remaining have consented to help us fight this evil organization, but that will take time."

"If they are back in their bodies, won't the organization know?"

"The two remaining souls are not in their bodies, but in the other dimension. Like Adam, they left enough behind to fill their own void, but can also keep communicating like Adam does with you. Adan stays in contact with them, and all of them are gathering information."

"That is all well and good, but I still want my soul as soon as possible."

"We will get to that matter next week. Don't worry, your spirit has not suffered. You and Adam were born with Sarah's power and access to the energy of the universe."

"Why did he take my soul?"

"To punish us for Sarah's betrayal by leaving the organization."

"They're going to be really upset when they find out we zapped one of their best, I thought out loud.

"It's a chance we took, and since we caught him off guard I don't know if they actually know who did it,"

"Hope not, otherwise we will have to learn to duck big time."

We took a pause. I had so many questions. "Zach, why

didn't you tell me about my mother earlier?"

"What for you were busy growing up, and you wouldn't have understood. Besides, I had looked for the man with ice cold eyes for fifteen years and never found him."

"I guess you're right. None of this would have been believable three years ago." Sitting quietly for a short time than added.

"You know, your mother would be proud and liked what you've done with your life."

"She probably knows. Maybe Adam is talking to her from time to time."

"I hope so, Son. Listen, Alex, I'm going to straighten up the basement. Care to give me a hand?"

"Can do. How come you've straightened up the study? It looks so spacious now."

"I see that you noticed. Well, I decided to air out the place a little. I've gotten over the past, and I want to get on with my life." He stood up, looked around the room, and smiled.

"So, I am getting rid of a few nick-knacks as well as unwanted memorabilia."

It was heartwarming to relate to my dad—man to man. "Good. Let's go down in the basement, I don't have all day."

"Well, I'm going to grab my soda. You want one, son.?"

"Yes, Dad, grab me an apple two, when you are in there."

I went to the basement door and turned on the light walked down the stairs, looked around. Boy, this basement was cluttered.

"Were do we start?" I wondered out loud.

Dad was not far behind me with two sodas in his hand, struggling with the apple and a book under his arm.

"Dad, where do you start. Gasoline and a match?"

"You are really funny. I asked you to help me, not to destroy the place."

"Just Kidding. But look around, it all looks lie junk."

"You should know. Most of the boxes are your toys. A few boxes are work related, and a couple of those are filled with photographs."

"What is the book under your arm?"

"Just a book I meant to bring down a long time ago."

We opened the cans of soda, shared the apple, and started to move the business-related boxes by the entrance. Dad had just enlarged his office and had more storage space in the city.

"Pat is supposed to come by and load up all of the business records around four this afternoon." These boxes accounted for two thirds of the basement.

"I hope he's got a dump truck or a van, something big," I commented

"He is bringing the company van. We'll load tonight and take the business boxes to the office before he comes back to get the rest tomorrow."

"Look, Zach, I found a pile of pictures."

"Let me see what you've got." There were pictures of him and Sarah as well as Adam and Me.

"I don't think I really want to look through them again, Alex. The pictures of Sarah still make me sad."

"Aw, come on, Dad, she was my mom after all, and want to know more about her."

"All right if you insist. Hand me a few."

I must admit, it was the best afternoon of my life. I learned so much about Mom. I learned about her patience and kindness. He told me how he met her, how they went horseback riding in the hills. He described how they would look into each other's eyes for hours, holding hands and not speaking. Words weren't necessary.

In the silence of the night lay their poetry. He would wake up early, before her and go down and make coffee. He'd go get a fresh flower in the garden and put it on the tray, went back upstairs. Then he would tickle her with the flower on her ear until she woke up.

One day, Sarah told father to be home early, because she wasn't feeling well. When he got home, the patio was set up for a dinner for two. A four-course dinner was served to them by a chef in full uniform.

Another time, Dad left her a note to be ready at three o'clock in the afternoon. At three sharp he pulled in the driveway and picked her up. We wouldn't tell her where they were going. They drove in a large field with a hot air balloon, and they rode above the countryside. The stories went on and on.

The best one, I thought, was the way he asked her to marry him. He taped a red rose to the kitchen window. She went out to take off the rose, and there was a note saying.

"Go to the car." She went to the car to find another rose and a note. "Go to the yellow house with the green trim." It was a house that had not changed colors since 1921. She drove over, and, of course, there was another rose and note. This one said, "Go to our special church."

When she went to the church, she saw a whole bouquet of roses. Thirty-six of them, thirty-five red, one white. The note read, "You are one of a kind. Will you marry me?" On the corner of the note it said, "over please," She turned it over and the message continued.

"If you want to marry me come inside the church, and if you don't come inside, I will settle for a kiss."

"Dad, I didn't know you were such romantic."

"I haven't told you even half of the stories. There were so many special moments. We both had to work at it, but I think we were the happiest couple in America."

"Look at this photograph, Dad."

It was Adam and I sitting on a donkey, on our way down in the basin of the Grand Canyon. That set off a whole new round of stories mostly about Adam and me. One of my favorites was when Adam and I thought we were drivers having learned to drive the tractor. We got it started without permission and promptly drove it in the ditch and broke the neighbor's fence. We didn't tell anyone, but three days later when the neighbor towed it out of the ditch, we finally had to tell Dad. He wasn't too happy, but quickly got over it.

After so many stories, I was surprised at how fast four o'clock came around. I didn't know how special Zach really was until this day. He is a romantic. A warm, creative, and generous man—he is my father.

"Dad, you are quite a character."

"Well, I was in my time, you're not too bad yourself."

At that moment Pat pulled in the driveway with the truck. It was large, so we helped him back it in the driveway. We helped him load up all the boxes that were going in storage, and between the three of us, it went fast. Afterwards he came in for refreshments. Before he left, he said he'd be back the next day at eight.

~~~

CHAPTER 37

B oy, my dad was punctual. I looked at the clock—seven thirty in the morning. Just time to dress and eat before Pat was to arrive.

"You better get moving. Pat's never late." Zach stuck his head in the room and left.

I just grumbled and pulled the sheet over my head. He's got to be kidding, this bed feels too good to leave. Five more minutes, that's is all I need.

"Alex, it's 7:50. Get up."

I must have dozed off again. Dad is standing over me, pulling the sheet. The sun in my face. I guess there's no escape, so I smile at him.

"Good morning, Dad. What's for breakfast?"
"Nothing if you don't get up right now."
"Be right there."

He walked out of the room. I jumped up and slipped in yesterday's pile of clothes, brushed my teeth, comb my hair, and went to the kitchen. An orange juice was waiting and the toaster working overtime. The whole morning was happening. Pat arrived right on time, and Dad went to open the door to let him in.

"Sit down and have a cup," Father greeted him. He joined me at the table while I finished my breakfast.

"How is everything, Pat?"
"Not bad. Ready to go to the big town?"

Trying to wake up, I slurred, "Think so."

We finished our food and got in the car, we headed for the Glimmer of Hope shelter. Peggy was waiting for us.

"Morning, Gentlemen. Rick is waiting for us. I'll tell him that you are here."

Zach nodded his head. Almost immediately Rick came out of the shelter and walked up to us.

"Gentlemen, we have to meet him at the 'Laughing Oyster' downtown across from the library. He said he'd meet me at eleven." So off we went.

We got to the place just before eleven and sat down at a table. The place wasn't terribly busy, and we sat down at the back of the restaurant. A voice popped in my head, out of the blue.

"Morning, Alex. You thought I had disappeared."

"Dad, could you sit somewhere else with Pat and Rick?"

He understood immediately and asked Pat and Rick to follow him.

"What's is going on, brother?" I asked.

"Listen, Alex. This going to be tough but follow your instincts and let the flow of energy guide you. I will be right here in your heart and head." Adam had been gone for two or three days, and he'd come back unexpectedly.

"Where have you been, anyway?"

Adam quickly said, "Never mind. He is coming."

"How will he recognize me?"

"Just call him 'Nails' when he passes you."

A young man came in the restaurant. He looked around, walked pass Zach's table, and continued without hesitation toward the back of the place. Having not seen Rick, he turned and made eye contact with me which gave me the opportunity to address him, "Nails, sit down."

He looked at me surprised and with caution, suspicious of a clean guy knowing his name.

"I said, sit down," and I showed the chair. My voice

had a commanding tone.

He just looked at me, sat down, and stared me in the eyes with disdain.

"Tell me, Nails, what are you doing here?"

"I was supposed to meet Rick. I ain't talking to you, just Rick."

"Relax, I'm here instead. Rick is over there at the other table."

"I don't know you. Get lost." He made a move as if he were going to get up and leave.

I looked at him. His eyes met mine, and he was literally thrown against the back of the chair. I had felt the energy go through my body.

"Let's talk," I said calmly, but with authority."

"Who are you?"

"Alex. Please to meet you, Nails. So, tell me again, why you are here?" Still suspicious he answered. "I want out of the gang life."

"Any particular reasons?"

"I'm tired, and I met a woman."

"Millions of people meet women," I pushed.

"She's pregnant, and I want my son to get more than a gang life."

"Why are you here?" I asked again.

"What is the matter with you? Are you deaf?" He squirmed in his chair still wanting to leave.

I looked at him straight in the eyes, grabbed his hand and held it tight. Something was guiding me; it was beyond my control. I whispered.

"The real reason, Nails?"

"I'm scared," He admitted.

"Scared at your stepdad. Mad at the way he abused you and beat you, and so you decided to become a gang member to hide your fears. The thing you didn't count on was that the fear didn't go away, and now you're a slave to your own reality. You're a slave to the fear, prisoner of the gang you founded, afraid to be called a coward."

Nails was looking at me like he was seeing me for the first time.

"Scared?" I pressed on. "We're all scared. There's no free ride in life maybe your stepfather was bad, maybe he did you wrong, but who cares? Nobody cares, not even your stepdad. It happened long time ago. He doesn't even remember it, but you allow him to control you by not forgiving and leading your own life."

"What do you want me to do?"

"I don't want you to do anything. If you want to do something for yourself, if you really want to get on with your life, first let go of your stepdad and the anger. Start fighting for yourself, no more hiding behind the tough guy image. Make your own decisions for a change."

"I make my own decisions," he insisted.

"You have never made a decision. You just imposed your though man rules, but you never feel good inside. You are a prisoner of your own rules, a decision is to take a stand, stick to it and never let go."

"How do you know if a decision is right?"

"When it feels good inside your heart, it is right."

He sat calmly now without a word for several moments. Then he looked at me and asked,

"When do I start?"

"One you stand proud of who you are. Two, stand up for your lady. She deserves a man, not someone who hides behind his own fear. Next, stand up for your son when he comes into this world. Give him the love you never got, give him everything you never had—security, discipline, education, friendship, give him pride. GIVE HIM A FATHER, FOR GOD'S SAKE." I had raised my voice at the last sentence.

Nails had a hard time containing himself, "Maybe you're right. Just one rule. If you break it, we can't help you because support is the only thing, we can give to you.

It is all up to you."
   "And the rule is?" With hesitation Nails questioned.

~~~

CHAPTER 38

"You fight tooth and nails for a better life, and we help you."

"Deal."

"See those people at that table? I will introduce you to them. They will never let you down. They'll always be in your corner. Don't let them down. Remember your little lady and your future son."

"I won't forget."

"By the way, what's is your real name? Your given name?"

"Ralph."

"Ralph, I won't tell if you don't like it."

"Ralph it is. You just told me to stand proud." His back straightened as he spoke.

"All right Ralph. Let me introduce you to everybody. "

Just now I realized I was still holding his hand. They were sweaty. We went over to the table where the other guys were sitting, and I introduced him to everyone.

"Hi Ralph." Pat added.

"Sit down with us."

"Someone told me there would be two of you.""

"Don't worry. Rick. I will be bringing over many of my friends as possible, including my lady friend."

The restaurant was almost full by now. Everyone was there for lunch, we ordered our food and chatted about different rules regarding the "Glimmer of Hope" shelter.

I heard that all the homeless run the entire operation with only a little supervision?'

"Yes Ralph, we try to give people responsibility and give them a chance to show us their talent and determination. By the way, we expected a lot more trouble,"

"I snuck out early this morning and walked around until it was time to meet you," confessed Ralph.

"That was a good idea."

"For me, I don't care, but it's for Isabelle. I don't want to stir up any trouble for her." Zack inquired.

"Is that your lady's name?"

"Yeah, in the street we call her 'Cheetah.' You'll see when you meet her." He was relaxing and smiling when he spoke. Rick was experienced and adept at helping people developing their talents, so he wanted to get down to business.

"Ralph, what can you do or what would you like to do? We need to find you a responsible position."

"Not very much. I dropped out of school, I can read and write, my spelling is decent. I can drive and I helped on a construction site, mainly digging, and laying pipe. I also loaded and unloaded construction material."

"Would you like to become a bricklayer?"

"I can give it a try."

"Good. Take a few days to get settled in at the shelter. We have a room for you and Panther, or is it Cheetah?" That made us all laugh.

"Let's make it Isabelle," Ralph recommended.

"Do you need help moving your stuff?"

"Not really. I ain't got much worth getting. I just need to get my lady."

Good the shelter is open twenty-four hours a day. At night we close the door, but if you ring the bell, someone will open it and let you in.

Ralph got up immediately after eating and thanked us

for everything.

"You will have a few problems with Nails," Adam said to me telepathically.

"Why is that?"

"All the other kids will see it as a betrayal. They will get angry. Don't worry, I will be watching over him."

"All right, Adam, don't forget, I want to get my soul back."

"You sure are impatient. Brother."

Never mind. Be careful out there.

Zach looked at me. He had heard the inner conversation.

"Don't worry, Alex, your brother will take care of himself. Without thinking, he had spoken out loud.

Pat and Rick looked at him like he was nuts, "Zach your son has been dead a long time."

"I know, Pat, I still can think of him from time to time, can't I?"

"It just seems odd, you are bringing him up, never mind, I won't ask." Zach smiled.

We took a load to the Glimmer of Hope and visited with Peggy and whoever was there. As for me, it was time to see Maggie. *I am getting fond of my special friend,* I thought to myself.

There was a lot of activity going on. Gary was washing a car, two others were vacuuming out another over the building with another kid I have never seen before, yet next was a truck been buffered. Theresa was sitting in a chair watching the little kids. Butterball stuck his head out of a black limo as he pulled beside us.

"Hey guys. Are you going to give us a hand?" Zach and I just looked at him too surprised to answer. Another car was pulling in the lot and believe me, this was not a shabby set of wheels. It was a late model car with all the bells and whistles

"It looks like you need an explanation," Butterball

came over, shook hands with everyone.

"It would help," Butterball turned to Rick.

"Thank you for keeping a secret. Now you tell them."
We all turned and stared at Rick.

"You have been so nice to us, so we wanted to show
you that we were capable and dedicated enough to start
our own business." I immediately understood where he
was coming from.

"You started your own detailing business?" I said

"Yes, One Eye came up with the idea. We printed up a
lot of fliers and saturated the business district downtown
as well as industrial section. We pick up the cars before
noon, clean them up, and bring them back before the
business closes. It's going better than expected."

"How do you cope with insurance?"

"Twenty percent of what we make goes in a special
account for that purpose."

"And taxes?" I continued with the questions and
became impressed with their thoroughness.

"That's is your father's department."

"Well, we sent all the receipts to your accountant in a
shoe box, we don't know how to do the paperwork yet."

"I guess I will have to arrange it with my firm."

"We already did, Mister Zach."

"Who picks up the cars and delivers them?" I asked.

"We do. We're all dressed up, polite, and it's simply
great. Our first was the mayor. We gave him a discount,
and he's recommended us to his staff and all of his
friends."

"Keep up the good work!" was all I could say.

~ ~ ~

CHAPTER 39

Maggie was standing behind me, and I didn't even notice until she put her hand on my shoulder prompting me to turn around.

"Hi, Alex. Glad you made it. I've missed you."

"I missed you too, Maggie. I was hoping to see you."

I noticed that she had a duffle bag beside her as well as a large box. Pat was already grabbing the box and the duffle bag.

"What is in the box and the duffle?" Zach joined us.

"Son, she is coming out to the house to spend a few days with us."

"I don't understand."

"She had asked me if there were any openings at the office, so she is going to ride to the office with me four days a week to work in the morning while she is being trained, "

"So, that is why Janice and you have been straightening up the house."

Father blushed and gave me one of his don't say anything glares, "Never mind, Alex."

"And I was wondering who you were redecorating the guest room for. Guess I'll have to be a good boy and help around the house. All kidding aside, I'm glad you're coming for a visit." I grabbed her hand as I spoke.

She remained speechless during the whole conversation and gave me a hug, when I made it clear I was just as happy as she was herself about the plan.

Now let's go inside and see how Peggy is doing. Zach, Maggie and I walked in leaving the rest of the group working on the car detailing business. Each proudly doing their job building self-respect in the process.

Maggie pointed out the new plants that she and Mary had added to the hallway and dining room to make it homier and more informal. There was a dark, four-foot fig tree, a couple of hibiscus plants and at least six or eight large ferns hanging from the ceiling. I noticed all the original pictures on the wall and asked, "Where did all the artwork come from?"

"Theresa has started a contest for all age groups, and we display their work here," Maggie explained.

"How does it work?"

"They are different categories not only age groups but also for subject matter, design and medium. Mostly it's just a way to reward their creative efforts."

"So, what is the grand prize?" my curious nature showing itself.

"It depends on the category. Why do you want to know so much about it?"

"I don't know, maybe, I want to enter," I am teasing her.

Kinda depends on the age group. There are movie tickets, Rollerblade for the arena, new t-shirts, video games, coupons for free hamburgers, and we are still collecting donations."

"How do you get donations?"

"We explain to the merchants what we are trying to do for the kids and young people, and ask them to help us out, After all they gain also from getting the kids off the streets—less shoplifting and petty theft, so most of them give graciously," Maggie explained putting her hand in mine again.

Father interrupted. Alex why are you asking so many

questions?

"I'm excited, and I'm looking for how I can participate."

"Good then participate, but don't talk her ears off."

"It's okay, M. Beard, I know how curious he can be."

"Listen, Maggie, it's Zach and not Mr. Beard, and he's my son, but he has to learn to be patient."

Peggy saw us in the dining room and walked in our direction her hand in her white apron, her hair pulled back except for a few wisps hanging down around her face, smiling as usual.

"Good Day, Zach."

"Peggy, you look ravishing."

"You could charm the devil, I know it's not true since I worked all morning, but any compliment is wonderful to hear."

"I've got many more, Peggy, you inspire me."

"Dad, stop you are going to make her blush."

"Make me blush, Alex, I'm too old to blush." She laughed as she came over and took me in her arms. Her gentleness had magic to let you know that you were loved.

"I heard that Maggie is going to stay at your house?"

"Yes, in fact I just found out the plan," my pleasure showing in my face as I spoke.

"You treat her right or you'll have to answer to me. Now go on with Maggie. I need to talk to your dad."

We walked out back to watch the detailing car operation; they were down to the last three cars with someone just pulling the next car around. We held hand while waiting for Dad. One of the teens started a sponge fight, and we decided to back off before we got soaked. Dad and Peggy came out of the building still talking.

"Alex, can I talk to you a moment?" a voice beckoned me from behind. I turn to the left and Rick was standing behind me frowning. I excused myself from Maggie and walked over to joining him.

"What's going on?"

"It is Bill. He is starting to act strangely again, and I spotted Simon snooping around."

"I will talk to my dad, and within the next ten days we will do something about it."

"I appreciate your concern," Rick seem relieved.

"Glad you brought it to my attention, and I'll also will talk to Bill."

"He is right over there." Rick motioned toward the building.

"I guess right now is about as good as any. Hey Bill, Bill, got a minute?" I shouted over the screams of happiness from the water fight that had gotten out of hand.

He finally heard me and walked over to where we were standing, after tripping over the garden hose, losing his balance and almost landing in my face.

"Bill, what's is going on with Simon?"

"The turkey found me. I don't want to hide all of my life, and ever since I saw him the nightmares have increased."

"Hang in there. I am working on it with Dad's help," seeing his fear I wanted to let him know that there was hope.

"In the meantime, I'll just stay around the shelter."

He looked scared, not as bad as when we found him over a year ago, but still very shaken. I reassured him as Zach was saying goodbye to Peggy.

~~~

CHAPTER 40

We got in the car and Dad and I talked telepathically about Bill's fear and the harassment from Simon before and deciding to talk about it more intensively at the house. Pat and Maggie had been chatting in the back-seat, so we joined in and enjoyed the scenery for the rest of the trip home. Maggie noticed the big white house with the gray roof, gingerbread trim, and the three-story turret on the side.

"I have never seen anything like this. Alex, look at least twenty columns on the side of the house with two round gazebos attached to the house, a balcony over the front porch, and a double carport on the back. "I wonder who live there," she commented.

We turned left, then went over the railroad tracks and drove by the yellow house with the green trim. The color of the house hadn't changed since1921, and now it was a classy grill eatery, Maggie is charmed by the picturesque aspect of the small town.

"I am going to like it here," she declares.

"We hope that you do." Answer Zach. "There is not much night life."

"I worked six night a week for almost four years, so I could use a little rest and enjoy evenings again. It will be nice to spending my days looking at trees, flowers, blue sky, and listening to bird's singing rather that sleeping in the daytime for a change."

"You will certainly find a slower pace in this town, my dear."

Once we pulled in the driveway, Pat grabbed one bag, and I picked the box. Zach led Maggie in the house and showed her the way to the guest bedroom, which had been prepared for her with new curtains and towels in the adjoining bath. He gave her instructions on how to adjust the window air conditioner to her comfort and told her to make herself at home.

Leaving her to get settled he joined us in the living room placing his feet up. "I am bushed. It won't be long before I am ready to retire."

Pat got up, I'm beat myself, so if you excuse me, I'll be on my way. He walked out the door after shaking our hands.

Zach went out to the back porch for a breath of fresh air while I turned on the television and watched the news. They were talking about a big industrial leader making multi-million dollar deals with the government revamping the computer system for the employee payroll.

"That is the man, the one with the black hair on the left side of the chief of staff to the white house." I will never get used to having, Adam popping in and out of my head and talking without warning.

"Hi, Alex did I scare you again?"

"Never mind, what did you said about the man with the black hair?" I asked him.

"That man right here," he pointed with my arm at the television. Without effort Adam was controlling it.

"You see this man, right there, his soul was one of the ones we retrieved from Lazlo. I returned his spirit and blended it back with his body."

"But he's a big wig."

"You bet, and they were blackmailing him for information," Adam reminded me.

"What is Lazlo's organization trying to do?"

"Lazlo was just one of the members of the secret society. We must find out who controls the power behind all of this mess."

"How can we do that?" Adam offered,

"I don't know but I am working on it, and Clayton had a few ideas of his own."

"You find out all you can, and father and I will be ready to help."

Maggie walked in the room, so I said goodbye to Adam. She sat down beside me, and we watched television while holding hands. Dad came back from the porch locked the door and said good night, then left for his room. She fell asleep in my arms while watching the program. I slipped my arm from under her head and got up to the refrigerator to get a glass of juice.

"Will you bring me back a drink of juice." "Coming up." I brought the glasses of juice back to the living room.

Not realizing how tired we were, we both fell asleep and woke up about two AM having not even touched our juice. Standing up and stretching I realized how sore my muscles were, and after a gentle goodnight kiss, we wandered to our individual rooms.

Toward the end of the week, Maggie wondered out loud. "Why have you never talked about your childhood, your dad, and the wonderful town you grew up in?"

"I had memory problems, but I would rather not talk about it." I realized that our relationship was deepening, and I couldn't avoid the whole truth much longer. Perhaps I would have my spirit back before I had to worry her.

"Was it related to your nightmares?"

"Exactly," I answered, just hoping that she would be patient a little longer.

"Well I am glad everything is all right, and we can forget about the past."

"Not really. I still have some work ahead of me. *That's*

an understatement, I thought to myself.

"May I ask."

If she pushed, I was prepared to be honest, I did love her, but please, please don't let her push for more detail, I don't want to worry her.

"Just trust me."

"I do, the pork chops are ready. Would you mind getting our drinks while I serve and put the sour cream on the potatoes."

"Will do." I went to the kitchen to get more ice relieved that she had changed the subject so fast. I didn't really want to explain until this ordeal was completely over. I returned with the glass in my hand. She had brought our plates out to the table, the food still steaming.

As we sat down, we were entertained by two squirrels defying the laws of gravity jumping back and forth from the branches overhanging the porch to the roof, to the guardrail back up the tree. I sat and she passed me the dressing for the salad. Eating in silence I could tell that she was a little miffed by my not telling her, what could I say not knowing how everything would turn out. Will I get my soul back, and how damaged will it be? Then what about explaining the communications with my dead brother! Talk about a perfect recipe to test a friendship, I decided to keep it to myself for the time being,

"Come on, Maggie, smile to me. The food is great, but I need the cook to smile at me to make me appreciate the flavor of it." She gave me a faint smile.

"You can do better than that. You're left side is still not smiling and that is your best side," I teased.

She pulled my head over to herself and gave me a kiss on the chick. "You better tell me all the details when it is over."

I promise, but for now you must smile.

The rest of the evening was spent listening to music and talking. Zach came in late and joined us. He had eaten earlier so he just sat down to share his day.

I signed a contract to help build the new arena attached to the conference center that I helped build two years ago. You know, in the north part of town.

I could sense his pride. "Sounds like a pretty good day to me."

"I would say so. I even purchased the adjoining building to the Glimmer of Hope."

"What for?" I asked, realizing immediately the answer seeing him as the magnanimous man who also was my father.

"Well, it dawned on me that there are only five rooms left with Ralph moving in with Isabelle, and so many more kids on the street, we are going to need more space shortly."

"Zach, you are such supper guy." Maggie exclaimed as she jumped out of her chair to hug his neck. Good thing I'm not the jealous type.

"Enough of that you two or I'll have to get another girlfriend," I teased. So, they laughed and hugged some more before she came back over to the couch and sat down.

Father proceeded to tell her a few embarrassing anecdotes about my childhood. He told them so well that he had both of us in tears from laughing so hard.

Around eleven o'clock we all cleaned up the kitchen leaving the crumbs for the squirrels for their morning snack.

~~~

CHAPTER 41

"Alex, it is time to get ready for action." It was late in the afternoon. Maggie and I had shared one of our perfect days, and I had just gone up to my room to shower and rest before dinner.

"Where have you been, Adam?"

"Gathering information as well as my strength. We are going to need it tonight."

"You mean we go after my soul tonight?" My entire being responded with anticipation.

"Yeah, there is no turning back now. Dad and you are driving into town tonight."

"I can't wait." My heart was jumping from anticipation.

"Well, brother I don't know how it will turn out."

"Swell, we are driving in the dark with no head lights. So why tonight. What make it so special?"

"Simon's been entertaining, and he told his maid that he was going to stay in and gave her the night off." He had been doing his homework.

"It sounds like you've been spying on Simon."

"Of course, do you want your soul back or not?"

"You know I do."

"Well, then get ready. We are leaving soon." His impatience showing himself as usual.

"Should I tell Dad?" As I slipped on my jeans, knowing the answer before I asked it, he answered, "He knows."

Zach knocked on my door on that precise moment to tell me to get ready. I startled him when I opened the door so quickly with my shirt in my hand.

"I see, Adam came to pay a visit," he observed.

"Yes, so when are we leaving?" My excitement had kicked in.

"As soon as you tell Maggie."

"Where is she?"

"Reading a book in the living room."

I went to the living room, and no one was there. Turning to leave I saw her sitting in the recliner, the light from the lamp shining on her face and book. I tenderly observed her through the open door for a moment.

"Maggie, sorry to interrupt you, but Dad and I are leaving."

"Will you be late?" she asked as she closed her book and stretched her arms over her head.

"Don't know, don't wait up for us."

"Have a good night." She blew me a kiss and went back to her book. I spent a few more seconds admiring her before pivoting on my heel and joining Zach in the car. He backed out of the driveway, and we were on the road rolling in the direction of the big city.

"Do you have any plans, Dad?" He was negotiating a rather sharp curve,

"Not really, but with Adam and Clayton's help, I think we can handle it."

"So, Clay is coming with us." I was watching the landscape change as we approached the four-lane highway, trying to keep my mind occupied.

"Yes, I phoned him about fifteen minutes ago and believe me, we will need all of his expertise to pull enough energy if we want to be successful."

"What do you mean if we want to be successful? We've got to accomplish our goal; I want back what is mine. I can't believe we're talking about it so nonchalantly."

"Relax, Son, we will all do our best."

"I sure hope so." I realized my reply was a little sharp. I guess I am under stress for having waited for so long for this moment to come to fruition and we are so close.

"Do you think that the snake is still alive?" Snakes have a long-life expectancy was an ample answer for my silly question.

"Man, that thing was large, bigger around than my waist and seemed like it was at least twenty feet long." I shivered just remembering. "I must say that Simon has a sense of humor—he called him Slider,"

Adam interrupted us. "Don't underestimate him, you two. You will need all of your mental capacity, so you two better pay attention and concentrate when you are in his presence."

"So, what do you want us to do?"

After all, Adam did have the most knowledge in these matters, and if we wanted to be successful, we had to trust and follow his lead. His answer kind of surprised us.

"I know that it seems crazy, but we are going to have to play it by ear. I mean that we must improvise again."

"Great, Adam, I don't think that the snake trick will work a second time, so I guess we had better be ready to tap dance." My stress level is among the stars right about now.

"Don't be so negative, Alex, I know you're anxious about your soul, we're all here so give us a chance. We've got to stay calm, work together, and have faith." Adam made sense.

I still felt like we needed a plan, "So, we just walk up to the door and ring the bell and scream 'Trick or treat'?"

"That's enough, Alex," reprimanded Zach, then he added. "On second thought, it just might work."

"You mean go to the front door and ring the bell. It is a rather bold approach," Adam mused.

"Why not?" Zach cradled his chin between his thumb

and index finger, rubbed his chin and continued, "the element of surprise just might work."

When he sees the three of us, he will lock the door and barricade himself inside. We are the blind leading the blind, I thought.

"Oh no, you forgot how pretentious he is and when you got arrogant, he lost his cool. Don't you remember my dear brother?" Adam reminded me.

"You have a point!"

"Nobody in their right mind would knock at their worst enemy's door with a smile on their face." Zach offered.

"Listen, Adam, I think you're crazy," I said, "but you know, it just might work. The last time I saw Simon, he had one hell of an attitude."

We arrived at the intersection right by the old fire station that had been transformed into a clothing store. Clayton had arrived and was waiting for us.

Zach opened his window while pulling the last few yards in Clay's direction. Clay greeted us as we stepped out of the car to plan our strategy, discussing a few options. At the end, the approach of ringing the bell seemed the most logical.

"We are a bunch of clowns and my soul is going down the drain."

"Don't be so negative." Clayton, Father and Adam, all shouted at the same time. I lowered my head.

All of us got in father's car and continued the journey to Simon's house. By now the tension was mounting. I asked if I'm the only one who was nervous.

"No, the anxiety is causing knots in my stomach," Clay admitted.

"Me, to, Son, if we weren't nervous, I'd think something was wrong with all of us."

"You bunch of chickens," Adam taunted, hovering above us.

"Be quiet you shadow," I replied, "All you have to do is fly away or go up the chimney like Santa."

"You made your point, Brother, I won't let you down. Just trying to loosen you guys up a little."

A couple of turns on the winding road and the driveway to the mansion turned off to the right sharply. We slowed down, and the car rolled down the slow incline to the front door. The silence is deafening, almost painful as we stepped out of the car. We've got to relax, I think, and Adam agrees as we all stretch our legs.

There was a light visible through the sheer curtains on the front of the house. I don't know about the others. I had a cold sweat running down my back. The light cast an eerie shadow over the holly bushes along the front porch. The silence weighed heavier as we approached the door.

"Who is going to ring the bell? I thought to myself. That's something we should have discussed before we all got here. Too late now.

An almost imperceptible squeak came from the door, which was open and still moving, we all focused on the front door. Our eyes riveted in the ray of light enlarging as the door swung on its hinges. Simon appeared in the doorway looking at us and shaking his head, a confident grin across his face.

~ ~ ~

CHAPTER 42

"**G**ood evening, you clowns. Oh, don't tell me, let me guess, you must be here to reclaim Alex's soul. Well, well, well. Come on inside. As you can see, I am not threatened by you, although I might observe that doesn't appear to apply to the bunch of you trembling in your shoes."

The energy around him was incredible. We could feel the evil in his voice. He was confident to the pointed arrogance.

"What are you waiting for? Enter. I have felt your vibrations for some time now. All of you together don't have enough power to overcome me."

The creep is going to trip over his ego. I felt a powerful blow across my head and found myself flat on my face lying in the center of the flowerbed.

"I heard that you little punk," Simon addressed me.

"Touchy, touchy, man get a life," I replied.

Simon looked at me and made me slide with great force out of the flowerbed, across the driveway and against the thick bushes.

"I will deal with you later." He turned around and entered the house.

Somehow Zach and Clay were mesmerized, following Simon in the house like they had been drugged. They disappeared from my vision, as I tried to regain my composure after having the wind knocked out of me.

Getting up was a chore, I forced myself to a standing position, walked up to the four steps to the porch, opened the front door and stepped in the hallway.

Dad and Clay were in the living room at the far end of the room, a lady was seated on the sofa. She is gracious in her gestures and her look is stunning. The snake curled up on the recliner taking the whole chair has seemingly increased in size since our last encounter several months ago. Simon stood facing them with his back to me unaware or uninterested in my presence.

"What is happening?" questioned the charming lady.

"Quiet," said Simon, "This won't take long." He turned his attention to Clay and Dad laughing at them.

"So, you are trying to reclaim what you think is yours."

"Yes, I have come to deliver the soul you are wrongfully holding." Clay answered.

A pristine serenity came to my heart, and suddenly I realized my power to harness the energy of the universe. We are so aware of our physical body, and totally ignore the power of our spirit. I acknowledged this truth and felt an unearthly peace as I anchored myself, gathering strength little by little with no limits in my mind.

Adam became conscious of my feelings and what I was attempting. He joined in my efforts pulling from the limitless supply of energy around us. Simon's attention was focused on Clay as he prepared to eliminate him as a threat. "Simon, why do you viciously terrorize people anyway?" I asked very convincingly.

"So, you've joined us," he continued, "because when I extract other people's spirit it not only keeps me young, it also gives me the power, actually supreme power, and I can control anyone I want."

"Big deal. So, you use other people's spirit because you are too weak to make your own power." If anybody has ever gotten him angry, it would be me. My arrogance ground on his nerves, and I just hit the jackpot for enraging him.

His face turned red, his fists tighten to the point of turning his knuckles white, his whole body was trembling out of control. I knew calling him inept to create his own power would infuriate him.

"Temper, temper, temper, there is a lady present," I said in hopes of aggravating him more.

Simon stayed in control, "You have no soul and are, therefore, insignificant to me."

Maybe, but you are still an incompetent man without the spirit of others.

I don't know why but I felt that his anger would make him lose his grip over the power he controlled, so I continued to nag him. His was as red as a beat.

The lady was getting impatient as well as scared from this strange conversation.

"I would really like to know what is going on?" Simon addressed her without taking his eyes of me.

"Claire, I told you to be quiet and not to interfere."

"I am surprised at your total lack of manners." I taunted him.

"I have a special punishment in mind for you later, for now I must take care of your friends," he said as he turned around ignoring me completely which is just what I have been waiting for.

I took a deep breath and pulled the energy from him. I pulled with all my mental strength calling upon the universe to help me. I didn't let go, I felt energy coming from the four corners of the universe.

Adam joined in, and we were now pulling together. For a split-second Simon stood very still, and an inhuman scream emerged from his lungs.

While turning on his heels the scream intensified as his face became hideously deformed. Adam and I intensified our efforts, and the miracle happened—like a blooming flower one soul emerged from his body. Simon's face was changing, the excruciating pain tore his body apart, his face had aged before my eyes by at least fifty years.

Simon tried to regain control a split second to late, Zach and Clay had already joined their forces to pull the spirits out of his body. He resisted for what seems an eternity, Simon's whole body started to convulse lightly, then it got more violent.

We gained strength as he weakened. One jerk from him and four souls emerged from the form that once had been Simon's body as it shriveled under convulsions. It started to dematerialize as we gave our last power in his direction, two more souls emerged as the hollow corpse disintegrated in a puff of dust as we watched.

We slowly let go of the energy when all that remained of him was a pile of dust. As the commotion receded, I ran across the living room crossed the large back deck, bent over, and belched over the rail. Father followed me.

"Is everything all right? Son." He handed me a pile of paper napkins.

"Fine, Dad. It must have been the effort of pulling the energy from the universe, go take care of the lady, I'll be fine in a moment."

Inside the lady is petrified, stuck in a long faint lamentation while closing her eyes in horror of this surreal scene. Clayton went over quickly to the open china cabinet, grabbed a bottle of sherry and a glass to bring to the lady, and poured her a glass.

"Drink it," he directed.

She did not move terrified by the developments. Her acquaintance had just been dematerialized; she had the right to be hysterical to say the least. Clay spoke softly to her while she returned to the reality that we were not there to harm her. She sipped the sherry as blush return to her cheeks.

I return from the deck as Zach spoke the first words

since the start of this ordeal.

"You can control a soul, but you cannot own it. So be it."

"Amen," we replied. For once we all agreed in unison.

In all the chaos the snake had not moved one inch, he must have been fed in the last week, so much for his loyalty to his owner. He even looked content curled up in his chair.

"Now let's take a look at the four souls." Clayton is back to business.

"Hold on, I saw five come out of his body as we were all pulling as hard as we could," We all looked at each other astonished.

Clay and Zach looked at me. "Are you sure they asked at once?"

"Absolutely, first three of them came out, then we put the rest of our strength and pulled as hard as we could and two more came out as a puff of dust exploded."

"I think that Simon's soul vanished in the commotion." I added in a gloomy voice. To top it all I was starting to get a headache. Also, we had no clue where to search for this missing soul. I was profoundly disappointed of Simon being able to escape in the commotion.

"I forgot about my spirit in the heat of the moment. Where is mine anyway?" As I spoke, I felt Adam's presence leaving my body. It was a strange sensation, tingling in every cell, every pore, from the follicles in the scalp of my hairs to my toenails. Everything seems to leave my body all the feelings—passion, peace, love, hope, tenderness, forgiveness, and joy just as it had entered some weeks ago. The sensations were all leaving at once, like roots of a tree being pulled out of the earth. I felt a shiver down my back.

One of the souls detached itself from the other three and moved toward my physical body, it hesitated for an instant, wrapped itself around me and started to seep inside of me. The process had been reversed and everything that I had felt leaving was now being restored. This time it was all my own feelings, it felt strange to say the least.

"Alex, I asked myself, "Are you here?"

"No, you're not entirely," Adam answered.

"What do you mean?" My anxiety was mounting. *Maybe my spirit got used up and shriveled from Simon's abuse,* I thought. Hearing my fears, Adam comforted me.

"Alex, your soul has been trapped for over four years. Now it will need to rest, so it has stored inside of you, and slowly it will start feeling your essence, remembering everything, and you will merge or blend."

"How long will that process of blending take?" I feel a twinge of joy in my heart as his words sunk in.

"Two, maybe three weeks depending on how damaged your spirit has been, so let it rest."

"How do I do that?"

"Stay calm and don't get emotional."

"Whatever you said. I'll give it my best. You know I will." I suddenly realize that I hadn't expressed my gratitude for Adam's help. Before I could tell him, he replied.

"What are brothers for, and now I've got work to do." He swirled and joined the three remaining souls.

He came back almost immediately to Clay and Father. I could hear him loud and clear. He was going to be able to bring one of the spirits to his original owner. It was severely damaged and weak. The others two were unrestorable, one was Jack's. While Adam was talking Jack's, spirit came to me, bringing along one of the severely damaged spirits.

I could barely see the forms, as it came closer it whispered to me,

"Here is Bill, I know that you can save him. Take care of yourself." Bill's spirit stood beside me as Jack's soul faded. Now he could complete his destiny and pass on.

Adam escorted Bill's soul to reunite with his body.

"Adam, tell Bill that I will see him at the Glimmer of Hope as soon as possible," I really couldn't wait to see, feel, and be myself and share it all with Bill. He would be the only one who could share the joy of experiencing the miracle.

Clay got up to refill the lady's glass and told Adam to give Bill his regards.

Dad was sitting with the lady comforting her, explaining our actions. I felt strange with my soul inside me, still not capable to communicate my feelings.

"Sorry to interrupt, Zach, but I remember a small detail from my previous visit here." My headache was now pounding.

"What is it, Son?"

"Simon mentioned that he had a box with papers that allowed him to change his identity at will."

"What papers are you talking about?"

"I don't recall exactly. The last time I saw him I was angry and wasn't thinking straight, and I ended up in a coma, I know that it seemed important."

Dad got up and took me by the arm leading me over to Clay after excusing himself to Claire. He explained to Clay my recollection of a stack of important papers.

"Alex, do you have any idea where that box could be?"

"Not really, however he did say that they were withing hand's reach."

Dad and Clay decided that the best course of action was to search the house. After all, there might be clues to other people in the organization or the identity of souls who were under the control of the secret society or even if they had targets in the future.

"What are we waiting for?" Clay said with excitement.

We concentrated our search in the study. The massive desk was probably too obvious, but it seemed like a good place to start, there in the second drawer on the left was a metal box. Opening it up, we found a stack of birth certificates, social security cards, and a deed to some property. Zach picked up the deed.

"This deed has never been assigned to anyone."

"What does that mean, Dad?"

"Well, Son, it means that this house can be deeded to anyone whose name we place on the deed."

Clay found other notes and files that don't make any sense. He picked up all the papers as well as notes and put them in a large folder.

"I'll go through them these later. I think it is time to get out of here."

"What about the lady?" We all turned around at Zach's words. She was sitting motionless looking at the sherry glass in her hand.

"We 'll take her with us."

"And the snake?" I asked as if I cared, it could give someone a heart attack or there was no telling what it would do when it got hungry.

"We can call the Zoo in the morning," Father quickly answered.

"Great idea," we all concurred.

"Actually, I was kidding, but you are right, we might as well make a donation to the zoo."

Zach stepped in the living room to offer to take Claire back in the city. She was still in a dazed state but seemed relieved and gratefully accepted. Clay and I walked out to the car and waited for them. Zach helped Claire into the car, and we drove in silence to Clay's car. He smiled as he got into his car.

"Good job my friends, I fear that there is much work to be done ahead. I'll call you in a few days after I've look over the papers."

"Thank you, Clay," was all Dad and I could say now.

~~~

CHAPTER 43

We drove to the shelter, Father and I exhausted and relieved. Claire still visibly shaken by the events of the preceding few hours. I could feel Dad directing his healing energy toward her, and I couldn't help but wonder who she was and what she was doing with us right now.

Why did he bring her here to the Glimmer of Hope? I asked myself. My headache continued to nag at me.

Although it was quite late when we arrived, the shelter was alive with activity, Bill stood outside. He could hardly contain himself when we drove up. We hadn't even come to a full stop when he grabbed the car door trying to open it thanking me profusely.

"Alex, I've got it, I feel it. I've got it back. The fear is gone."

"Calm down," I said still in the car.

"Why calm down? I feel too good."

As I got out of the car, I put my arms around Bill, "Yes, Bill, your spirit needs to rest, so chill a little, I'm telling you to just relax for the next few weeks."

Neither Adam nor I could have told him telepathically that his soul was damaged. Hearing my voice would have sent him in a downward spiral, and damage him even more. So even with my persistent headache I sent a large dose of my energy to calm him down.

"If you say so, it is going to be hard to calm down."

He went around to introduce himself to everyone as if

he had just arrived on the scene himself.

Father, Claire, and I walked in the dining room where Peggy was talking to a young lady with stunning blue eyes and brown hair to her shoulders. She had a soft voice, deceived by the hard look of the years in the streets.

Claire looked around the place as I spoke to Father telepathically.

"Why did you bring Claire to the Glimmer of Hope?"

"Son, that is the best place to convince her that we are no treat to her, including Clayton. Look around you, peace, trust and acceptance."

"I am glad that you know what you are doing."

"I am driving her to her apartment soon. She needs this time to trust me all alone in the car with her, you stay here for the night, and I will pick you up in the morning."

Peggy got up to greet us and led us to another table, "I will be right back with you." She went back to the young lady and whispered a few words, then called me over with a gesture, I excused myself and approached the table.

"Alex, have a seat. I want you to meet Isabelle, she's Ralph's friend."

"Please to meet you, Isabelle."

"How did you trick Nail's into coming here?"

"I have a pounding headache, and I don't need this. You can go," I snapped as I showed her the door, "Grab your stuff. You are free to go.

"I think I'll do just that," She reached for her bag.

By the time I stood up and turned around to walk back to Zach and Claire she called,

"Come back, Mister."

I turned around again and saw a woman who had obviously been toughened by the street with a tired and forlorn look in her eyes, both arms hanging by her sides.

"I have nowhere to go." She walked toward Father, his guest and me.

"Let's start again," I replied and extended my hand,

"my name is Alex. Welcome to the Glimmer of Hope. This is your new home, feel free to come and go as you please."

Isabelle apologized for being so rude while shaking my hand.

"No need to apologize, I was a street kid myself, and I know how hard it is to trust a stranger." I took her to an available table.

She relaxed as we sat down again and got to know each other better. She told me that she had been in the streets for four years. "I don't remember what it feels like to have a safe place to rest, clean sheets and somewhere to bathe."

"Great there is no more worry because here you will be safe. You will have your own room, and there is always someone here to answer questions and help you. When is your child due?"

"In a couple of months, I think. I came here because I want my child to have a better life than the one Nails and I have. There is no hope in the streets."

I looked around the room and realized a truth as I spoke, That is what this place is all about, Hope. Hope for all of us and your unborn child. By the way, I haven't seen Ralph.

"He'll be here in a couple of days. He is trying to convince Bumper to come here, and, if you don't mine, please call him Nails regardless of what he said. He still needs the respect of his followers and there is a chance that this way he will disassemble the gang, and there will be less violence in the streets."

"Isabelle, I cannot interfere in your private lives, we must discuss between the three of us, and we will call him the name you two choose."

"Any reason why Bumper needs convincing? Each person who comes here needs to be committed and responsible. We don't force anyone." I continued to question.

"Because he is scared like the rest of us."

"I understand." I had all my memories back and, yes, I could remember and understand the misery and fear of street living.

Zach got up and joined the table, "Everything okay?"

"Yes, Zach, just getting acquainted with Isabelle."

"So how do you like it here so far?" Dad asked.

"I don't know yet. It's all too new and seems to be too good to be truth," Isabelle answered.

"You have plenty of time. Nobody will force you to do anything. When you are ready you will find a way to help others like yourself,"

Dad had an amazing ability of giving people hope and a sense of responsibility. I sat there watching them with a lump in my throat. I was looking at hope, true hope.

My mind jumps to Maggie reading her book and could feel that now she has a future—we had a future.

Isabelle shook her head, I guess I have never experienced the honesty and kindness that you are extending. It still puzzles me. Her eyes filled with tears and spilled over as Zach moved over to comfort her by tenderly holding her hand.

"I am going to bed. My headache is not going away." Zach got up and shook my hand.

"Take tomorrow off, Alex. Maggie will come back here tomorrow. And the two of you can drive back home together on Monday morning."

"I think I will do that."

"I am going to take Claire to her place and see you Monday morning. See you soon." I waved as walked out of the dining room.

~ ~ ~

CHAPTER 44

Claire stretched as far as she could, barely catching the ball, hitting it as hard as she could while still trying to keep her balance, Gwen returned the ball. It brushed the net, catching Claire off guard. Too slow to catch the ball, she lost the game.

"This the first time that you have lost a game with me, Claire. What is troubling you?" Gwen asked.

Claire made a gesture of exasperation, obviously irritated, and laid her tennis racket against the net.

"Never mind. Let's just get to the showers. I am boiling!" It was unusually hot on the black surface; to top it off, only one tree shaded the four tennis courts—a joke by any standard.

"Listen. If you are in a jam, just talk to me."

"Thanks, but I have to handle this one by myself." She grabbed her sport bag and racket laying against the net and walked silently to the club house with Gwen. Claire got in the shower irritated, not able to put a finger on the anger nagging at her. The whole scenario seemed wrong.

"Listen, Gwen. I must cancel dinner. I'm in no mood to smile. As a matter of fact, I feel like I am going to explode." She told her friend as she stepped out of the shower.

"Suit yourself." Gwen had been her best friend for years and knew when to back off, insisting would have been a mistake.

Claire went straight home. After grabbing a snack at the local diner, she went immediately to bed. Unable to sleep she was lying in the darkness of the bedroom. Her life was not an easy one.

Born during the Vietnam war, she never got to know her father. She didn't even own a photograph of him. Walter was his name, the few stories her mother told her were the only memory of him. The call to duty to serve his country arrived seven months prior to her birth. His wife Betty got two letters from this far away land.

The first one told her about the lush growth in the dense forest, the good friend he made, watching each other's back, shared home stories, and keeping each other's moral uplifted. Heat and humidity as well as the relentless rain when it came soaked them to the bones. Most of all the love he didn't have the time to show her. There was no mention about Claire at the time of his letter. He didn't even know that his wife was pregnant.

The second letter came by way of an officer knocking at the door with a formal note clutched in his white gloved hand. After passing the letter to Betty, he said a few words of consolations and left her devastated and in shock.

Walter had vanished on the eleventh day of his arrival; the only explanation was that his chopper was shot down in the jungle. She got a note from an unknown official person saying that they were sorry, and a meager pension would follow shortly, after all he was only a private.

Claire's mother was a flower child growing up in the sixties. No skills or diplomas she could rely on, and to top it off not a single penny was saved for a rainy day. Life had not prepared her for a tragedy of that magnitude with a baby still not born at the time of the arrival of the second letter.

No job and no clue of what life was all about. Luckily, Betty had made up with her mother when Walter had to fulfill his call of honor. The bickering was never bad, just a generation gap—quarreling about difference of opinion —the color of clothes, wrong haircuts, music being too loud. It was nothing too serious. Betty went immediately to work, leaving the task of babysitting split between the two sets of grandparents. So, Claire grew up going from one family to another. Both sets of grandparents spoiled her rotten, to her delight. Of course, mother disapproved.

Betty went to evening classes to finish her GED, she immediately followed with the study of dental hygiene. However, the everyday struggle of laundry, school, cooking, shopping, vacuuming, studying, and changing diapers took their toll. She hardly had time to put on makeup.

One day she ran herself silly and didn't remembered which of the two grandparents she had left Claire with. Overall, her pride gave her the courage to fight and she did well for herself, passing her course with an average of B+, unfortunately the stress made her very bitter and cynical toward life.

At school, kids were nice to Claire. Everyone knew about her dad in Vietnam and him dying, and the difficult time Betty had to raise a child as a single parent, so the whole town participated, trying to help in their own way.

By the time I was sixteen, straight A's was a normal occurrence on my report card. I just didn't want to let my mother down with a B, or worse. By the time I was eighteen, the University became my second home.

My mind was made up, I wanted to become the best lab researcher from this part of the country. Unfortunately, my mother never came to my graduation or my wedding. Meningitis had claimed her life.

As for my husband, we parted after nine years. His insecurity made him terribly jealous of my better salary. He could not bear my success, so when I got promoted to the head of the laboratory in the firm that I was working for, he just left. I felt abandoned for the third time in my life.

I had three loves in my life. The first one was my mother, the others were my two sets of grandparents, whom I cherished with all my heart, the feeling of having someone of my own was denied.

A job opportunity came in the form of a large firm scouting for good, bright, talented decision-makers. I decided to take a chance. A notice of ninety days was given to my employer for them to adjust and hire a new candidate.

After all, they had been good to me. The movers came on a bright, crisp day. They packed everything in a great big truck and moved me half across the nation, or so it seemed.

I was two months in this town. It was larger than I expected, with never-ending streets. One section of the city was larger than my entire town, wealthy people and poor ones, traffic in every direction, homeless people, expensive cars, abandoned pets, trash piled up, well-groomed parks in the city, and government buildings. It was all intimidating, and it made me morose, too scared to explore the town.

I stayed home most of the time. The only thing I knew was going to and from work. My co-workers were my only human contact. The city's unfamiliar pace made me uneasy. Even the radio stations were difficult to choose from, with too many of them, all talking too fast.

I unfortunately got a flat rear tire on my way back from work, it took many cars zooming by before one finally stopped. He took out the scissor jack as well as the spare and changed the tire without a single word as I sat a few feet away on a guard rail.

"Your tire is a doughnut so don't go over fifty miles an hour, those spares are useless so I will follow you home to make sure that you are safe and if you want I could come back in the morning so you could get a new tire, have it balanced, remounted. If that is convenient."

First, he was a gentleman, warm, witty, and honest looking, he inspired trust, who was I to refuse his gallant manners.

John Languish was his name, he was very proper. Every time he asked me out to lunch or a dinner date, he pulled out the chair and waited for me to sit down before he himself would take his place.

He became my guide to sightseeing the city, and after a few weeks of knowing him, I agreed to visit him at his house. I sat on the sofa while he prepared two homemade lemonades as we sat together on the sofa.

Almost immediately John stood up.

"Will you excuse me there is someone at the door." I had not heard a single noise, but apparently there was, the doorbell rang, shortly after he came back with two men. One was old with white hair, distinguish looking. The other much younger, John was obviously agitated, and they argued, the younger called him Simon.

"Zach, Clayton you come to claim a few spirits?" John was arrogant and defiant as well as obnoxious. I was getting scared when a young kid appeared out of the blue in the sunken living room.

"Hi Ghost, long time no see. His arms were raised." John turned around suddenly, yelling, while the others sucked the life out of my friend. He just vanished in a cloud of dust. It was like I was watching an episode of "The Outer Limits." Too terrified to scream, I just sat there on the sofa paralyzed from the terror of witnessing this phenomenon. Three men had just erased a human being in front of my eyes, and the only remains were a pile of clothes.

The older gentleman poured me a glass of brandy and told me not to worry, but at that point I had earned the right to be hysterical. They took me out of the house. Here I was two days later in my bed, lying down, wondering if life had more surprises to throw at me or dragging me in some scary adventure?

Nothing in my life came easy, but now I was involved with some unknown phenomenon too weird to be explained. What if it was a Hollywood special effect movie? Maybe grown men who never got out of their weird college mentality. How can I go to the police and explain that they killed someone and made them vanish in a puff of dust and cleaned the crime scene with a dust mop.

Talk about making a fool of yourself? I just wanted to die —to die from fear of getting involved, to die from being tired of living, to die for never feeling love and for being unimportant or useless. I wanted to die with all my heart. I demanded to the universe to let me die.

I could not live like this anymore. Nothing in this world had any purpose for me, and not one ounce of strength was left in my body to get up. With my mother gone, a father I never knew, all my grandparents resting in peace, no children of my own, and no sweetheart to come home to, life seems so futile, like a meaningless exercise done again and again without any result whatsoever. Getting up seemed pointless.

The only rational thing was to fall asleep and never, ever wake up. I ached too much to fight. "Someone please let me go." My heart was imploring an end to the agony of my mediocre life.

The shadows in the room were gently softening; every corner of the room was slowly lightening up, getting brighter. It did not seem to be coming from a light, it came from all corners of the room, like a soft mist rising from thin air. There was no trace of shadows to be found.

By the time I noticed the glimmer it became a full-fledged bright light, so incredibly soft. The peace, love and warmth emanating from it were too overwhelming to be described. *Is it a dream or am I awake?'* Tears of pure joy rolled down my face. I felt so special, accepted like I have never felt before. A gentle voice addressed me.

"Claire do not be afraid. I come to grant your wish."

I accept the voice as naturally as one would accept the air that we breathe.

"Who are you?" I asked with a calmness I had never experienced before. With no fear, no threat, it just felt right.

"Please to meet you Claire, I am Sarah, and I am an ancient soul. I have been chosen to come back to earth, to finish a task I started years ago. "

None of this seemed real, I was not scared or terrified like the last few days, on the contrary I seem to accept this strange phenomenon, and the only thought going through my mind was to play along.

"How do you expect to accomplish your work?"

"Let me explain," said the voice.

"Very few people know about spirits like me. We are what you call us in your world a 'walk in,' but actually we are just souls coming back on this earth to take care of unfinished business, and to teach our knowledge to the ones who want to listen." The soft glow shifted and seems to approach the bed, it went on.

"We ask permission to take the body of the terminally ill people or with an accident that nobody believes would survive. In exchange, they make a miraculous recovery. As far as your case is concerned, you seem genuinely tired of living, so I came to get permission to grant your wish."

"I might be desperate, but I do not want to get killed by a ghost!"

"Nonsense! Claire. I will not do such a dreadful act, I merely want to exchange bodies, you will be going in a place of your choice, then your memory of this moment in time will be erased, and you will begin the life of your choice."

"How will you do this exchange?" I asked.

"I just come inside of you and release your spirit, then you will go where I just came from with no feelings of pain, sorrow, or sadness. Just love, joy, and peace."

"You are kidding me," I said in a trembling voice.

"You are welcome to come with me and see for yourself. If it is not to your liking, just refuse by saying no. You will wake up, never remembering what happened during this night, and go back to your daily life." Again, the glow shifted.

"If you agree I will keep your position as head of the research laboratory as well as all of your memories. Everything will be the same except you will be in another world where nothing is of importance until you choose a new life of your convenience. As for me I simply take your place, do we have a deal?"

There is no commitment on my part, none?'

"None whatsoever."

I woke up early, even before the alarm had the time to do the job. I felt strong and spirited. *I could conquer the world as I feel invincible, and it is going to be a perfect day,* I thought, stretching between the warm sheets for a few minutes.

"This must be the best part of the day." I shouted while experiencing a feeling I had not felt for a long time. Stretching between the sheets with my eyes close trying to captive the moment.

I was indulging before getting on with the day. I walked in the bathroom and looked in the mirror. There reflected a perfectly shaped body looking at me, not one ounce of fat in the wrong place; the curves were smooth. *It is too bad if someone does not like it,* I thought smiling.

A quick look at the face revealed that not a single wrinkle was on the face, other than a few minuscule lines under the eyes.

After a quick breakfast drink and a breath of fresh air while stepping outside on my way to work, for the first time in many years I felt the warmth of the sun on my skin. *It's good to be back!*

~~~

CHAPTER 45

I had no contact with the Glimmer of Hope, except for a few conversations over the phone to keep informed with Peggy. Bumper the friend of Isabelle and Ralph made the transition from Gang life to resident at the shelter and progressed nicely. Having my soul reunited, I made the decision to take time for myself.

I stayed at home getting to remember the town that I hadn't strolled through in so long. Over three horrendous years had just been battering my body and spirit beyond normal human conditions, so what could be better than to spent time getting to rediscover my father?

He was turning out to be more of a friend than a dad. The respect was the same, but the rapport and friendship for each other needed private space to become more defined.

I also spent time by myself, meditating on the lake and reflecting about my brother's accident. Nothing could have prevented it. Knowing Adam, he was fulfilling his own destiny. The sadness and happiness blended and became total acceptance. I was resigned to my destiny, although I didn't fully understand the sadness of life.

Clayton promised to help me bettering myself through mental exercises to get strong and getting ready to help others, I had to recover first and mend the soul. The lake helped me to accept the past and the pain to let it go.

I finally took of my driver license. It was now official,

safely tucked in my back pocket. From now on, I could drive around without worrying about getting pulled over.

After a few weeks, Clayton came to my father's house. He, too, had been resting for a while. I guess we all needed time to ourselves after an ordeal that left us all a little shaken. We walked through the door, Maggie, and I, as Clay was laughing with Zach and Ray our foreman.

"Alex, Maggie, how are you?" He asked in his jovial voice.

"Clay." I replied. "Is that your car parked in the driveway? It is neat! Where did you get it?" The car was impressively big, even by today's standards, and chrome from bumper to bumper. The steering wheel was over-sized. Wheels and tires were impeccable, the white walls perfectly clean.

"My uncle gave it to me twelve years ago. I took care of polishing it, cleaned it, waxing it, and changing the oil, ever since he handed me the key."

"Can I drive it sometime?"

"Yes, tomorrow we have to go to town, you and I." The look on Maggie's face changed in an instant. She knew by instinct I would be gone for some time. It is strange how a woman's intuition works and is ninety-five percent correct.

"Why am I going to town?" I asked, looking at Zach.

"To fulfill your destiny, son." Father had not called me, "son" in quite a while, it must be of some importance for me to go to town. Little did I know how important my task was to become.

After packing a toothbrush and a couple of changes of clothes, I gave a hug to Maggie, went to the car, and threw my possessions on the back seat. I caressed the chrome. The chassis felt good, smooth under my fingers. I looked inside.

To my amazement there was not a single crack in the leather seat or the dashboard. The tachometer was the biggest I had ever seen. The steering wheel took half of the front seat. All components were electrically powered. A slap on my shoulder brought me back to reality. I peeled my eyes off the navy-blue car.

Clay put the key in front of my nose. "Take it, Alex."

"You really mean it?" I asked, snatching the key, just in case he changed his mind. How about that!

A Ford Edsel, a car named after his own mother—it was the pride of their dynasty. I jumped in the car, started the engine, and listened to the enchanting power.

Clay got in and I backed the old Ford out of the driveway, put it into drive, and slowly rolled away. We forgot to wave goodbye to Maggie and Zach.

~~~

CHAPTER 46

After a good night' sleep at the Glimmer of Hope, where there was always a room ready for me, I was ready to face the world. Peggy was in the dining room and asked, "When did you arrive, Alex?"

"I arrived late last night, so I went straight to bed, I didn't want to disturb anyone."

"Come and sit down so I can tell you the progress we are making here." My head was a little light as she filled me in on what had happened in my absence.

"You are a bit pale, Alex."

"It is all right, I just got up earlier than usual," I explained.

"So, you are still not awake?"

"No, ma'am, I am not."

Clay picked me up shortly after that to start the training—which, by the way, I had no idea what it was all about. By seven we were driving to his place of residence. He handed me a fresh, hot brew, and two jelly donuts in a bag with a few napkins.

"Great service, Clay! You should have been a butler."

"I am too old to start a new career, but thanks for the vote of confidence."

We drove to his place in silence, with him thinking and me chomping at my donuts and sipping my coffee. On our arrival we started immediately to do our training, consisting of learning about telepathy.

Through his knowledge and from books I learned how to harvest energy from the universe, how to guide it into the proper direction and release it again, He made me promise never to use the energy for negative purposes or hurting anyone.

"Do not wish anything bad; it will come back tenfold. The only resource of the energy is to help someone to restore goodness, or to better yourself.

When he slowed down his teaching, I pestered him with tons of questions, and when I got tired, he encouraged me. I learned to heal, as well as to ease the pain, and how to talk to people to give them the spiritual knowledge to fight back.

"However." He added, "If they are not willing to change, don't force your belief on them."

"Just ignore them if they don't want it?" I asked.

"They will always return when they are good and ready."

I read books about 'Walk-ins,' healing, self-awareness, positive thinking, Rune stones, channeling, crystal healing, and how to listen to people. It all came easy to me, but it didn't always make sense.

Remember, Alex, the key to all power lies withing. You never stop believing in yourself.

I have heard this sentence a thousand times. It is engraved in my memory.

"Clay a part of my life is not clear to me."

"Ask. If it is anything I can answer, I will be glad to?"

"How when Simon, the ghost, sucked out my soul, I did not collapse?"

"It goes back many centuries. As soul travel gathering knowledge over time, you have the privilege of being ancient, also. It had remained relatively pure over the centuries, so it is so strongly planted into you that it is almost impossible to be destroyed. Besides, a lot of people are protecting you."

"Like whom?"

"We have no idea, however, in time you will find out, as a matter of fact. We will all find out."

One afternoon as we were training, Clay asked me to take a few minutes' rest. We sat down. At that moment, I remember the friendship between him, and my dad Zach went a long way. My mother and Adam's passing, as well as spending over two years in three years in the streets made Zach a father figure, but as far as knowing him, I kind of missed the boat in his department.

I never asked how I grew up, how I behaved in class, or whether he went to the army or other past lives he led. I only recalled that he was a good father, played with Adam and I, fed us, and provided us a good education. To put it bluntly, he was a total stranger. His obligations did not leave enough hours in a day for him to show us his human side.

Clayton, how well do you know my dad?

"Actually, not very well. I knew your mother much better than Zach."

"How so? Dad never told me."

"I introduced Sarah to your father a couple of years before they got married. I even had the honor of giving your mother away at the altar. Since she was an orphan and had no father to give her away, she chose me."

"You don't say! I want to know more about my mother."

"Let me see... It started many years ago. When I was thirty years old, after finished my studies, I decided to go to South America to bum around for three months. If you don't realize your dream when you are young, before you know it, the responsibilities get a hold on you, and all yours dreams vanish in smoke." Clay seems to gather his thoughts.

"About five weeks into my trip, hitchhiking through Venezuela, Ecuador, Peru, and Argentina, in a small village south of Asuncion in Chile, as I was walking a small church built of roughly carved stone caught my eye. It stood in the center of a village, with the back of it built against a mountain, dominating the surrounding houses on front in a half circle. It was the only attractive building for twenty miles around. "

"I decided to visit it. As I stepped in the church, I had an overwhelming feeling of serenity. I wanted to run away, but my feet felt as if they were nailed to the floor. A voice came from behind the column."

"Don't be frightened young man. We have been expecting you."

"I just stayed there with my mouth open, my eyes getting slowly accustomed to the darkness of the church, after being out in the bright sun. A light footstep was coming toward me, and the shadowy shape gently took my arm."

"Follow me, please." It was a young woman.

"She brought me to a man in his thirties, strong and slender with a black beard and a rosary entangled between his fingers, as I approached him, he smiled."

"Welcome to our humble residence. My name is Minos."

~~~

CHAPTER 47

"I introduced myself, and the few spoken words ended up in a fourteen-month ordeal. I stayed at the old stone church. With his eyes, Minos could persuade any human to do whatever he wanted. It was during this fourteen plus months that Sarah and I became best of friends. Every day, Sarah Minos, and a few other members, all from different nations, gathered." Clay closed his eyes.

We did our morning exercise, after that we went to our meditation hour, then came the chores to keep the place clean, did repairs needed on occasion, and gardening, simply basic tasks. In the afternoon, we were learning how to harness various energies, as well as mastering telepathy. Telekinesis, and out-of-body experiences, touching other people's minds. We had one day a week off. Clay gather his thoughts.

I forgot, there was a beautiful house in this small hamlet, it was supposed to be for special guests or dignitaries, but it was never used. Sarah and I had the task to cleaned it once a month, we stopped our exercises and did the cleaning of the house, strangely enough no one ever lived there, we only dusted the furniture and mopped the floor.

"I found out one year after my arrival the real meaning of this house being there. You see Minos lived in the mountain behind the church. There was a secret passage leading into a large cave. He lived in there for protection, every person leaves vibes with most of them too weak to be detected. Others like, Minos happened to be phenomenal, he was only safe from sending vibes inside the church and the grotto in the mountain, so he never went out and the house we cleaned was actually a decoy."

"Once before I left, Minos show me his inner sanctuary. Behind the vestibule at the back of the church was a small holy stoop built in the wall. Minos grabbed it with both hands, pulled it hard and twisted it to the left, the wall in the shadow moved without a hint of noise. Inside his sanctuary were shelves buckling under books after books of knowledge from astronomy, medicine, philosophy, and architectural concept," Clayton took a breath.

"His bed, couch, and all his furniture were centered in the middle of the cave, exquisitely arranged, a cascade ran down a wall making it a natural shower. Further in the depth of the grotto was a small chamber, this small room had a hole in the rock formation opening to the sky, two items only were inside this room. A chair and a telescope. It is the only time I went inside his sanctuary." I did not move to scared to lose one single word from his narration.

"I got to know Sarah better in those times off. We went fishing, took walks in the forest, and had long conversations. We giggled a lot during the morning chores. She took a liking to me. Her drive to learn English was immense. Minos spoke several languages himself, but he had no time to teach her English. He was constantly meditating or consulting the elder students. The entire course lasted five years."

"One day Sarah turned to me for help and asked, 'Will you teach me English?' No one has the time or the patience." I felt honored. So, I became her big brother. She told me about her life, and about how her parents left her enough money to live, as well as a house."

"She liked me, as a second priority. First, she wanted

to see the world before settling down. Getting married and being tied down raising children were not exactly her cup of tea. After fourteen months, I felt that it was time for me to go."

"Minos started to talk about 'Walk-Ins' people changing bodies. It spooked me, and after giving my home address to Sarah, I left. Her English was good, emerged herself on this course she wanted to follow to the end, and I had no more reason to stay and my father was getting old, which prompted me to get back home. To top it all she had only a few months to complete her course."

"Clayton, you just took off like that?"

"At the time, I didn't know better. Minos was so knowledgeable that it spooked me. I wrote a diary about the time I spent in South America. When I find it, you can have it and read all about your mother."

"Is that it? Nothing more about my mother?" I asked frustrated.

No, there is more. Upon my return to the States, my thoughts went often to Sarah, but they slowly faded away. One day she just vanished from my mind, as if every thought were erased. I helped my father with his antique shop.'

"The flower children started to get in crystals, metaphysics, and just being into themselves, so I decided to use my knowledge that I learned in South America. I set up shop. It was hard at first, with my dad selling antiques during the day I managed. When the candles, crystal, and other items got accepted, it paid the rent. I started an awareness class."

"One day your father, Zach showed up. He was having a strange dream occurring from time to time; also, his hands would get hot and tremble, so after talking to him, I noticed his natural energy power and asked him to become a healer. He started class immediately. We became friends"

"It was approximately twelve years after returning from Chile, as a was setting up for the evening class. I was always rushing because my father was getting old and it was my duty to close the antique shop, so it always created a mad dash to prepare my own shop. As I was running frantically, I didn't hear the lady entering behind me. As I turned around with a candle in my hand, I saw her standing in the middle of the room."

"You scared me? Don't you knock before entering someone's home?" I said, more shocked than angry, with goose bumps all over my body, and catching my breath.

"Sorry if I scared you," she replied, "I need your help."

"Sarah!" I was in shock. She came in my arms and held me with all her strength.

"Please help me." She whispered and cried. She was totally exhausted. I canceled the class immediately, took her home and put her in bed without asking any questions. She slept sixteen hours. Are you still with me, Alex?"

"Yes, Clay. Go on." I was drinking his every word.

"I let her stay in my apartment," Clay went on, "She recuperated for a few days, and on my first day off she told me her whole story. She was genuinely scared. I had to calm her down to understand what she was talking about. After I left Chile, she completed her course and went back to her home in Thailand."

"Born of Dutch father and a Thai mother, she didn't look like a native; she was tall and brunette, with long slender fingers and a light complexion. She wore thin gold-rimmed glasses for reading"

"Upon her return, she started volunteering work in a local orphanage. Later, she helped at the Red Cross and made frequent trips into the slums. She got heavily involved with her work, and one day she met a gentleman, Lu-Kim-Bog, whom she later married. It was a perfect union, just like a dream."

"He treated her right, a meticulous romantic, and gave her a lot of attention, never a harsh word or raised voice. He went on many trips, never failed to bring her something when he returned."

"The only time he ever raised his voice was the day after their wedding, when they were on a Sampan on a romantic outing. The driver of the boat made a false maneuver and hit an incoming Junk. The impact threw Lu-Kim-Bog against the hull of a boat. He tried to keep his balance; his pinky was crushed and severed, finally falling in the water, never to be found."

"That day made him swear like craze, he quickly regained control of himself. He wrapped his injured right hand and had it taken care at the hospital."

"The romance lasted one year; slowly, afterwards he made hints for her to spend more time at home. It soon turned into remarks like, 'You like your kids more than staying at home. Or do you have to be with them all the time?'

"One day her husband came home with a friend. His name was Lazlo. They were introduced and he spent a couple of months at their house. One night as she could not sleep, she went downstairs. It was about three AM and Lazlo and Lu-Kim-Bog were still up. Both men were making exercises, talking about South America. Sarah stood there; it was impossible for her to move."

"Her honey had been to the same person and endured the rigorous training, but he never told her! It seemed odd. Lazlo was making different moves from those that she knew, blended with moves she had learned. Lu-Kim-Bog asked what they were for, and he said they were to take the soul out of an unsuspecting person and to stay young. I was totally flabbergasted by this narration of my mother's life.

"Lazlo was much older than her husband bur didn't look it, so he was learning the way of energy in an evil way. She stood there over an hour, standing in the hallway, not making a move, too scared to breath, with her drink on the stairs. She was horrified by the conversation her husband was having. He was part of the secret police, which she never knew. Lu-Kim-Bog had been using his power to torture innocent people, was also involved in drug cover-ups, selling woman in nearby countries for prostitution and laughing about it nonchalantly."

"She silently went to her room with a cold shiver running down her spin. Sleeping was out of the question, being greatly disturbed by those revelation. At the first light of dawn, she left for the orphanage without saying goodbye to Lu-Kim- Bog who was still sleeping."

"That night your mother got home and went down to look in her husband's desk. It was something she had never dreamed of doing, but the chilling revelations were too much. She had to double check. The photos she had seen of tortured people made her stomach turn. Refusing to be involved in such despicable, violent activity, Sarah returned to her room, upon her husband coming back home, she had no time to prepare herself."

"He stormed into the house and went straight to her. He proceeded to beat her, calling her vile names. He didn't stop until she was swollen all over, bruised, lacerated, and had admitted to listening to the conversation. She later found out how he knew about her being behind the door on the staircase. While stepping out of his office in bare feet, he had stepped in the condensation from the glass she had left resting on the stairwell." I had tears wetting my eyes while listening. Clay went on without noticing.

"Immediately Lu-Kim-Bog. Called Lazlo, who came over immediately. They grabbed Sarah, dragged her into a car, drove all night on a dirt road, and threw her in a rice field on the edge of the jungle. By instinct, she raised enough energy to shield herself before Lazlo zapped her with his negative energy and left her for dead. He didn't even look back because he was so confident of his capability. Sarah was discovered by the owner of the rice paddy at the break of dawn. She looked dead.

"He and his wife nursed her back to life in their humble hut over the next four months. The gentleman who found her also helped her to leave the with his cousin, a small-time smuggler making frequent trips to Singapore. Having nowhere else to go, she looked for her best friend who was living in the city."

"Sarah started reconstructing her life from scratch, she did not realize that if you didn't shield yourself, your energy will travel in any direction and could betray you over time. Lazlo did just that. He picked up the vibes and located her. She already had made her application to come to the USA. She left the week before he arrived in Singapore."

"Sarah found out when she called her friend to thank her for all she had done, and she had arrived safe in the good old USA. That is when her friend told her a man was looking for her, and it was the same man that was on the picture from her wedding day, so Sarah had the picture sent to my address to show me what this evil man looked like. She was constantly shielding herself in fear of getting tracked down."

This story was getting stranger by the minutes, and I communicated my feelings to Clayton.

"You are not pulling my leg, are you?"

"Of course not, Alex. I have the picture at home of your mother in full traditional wedding attire with Lu-Kim-Bog and Lazlo. I'll bring it over tomorrow if you want me to, I must look for it."

"I'd like very much to see what she looked like when she was young."

"Well, Alex, she didn't look the same as she did in the

picture. She colored her hair to keep from being recognized."

"What about Mom and Zach?"

"At first, she was overly cautious, but your dad felt the chemistry and didn't give up. He was nice about it; he never insisted, giving her plenty of space to be herself. One day Sarah came to me. Zach had proposed to her and she wanted to know if it would be possible for me to be the father she didn't have and walk her to the altar. I was not about to let such honor escape."

"Listen, Clay. How were they together?"

"At first it was very slow for them to trust each other, It was funny—she came to ask me questions, 'Is it all right if...,' and then Zach would phone me and asking, 'Do you think that she would be offended if... 'Both were asking my advice. Imagine, me a lifetime bachelor! I wouldn't know to date a lady for the life of me, after a while both let their guard down toward each other and love took its course. The rest became fun and games."

"Every day of their life was laughing, caring for one other. During the daytime, Zach worked at building his empire, making deals, going to company lunches, verifying workmanship on the job sites, doing inventory and bidding. She in the meantime, came and worked with me for about a year until she got a little more confident in mastering English. After that, she worked part time to help batter woman, she never forgot to poise a protective shield every morning. She was scared that Lu-Kim-Bog or Lazlo were looking for her."

"Never once did she go back or phone her friend. She was terrified to leave a trail, in the evening and weekends, they were totally into each other, going to sport events and on picnics; they visited all the national parks withing a 500-miles radius, as well as movies and the theater, and they went to the flea market as well as festivals. Your father had an old Indian motorcycle, an absolute beauty in black and burgundy." Clay took a breather.

"Now, Alex, let's go back to practicing."

"Don't you have more to tell me?"

"What do you expect? It happened many years ago, and by now my memory is getting rusty. When I remember, believe me, I will tell you. Until then let's practice."

"Clay, have you looked at the time? Maybe we should leave the work for tomorrow. I cannot believe we took such long break! Tomorrow it is."

~~~

CHAPTER 48

The doorbell rang and Clay went to answer it while I tidied up the place. I could hear the voices, the column in the center of the room blocked my view. He chatted a couples of seconds and then I heard Clay's voice say,

"Won't you come in?" Clay backed up to clear the way. Two midgets walked in, both men about three and a half feet tall. They were well dressed, with three-piece suits, impeccable ties, and well-polished shoes.

Clayton closed the door behind them and asked if they wanted some refreshments. Suddenly, in perfect harmony their eyes closed halfway, and a bolt of energy went straight to Clay's stomach, through his body and out of his head.

"No!" I screamed.

A bitterly cold wind entered the room in an instant. Dozens of lights swirled around the two midgets. Both started immediately to choke and ran out the door, screaming. Clay was lying on the floor. The cold dispersed.

I ran to my dear friend and mentor. He was just coming out of his shock, a little blood coming out of his nose and saliva running out of the side of his mouth.

"It is too late, son. They caught up with me." He reached in his pocket, pulled out his key and put it in my hand.

"Sorry I arrived too late." I started to weep in silence.

The spirit of Adam, my dear brother, was standing in front of me in all his majestic splendor.

"What is going on? This is senseless!" I cried. The anger and frustration were wearing me down. It all happened too quickly for me to understand.

"Listen, Adam, I want no part of this! I am too young to go out there and face whatever it is that I am supposed to fight. Why me? Why can't I grow up like anyone else and have a good time. Who decides what is going on? I didn't sign for this crap." I did not realize that I was screaming. I walked out of the house for a few minutes and stood in silence. Words were futile.

Adam respected my pain and waited for me to regain some control. The thought of Clayton laying alone on the floor snapped me back to reality.

"Alex, listen to me. There are many more facets you have not learned yet but protect yourself at all time."

"Wait one minute, brother. Right now, I am too shattered to listen. First, 911 must be called, then Zach." I walked back up the stairs like a zombie. One thought was in my mind, '*Clay, you did not die in vain; I will make sure of that!* The key to the Ford Edsel was still clutched in my hand.

~~~

CHAPTER 49

Claire walked in the laboratory, after a dreamless night, feeling like a million dollars.

"What is going on with you, boss?" Asked Gwen.

"Had a good night's sleep. What is on the agenda?"

"Nothing much, we are doing routine work, waiting for all the samples to develop. You know the waiting the game."

"Well I am going to catch up with the paperwork." The entire morning Claire was humming, smiling, and walking around the lab like she was on a cloud.

At eleven AM. A delivery boy arrived with a dozen roses, all of them yellow, the sign of friendship. By now, the whole lab wanted to know where the roses came from. Claire stood her ground and never answered. How could she answer, the circumstance was too bizarre for anyone to believe her? So, she told them the minimum.

"A gentleman by the name of Zach sent them, I met him under strange circumstances last week, and he sent them to apologize."

"I guess that is the reason, you are off the wall today?" Gwen asked with a candid smile.

Claire was happy. "*Yes, he was a nice man. How can I tell them that I have never met the man and was only assuming through a memory from another person as I was myself 'a walk in.'? If I open my mouth, it will sound unimaginable. I surely would get my pink slip. In any case, I would be ostracized for the next one hundred years, so no answer is better than making up lies I can never get out of or explain,'* thought Claire.

"Listen Gwen. I am going to freshen up. Would you like to join me for lunch afterward?"

"It sounds great." She replied, I will be glad to stay away from the cafeteria food for one day." Gwen walked back. Claire went back to the rest room and for the first time she looked in the mirror. *'Well, Claire, that is what you look like,* she said to herself. *'You are one lucky lady.'* The figure reflected in the mirror was one tall, slender lady. The auburn hair cascading over her shoulders made a perfect balance with the tone of skin.

Just a little makeup was enough to underline her features as well as leaving her natural beauty exposed. *'I am ancient, and fortunate enough to be in the body of a perfect lady, with all the power of a goddess. I am going to like my tasks in this world.'* she thought, smiling while moving like a graceful swan back and forth in front of the mirror—fluffing her hair, making silly movements and dance steps.

After all she had not been here for many years, and even when she was here many years ago, she lived in fear, watching over her shoulder, never knowing the pleasure of relaxing. She didn't even have the luxury to say goodbye to her loved one.

"All that is behind me, for now." She brushed the memory aside with a gesture of her hand. *Now it is time to get used to this new body.*

She went to Gwen with a smile splattered all over her face. "Let's go to lunch."

Gwen lifted her hand from the microscope. "Be right with you, Claire." She finished observing the slide, unbuttoned her lab coat and noticed the smile on Claire's face.

"Claire, with a grin like this on your face, you are

planning something mischievous." Gwen didn't wait for an answer. She knew better.

A few moment later, they walked out of the building. Men and Women were turning their heads at this towering auburn hair lady. *'I am a lethal weapon,'* she thought, walking straight into the sunlight.

~~~

CHAPTER 50

Everyone showed at the funeral, from Dad to the family and friends of Clayton. Adam's spirit came down to pay his last respects, whispering his sorrow and condolences telepathically to Zach as well as myself. Despite the pain, we were all trying to make sense to this senseless killing.

Why would someone wish to harm Clayton? No evidence could be given to the authorities. Of course, an APB was sent to various police stations to look out for two midgets, even then it would not stand in court, the prosecutor had warned us.

The autopsy revealed only a heart attack; there were no drugs, no injury, no evidence of any strain. It was a closed case. If we had insisted, it would have been sheer suicide, a bunch of fools trying to explain the unknown, something nobody can see or feel.

Energy of the universe is constantly swirling around us. Yet it is also never there, just like the wind, you can describe it from moving objects, dust flying, flags showing its direction, but no one can see it. Yet it is there, sometime as gentle as a loving kiss, other times creating unthinkable havoc. It is always around us, without ever being seen. With this theory, to face a jury would be a first-class ticket for all of us to end up at the funny farm.

Everyone from the Glimmer of Hope showed up, including Peggy, our chef de cuisine. She left her pots and wonderful simmering soups for this sad day. Of all the people gathered here, she understood the most how much Clayton and Dad had helped the homeless, and to realize the dream of building this wonderful shelter.

The padre mentioned Clay's accomplishments in life and read the epitaph, we all took a minute of silence to express our last respects.

After the crowd thinned, a very distinguished lady wearing a veiled hat came over to Peggy and me and proceed to excuse herself.

"Sorry to intrude. Are you Alex?"

"Yes, ma'am."

"I would like a word with you." She looked at Peggy for a silent permission to take me away.

"I will see you at Glimmer, Alex. Your father is going to drive me back." The lady took me by the arm. We walked a few paces to the next stone monument.

"Let me introduce myself. I am Iris, Clayton's sister. He talked to me a great deal about you." She paused.

"All good I must say." I noticed tears in her eyes as she spoke. "He had great respect and told me a lot about you, you are a special gentleman." She stopped a second to regain her composure. She wiped her tears and went on.

"Even though I do not always agree with his theory of harmony of the universe, my brother wanted you to have this," She handed me a large envelop, shook my hand, turned around and walked away without a word. I returned to Peggy and mingled with the rest of the crowd, then I excused myself and went to the car, putting the envelope in the glove compartment.

Zach knew that his friend and mentor Clay had gone to other tasks in a parallel world, probably having fun with his son Adam up there somewhere, but it still was hard to lose a friend. Theresa and Maggie, as well a few others, were having a conversation, catching up with the past couple of weeks when they didn't see each other. Girls can talk a mile a minute.

I was about to go back with everyone to the Glimmer of Hope after a last goodbye to Clayton, when from the corner of my eye on the left, about a hundred fifty yards away, was a tall lady standing between all the tombstones, just beside a mausoleum. As I noticed her, she waived at me, imploring with her gesture to come over. I rushed to my father and said.

"Listen, I will join you in a moment,"

"Anything I can do, Son?"

"No, you go ahead."

"Don't be late. We have the wake in the shelter's dining room."

"I'll get there as soon as I can," I replied while walking toward the waiting lady. As I approached, she started walking toward Clay's resting place, so I slightly changed my angle to meet her in front of my dear friend. *Do I know this lady and what is she expecting from me?* As I came closer, the face became familiar, still I could not quite remember from where.

She stopped between the flowers and the grave. She observed a minute of silence, took a handful of dirt, and threw it on the coffin. "We will miss you," turned around, lifted her veil.

"Sorry for what happened, Alex. First, it could have been prevented, but it happened so fast with those two men."

I looked at her, spooked. *'How does she know about the two men? No one had a clue who sent Clay the bolt of energy; the coroner had declared it as a heart attack. Nobody believed us about the two midgets, and here she was talking like she was there during the ambush'*

"Excuse me, who are you?"

"How rude if me! I forgot to introduce myself. I am Claire."

Now I remembered, she was the lady freaking out a

while back when we zapped Simon. Zach sent her a bouquet of roses after the incident to apologize for scaring her out of wits, still how did she know about Clay, the funeral, the incident and our whereabouts? She must have been reading my thoughts. She addressed me like she had always known me.

"I need to see you, Alex." She handed me a business card with an address on it. A couple of words were scribbled on the back. Tomorrow, 11AM. Please. She smiled sadly.

"You have to go now. They are expecting you at the wake, please be there tomorrow. I am counting on you and keep practicing like Clay asked you." She pivoted on her heel and walked away in silence, her dress caressing the tombstones as she glided by.

I barely remember walking toward the car, shaking my head in disbelief. *'I better ask Zach what is going on,'* I thought while driving to the wake.

I arrived at the wake before anyone had the time to sit down. My encounter with Claire was too brief for me to arrive late, something must have been showing on my face. Rick stopped me as I walked in the door.

"You are looking pretty pale, buddy. Are you all right?" he was carrying two pitchers of ice water.

"Let me put these down and we can talk. Hey, Nails! Grab these pitchers. I have to go."

Nails came over, took the pitcher, and put them on the end of the table at the far side of the dining room while Rick gently took me by the shoulder and dragged me outside to a quiet corner. "SO?"

"I am okay, Rick." I was not about to spoil the wake, his asking of my stunned look, shook me out of my stunned look.

"Have it your way," he said, "Remember, we are always here for you, and for everyone as a matter of fact. Now, come inside and have pizza."

"Pizza." Now I understood why Peggy left her kitchen. "Who came up with the idea?"

"Your dad. You know he never miss a beat, even in the toughest of times. He even ordered them with the works and extra cheese."

"That is a feast not to be missed!" I said, dragging him back inside the hall. My mind was wondering, still affected by Claire who had approached me in such a peculiar way.

"Nails, do you speak other languages beside English?" I asked for no reason.

"Yes, Spanish. My parents are from Spain. I learned it when I was little and kept it up in the street with all the Mexicans. Why do you ask?"

"No reason, just curious." *Why did I ask?* I questioned myself. A young lady walked through the door, her legs buckling under the weight of all the pizzas. Nails saw her coming first and jumped like a cat to go to her rescue. He took half the pile, *Boy, this guy is turning into a gentleman* I observed.

"I see this too should have been delivered, judging by the way everyone was grabbing the food." She smiled. "There are seven more in the trunk," she added. "Want to get the rest, please?"

Nails had already gone to the dining room, mobbed by a dozen hungry kids. I looked at the young kids one more time and went to get the rest of the food. As I walked toward the building, out of the corner of my eye, I caught a brand-new Japanese car, driven by two midgets looking at the building. Having my face buried in the pizza boxes shielded me from them, so they didn't notice me, but I saw them as plain as day.

Zach was taking care of the bill while the delivery girl was waiting patiently. She left after shaking father's hand.

I sat across from father on the bench. "We need to talk."

"Yes, Son," he turned around and gave me his full attention. "I was outside helping to bring in the pizza when from the corner of my eye I saw the two midgets drive by."

"Are you sure?" he replied. Almost jumping out of his seat.

"Positive. It was fast, still my eyes are keen, and I will never forget their faces. They killed Clayton, and I intend to find out what they want?"

"You know that all of us will be ready to work with you, but for the time being, we better tell everyone to be on their toes."

"Who must be on their toes?" Maggie asked holding me gently around the neck from behind.

"Maggie, I see you are finished with the kids," I lovingly, held her arm while she places a kiss on my neck.

"So, tell me who must be on their toes."

I asked her to sit with me and took the time to explain what I had just seen. "From now on, we all are to be extra vigilant." The rest of the night went quietly, a few were reminiscing, others cleaning up the dining room, helping the kitchen staff, sending the small children to bed. I personally hit the sac after a good shower.

~ ~ ~

CHAPTER 51

Four in the morning a nagging feeling woke me up. Lying in the dark, I remembered Clay's sister Iris gave me an envelope, and I forgotten all about it. The first impulse while getting up was to make a beeline for the envelope.

It was still in the glove compartment, so I ran to the car in my pajamas and feverishly grabbed the knob on the glove box. There it was a beige envelope with my name on it in bold letters. I opened it and found that it contained pictures of Lazlo and a gentleman whom I presumed to be Lu-Kim-Bog, as well as a young lady, all standing in front of an old temple in an exotic country.

The young lady was wearing a traditional Saran, probably from Thailand. *'I will have to look it up,'* but for now, I must get ready to go to my appointment with the 'lady who knew too much about me.' I returned to my room with the photograph, put it on the nightstand, jumped in the shower, and soaped my body.

I was getting impatient, wondering what she wanted from me, I wanted to know how much more she knew about this whole charade. I got out and realized I had forgotten to rinse my hair.

"Now I can tell the whole world that I am a smart Alex," I expressed loudly while returning to the shower laughing.

At 10:45 I was in front of a massive building, it was

very impersonal, with no architectural beauty and hardly any landscaping in front, only grass. I classified it as a 'Concrete anonymity' not the place I would want to work in. At the front desk, a security guard stood, she asked me the nature of my visit, so I showed her Claire's business card.

"I am expected at eleven."

"Please sign your name and time of arrival" She gave me a visitor pass and picked up the phone all at the same time. She dialed the extension number to announce me.

"Mr. Alex Knight is here to see you." After a slight hesitation she continued "Right away." She put the phone down and asked me to go to the conference Room 311, using the first elevator on the left. I walked to the elevator while clipping on my visitor pass.

The door was open and waiting for me. I pushed three and arrived at my destination in a few seconds. I turned left in the hallway and spotted 311 in front of the door of the conference room.

My heart started to feel funny. I had to put my hand on my chest to stop it from jumping out. *"What is going on? I am scared! I worried before anything happens!"*

As I knocked on the mahogany door, her voice came loud and clear. "Come in." She was looking out the window with one hand clutching the heavy curtain. It was just like in a movie scene. She turned around and said to me.

"You see, Alex, I have been waiting for you forever."

I stayed right there in front of her like an idiot. I was looking at her, feeling uneasy. Claire was looking radiant and happy at the window.

She stood only a few feet away, I had the impression that thousands of miles were between us. As she inspected me from head to toe, a feeling of awkwardness paralyzed me, I must have looked intimidated with a pearl of sweat running down my temple, standing like a child caught with his hand in the cookie jar.

"Don't be frightened, Alex. Come to me." She opened her arms.

I crossed the room and she took me in her arms and kissed my cheek. *'This is beginning to feel awkward!'* I thought. I didn't know this lady, but it felt comfortable, so I let my feelings take over.

An atmosphere of peace and tranquility surrounded us. I took one step back and looked into Claire's unusual blue eyes and said calmly.

"Who are you?" She did not answer, she kept smiling. Suddenly it all became clear to me.

"You are my mother." Tears of joy, surprise, and total disbelief flooded down my face.

"Through the years, I have been the mother of many. Yes, Alex I am your mother." She herself let the tears stream down her face.

Thank goodness there was a chair in the vicinity, the news was too stunning and hit me like a ton of bricks. The lump in my throat kept growing and rendered me speechless.

"Are you okay, Alex?" She did not give me time to answer.

"I know that this news is coming to you as a chock. I could not wait any longer to hold you in my arms. By the way, do you mind if I call you Alex?"

"No, it is perfectly all right," I said. At that point I had other concerns other than what I wanted to be called.

"This is one hell of a spicy meat ball to swallow." I said in a trembling voice.

"Do you want to go for a walk, or do you prefer me to explain over lunch?"

My mouth was dry and all I could say was. "Who are you?" She briefly filled me in on being a 'Walk-in' and traveling back and forth as a spirit. Meeting my mother twenty years after knowing that she was dead was a shock to the system to put it lightly.

"Should I put garlic around my neck and in my pockets?" I asked with the most serious face in the world. She exploded in a hysterical laughter that brought tears to her eyes. She could hardly contain herself; I was glad that she took it so lightly, it took a few minutes for her to regain her composure.

"Alex, you are not inclined to make a decision, so let's go. Lunch is on me, and we can talk about the surprise I sprang on you."

Boy, she was not kidding! A surprise called dynamite would be more appropriate. She grabbed my arm and gently pulled me out of the chair with a smile.

"Come on. I am not dangerous," We went back to the hallway and walked through a bright office that was very elegantly decorated. Claire took her purse, and we went out after she told her assistant Gwen she'd probably be back late.

We walked out of the building, her full of vivacity, and me with lead legs. I dragged them like someone who had not slept for four or five days, so she took my arm.

"Alex, I promise no harm will come to you."

TO BE CONTINUED

~~~

ABOUT THE AUTHOR

I was born in Geneva, Switzerland. and grew up in the small town of Carouge. I have three brothers and two sisters. I was known as a super active kid. My parents shipped me to Lucerne when I was 15 years old to learn the Swiss German national dialect. I worked in an old age home run by monks, and I was chaperoned by Brother Dominicus who also taught me to cook for six hundred people daily including the staff and patients of the nursing home. Upon my return to Geneva. I started the apprenticeship of Chef de Cuisine. It was a two and a half year of commitment. I finished third out of ninety-seven apprentices and accepted a contract in Scotland. When I reached the end of that contract, my next location was Toronto, Canada.

This was the beginning of my love of travel mixed with my profession. I have been in thirty-seven countries; speak five languages as well as Swiss German, our national dialect. My travel in the United States were combined with the ability to speak English as well as the ownership of my motorcycle, permitted to visit many States. I believe that I only missed 8 or 9 States and I am working on those since I am retired and writhing full time.

During all my travels and for all my adult years, I have recorded my experiences and memories of people and places in "My always handy composition book" which became the source of stories and books.

Twenty-three years ago, I met the most wonderful lady in the world in my eyes for sure, my wife Diane, and here I am writing books and not letting my Parkinson disease slow me down. Please never give up!

Merci, François Sigrist

~~~~~

Made in the USA
Monee, IL
29 December 2021